Golden Eyes

Love can tame the wildest heart...

After Duncan Kennedy stumbles across poachers in his mountains, he is understandably angry. His discovery of an injured cheetah makes him even more furious. He takes the cat home until he can summon the local vet, only to get the shock of his life. When he checks on his charge, he finds not a cheetah but a gorgeous, very naked woman.

Aliyah Carter spent the past six months trapped in cheetah form, a prisoner of the poachers who took her to use in an illegal exotic-game hunt. Finally she's escaped, but now she faces another problem. A devastatingly sexy sheriff who knows her secret.

Warning: This title contains explicit sex and adult language.

Amber Eyes

Their final mission will be to win her love.

A beautiful, vulnerable woman appears at the high country cabin where Hunter and Jericho live between assignments. They are captivated by their stunning, reticent visitor and vow to protect her—and uncover what she's hiding. Neither is prepared for the unbelievable. Their beautiful innocent is a cougar shifter who's spent a lifetime alone.

In the shelter of their love, Kaya blooms, finally willing to trust—and embrace her humanity again. Then Hunter and Jericho are called away on a mission that goes terribly wrong. Now, pregnant, and alone once more, she must find her way in a world she doesn't belong to—and hope that the two men she loves will find their way home.

Warning: This title contains explicit sex, adult language, sweet lovin', multiple partners and ménage a trois.

Look for these titles by
Maya Banks

Now Available:

Seducing Simon
Understood
Overheard
Love Me, Still
Undenied
Stay With Me
Amber Eyes
Songbird

Brazen
Reckless *(stand-alone sequel to
Brazen)*

Falcon Mercenary Group Series
Into the Mist (Book 1)
Into the Lair (Book 2)

Print Anthologies
The Perfect Gift
Caught by Cupid
Unbroken

Print Collections
Linger
Wild

Colters' Legacy Series
Colters' Woman
Colters' Lady

Free Download:

AT
My Bookstore and More
Colters' Wife

Coming Soon:

Colters' Legacy Series
Colters' Daughter

Wild

Maya Banks

A Samhain Publishing, Ltd. publication.

Samhain Publishing, Ltd.
577 Mulberry Street, Suite 1520
Macon, GA 31201
www.samhainpublishing.com

Wild
Print ISBN: 978-1-60504-512-2

Editing by Jennifer Miller
Cover by Anne Cain

Golden Eyes, ISBN 978-1-60504-704-1
First Samhain Publishing, Ltd. electronic publication: April 2010
Amber Eyes, ISBN 978-1-60504-466-8
First Samhain Publishing, Ltd. electronic publication: March 2009
First Samhain Publishing, Ltd. print publication: July 2010

Contents

Golden Eyes

Chapter One

A long hiss escaped the jowls of the cat as she hunkered down amongst the rocks and thick shrubbery. Low chirps echoed across the fog-laden ground, and even the human inside the beast could not call back the frightened sounds.

She panted, her breath forming puffs in the frigid morning air. The burst of speed she'd needed to escape her pursuers had drained her. She lacked the energy to go much further, but it was imperative that she find safety.

Her gaze focused on a ponderosa pine several yards away. Cheetahs were ill-equipped to climb trees, but there were enough low-lying branches that she could scramble toward the top and hide in the dense foliage.

She sprang from her hiding spot and ran for the tree on stealthy paws. Fatigue burned every muscle, but she couldn't succumb to the need for rest. Not yet. They were coming for her, and they would kill her.

With sagging energy, she jumped to the lowest branch. Her claws dug into the bark as she fought for balance. Her ears twitched and shot upward as a sound in the distance caught her attention. Higher she climbed, desperation bleeding over into her movements.

When she'd gained enough height to not be easily seen from ground level, she stretched over the limb and flattened her lithe body as much as possible.

Even as she swallowed against the involuntary chirps of fear, she felt the change radiating over her body. Pain, welcome pain, locked into her bones, seized her muscles, and shot like fire through her limbs.

She clung to the branch, desperate not to plummet to the ground. Paws became human fingers. The spotted fur rippled away and was replaced by pale, naked skin. The soft tuft of hair at her nape became long strands of honey gold hair.

For the first time in months, she was human again.

She closed her eyes and wrapped her arms around the rugged tree branch. Time was something she didn't have, but she needed the rejuvenation her human form would bring, if only for a few minutes. The cheetah was spent.

Perhaps she slept. She had no clear idea of how much time passed, but she was alerted by a rustling in the distance. Voices. Familiar voices.

They were coming for her.

Fear swelled in her throat, blocking out her breath. Panic raced in her veins and prickled like razors over her skin. They wouldn't take her prisoner this time. They would kill her.

Pulling every thread of strength within her, she concentrated on becoming the cheetah. She would run once more.

Her human side cried out in protest, but she gave free rein to the beast, allowed it control as her body conformed to the parameters set by her mind.

She blinked to adjust to the difference in visual acuity. The landscape sharpened, and she focused on the most expedient route away from danger.

Slowly she inched further out onto the branch, her intention to leap to the neighboring tree. She slid on her stomach, her claws gripping the wood as she prepared to spring.

A light sound riled her instincts, and she shot forward. Pain seared through her hip, and she was left gripping the air. Seconds later, she hit the ground with a resounding thump.

"Fuck! She jumped the string. I didn't get a good shot."

The voice was too close. Agony wracked her body. She lifted her head and glanced down her body to see an arrow protruding from her haunch. She panted heavily, trying to squeeze oxygen back into the lungs that had been severely jarred by her fall.

If she hadn't jumped, the arrow would have sliced through her heart and lungs. She'd be lying on the ground, bleeding out.

She struggled to right herself, to heave her aching body from the hard terrain. Then she looked up to see the hunter standing just thirty yards away. Notching another arrow. Terror lent her adrenaline, and she rocketed away, the hunter's curses ringing in her ears.

Duncan Kennedy hoisted his rifle over his shoulder then shifted his backpack into place. He stepped away from his truck and surveyed the wooded area he was about to venture into.

With a shake of his head, he tucked his chin down, buttoned his jacket, then headed out. He felt ridiculous, but his job as sheriff was to check out sources of possible threat, and he'd had three reports from locals of strange, wild animals roaming the area outside his small Colorado town.

The first he'd ignored because old man Hildebrandt had been known to spin a yarn or two. But then Silas Maynard had reported seeing an animal he swore looked just like a tiger. A day later, Mrs. Humphreys had called to tell him she'd seen an honest-to-goodness lion, not a mountain lion, and then she'd heard shots.

Hunting season didn't start for several more weeks, but Duncan knew that didn't hinder overzealous hunters. He'd get out, do a little tracking, look around and hopefully quiet any fears of strange beasties running around the mountains.

He walked a straight line behind Mrs. Humphreys' house, his gaze darting along the ground for any fresh sign. He wondered if the shots had been people merely target practicing and if the animals were just mountain lions or even large bobcats.

Not that he really thought he'd find the answers, but he would do his job and reassure the people of his town. Even with their quirks, he wouldn't want to live anywhere else. His parents had died when he was young, just in high school, and the townspeople had stepped in, taken care of him and later made sure he could go to college. He owed them more than he could ever repay, and returning here to act as sheriff after gaining a degree in law enforcement seemed the least he could do. These were his mountains. His home. These people were his family.

The terrain had begun to slope more sharply upward, and his breath came a little harder as he climbed in elevation. He stopped and dug a bottle of water from his backpack and rested for a moment as he sipped.

He reckoned he was about a mile from Mrs. Humphreys' now. He'd go another at the most. She'd said the shots sounded distant, not close. He capped the bottle of water, tossed it back into his pack and resumed his hike.

When he topped a slight rise, he caught movement out of the corner of his eye. A group of men, one holding a compound bow, the others carrying rifles, moved stealthily through the craggy underbrush.

Duncan crouched and took out his binoculars so he could zoom in on the group.

They appeared to be tracking, their heads down as if following a blood trail. Anger tightened his muscles. Friggin' poachers.

He noted their appearance, took mental notes of their characteristics. No way he'd approach them blind. He was outnumbered, and more than one wildlife officer had been killed when crossing an illegal hunter.

Instead, he pulled his rifle around and uncapped the scope. He brought the gun up and stared through the crosshairs until he found his target.

He resighted a good twenty yards in front of the men and squeezed off a warning shot. They jumped back and sprawled on the ground, guns and bows flying everywhere. Duncan grinned. City slickers.

After a few seconds, they warily rose then scrambled for their weapons. They took off in the opposite direction, and Duncan could hear their thrashing all the way from where he hunkered down.

Duncan waited. He pulled out a snack and ate it in silence. Half an hour later, the poachers hadn't returned, so he made his way down to the area they'd been scouring.

After a few minutes searching the area dotted with their boot prints, he found the first sign of blood. Son of a bitch. They *had* been tracking a kill.

He shook his head in disgust and began following the sign. There wasn't a lot of blood, which told him the shot hadn't been clean. He grimaced at the idea of having to put down the animal. If he was even able to find it.

It wasn't an easy trail to follow. Several times he had to backtrack to the last spot he'd seen blood and circle out to pick up the trail again.

The sun rose higher overhead, breaking through the canopy of trees and whisking away the damp coldness of morning. Duncan unbuttoned his jacket as he walked on.

He followed the spots of blood to an area where brush was thick and bushes huddled, their leaves and limbs twining together. He glanced ahead, hoping to find the animal rather than wade through the thick growth. A warning hiss stopped his foot in midair.

He stood there a moment, paralyzed by what he'd almost done. Feral eyes stared up at him, glazed with pain and warning.

Holy Mother of God.

He scrambled back, putting at least ten feet between him and the... What exactly was this animal?

The cat lay panting, an arrow protruding from its left haunch. Light chirping sounds ripped from the cat's mouth, intermixed with hisses and growls.

His mind raced to absorb the scene. A tawny cat with black spots. It wasn't a bobcat. The tail was too long. Was it some bizarre mountain lion hybrid? No, the body structure was all wrong. God, if he didn't know better, he'd swear it was a cheetah.

What the fuck was a cheetah doing in the Rockies? Had someone's exotic pet escaped? Suddenly the reports of a tiger and a lion didn't sound quite so farfetched.

He frowned as a possible solution occurred to him, one that fit the scene he'd interrupted earlier. Could the animals have been illegally imported for the specific purpose of hunting? Or could someone merely have spotted the escaped cheetah and decided to hunt it down?

There had been no reports of any missing animals from the Cheyenne Mountain Zoo or the zoo in Denver, and he wasn't sure either housed any cheetahs.

The cat continued to stare at him just as he stared at it. It looked to be a female. Her stare eased and her eyes lost some of the wildness. Her lids relaxed, though she continued to observe him cautiously.

"I'm not going to hurt you," he said soothingly and then felt like a dumbass for cooing at a wild animal. One that could outrun his damn truck. She could chase him down and have him for lunch in ten seconds flat. If that long.

He reached for his rifle. The stock cradled in his hand gave him a measure of confidence.

But she didn't move. A low sound emanated from her, and after a moment he realized she was purring. The vibrating rumble grew louder as he stared at her in amazement.

He had no idea what to do with the cat. She didn't *seem* threatening, but then only a moron would assume a wild animal could be reasonable.

If he left her to go back and get help, he risked the hunters coming back and finding her. If he could get her to a vet, he knew she could be saved. She hadn't lost an enormous amount of blood, and the wound wasn't mortal.

What he needed was a tranquilizer dart, and gee, it just so happened that wasn't standard issue for a sheriff to be carting around in his backpack. Water, bandages, flares, basic survival gear? Yes. A buttload of kitty Valium? No.

He circled around the cat, who still hadn't moved so much as a muscle. Maybe she was conserving her strength to attack him. Not a very comforting thought and one that had him backing away even further.

Then she moved. He froze, not wanting to excite her. She struggled to her feet, collapsed back to the ground then pushed herself up again.

He gripped his gun tighter as she limped very slowly in his direction. His thumb flicked over the safety, and the click echoed loudly in the stillness. The cheetah stopped and stared at him, her big golden eyes dripping with sadness. And fear.

His eyes narrowed as she started forward again, her steps measured as if not to startle him. Yep, he was losing his mind. He was standing in the middle of nowhere having telepathic communion with a cheetah.

She bumped her head against his leg and rubbed the side of her jowls over his jeans. She circled around him, rubbing up against him just like a domestic cat begging to be petted. She kept the arrow pointed outward, but she circled him three times.

Still keeping the rifle gripped tightly in his left hand, he reached down with his right, tense and prepared to fight for his life. His fingers touched the top of her head, and her fur, coarse and downy, spread over his skin.

She stilled and arched into his hand. He relaxed just a bit as her purrs filled the air. She twisted her head and licked his palm then scrubbed her face against his hand once more.

Was she tame? Had she been someone's pet? It seemed the only reasonable explanation.

Her back leg buckled, and she sank with a thump onto the ground. His chest tightened with compassion. Such a beautiful, regal animal.

"I need to get you back to my truck," he murmured. "Any bright ideas on how to do that?"

She continued to stare at him, her throat rumbling with her soft purrs. It was an intoxicating sound. But deceptive. It made her seem less wild, and Duncan couldn't afford to underestimate the cat.

He shrugged out of his coat, careful to keep his movements measured and non-threatening. Maybe if he spread the jacket on the ground beside her, she'd crawl onto it and maybe he could drag it back to the truck. Or maybe he was losing his mind.

He crept forward and gingerly arranged the coat on the ground next to the cat, who regarded him with half-closed eyes.

"Go on then," he muttered. "Get on the coat." He could grab the sleeve and still position his body as far away from any teeth or claws as possible.

To his surprise, the cat heaved herself up and padded onto the jacket. She made a tight circle before settling down.

Well, that had been easy.

The cat watched him with uncanny intelligence as he gathered one sleeve in his free hand. The other grasped his rifle, but he knew dragging the heavy cat off the mountain was going to take more effort. He was going to need both hands.

He stood there for a long moment, judging the cat's mood. She seemed complacent enough, but what would she do when he started pulling on the jacket?

The cheetah extended her front paws then laid her head down on the tops and closed her eyes. There was trust in that gesture. Even as the absurd thought crossed his mind, he couldn't discount it.

He took the strap of his rifle and pulled it over his shoulder. He reached behind him to touch the stock, positioning it so he could reach it quickly if needed. His pack would have to stay.

Keeping a wary eye on the cheetah, he bent down and picked up the sleeves of the coat. He gave them an experimental pull, but the cat never stirred.

This was going to be one long-ass walk.

Chapter Two

Duncan stopped to rest and catch his breath. It wasn't that dragging the cat was too arduous, but having to bend over while pulling *and* navigate all the rocks and rises was hell on his back.

Just as he bent to pick up the sleeves and resume the hike to his truck, he heard the snapping sound of someone stepping on a twig.

He automatically reached for his rifle.

"I wouldn't do that if I were you."

Duncan turned warily to see one of the poachers ten yards away, looking at Duncan down the barrel of a rifle. Fuck. He glanced down at the cheetah to see she was still undisturbed, either sleeping or unconscious.

"I just want the cat. Cooperate and you won't get hurt."

Duncan scowled. At least his badge was shoved into his pocket and not visible. That little piece of information would probably get him shot on the spot.

"This your kill?" he asked casually. "I found her about a half a mile back. Wondered how a cheetah got in these mountains."

The man chuckled lightly. "That doesn't concern you. And yes, she's my kill. I'd appreciate it if you backed off."

Duncan kept his hands up and nonthreatening as he took several steps back. An injured cheetah wasn't worth his life, but the fact that this asshole was holding him at gunpoint in order to claim a hide pissed him off to no end.

The hunter moved forward, motioning for Duncan to stay back. "Toss your rifle into those bushes over there," he directed. "And keep moving."

Duncan eased the strap off his shoulder, wrapped his hand around the butt of the stock and tossed the gun as gently as he could into the bush.

"Now, down on your knees. Hands behind your back."

Duncan gritted his teeth but complied.

A few moments later, Duncan felt a coil of rope burn around his wrists as the hunter tied his hands together.

"Just in case you get any ideas about going for your gun," the man murmured.

Son of a bitch. What a mess this had turned out to be. And all because he felt sorry for a fucking cheetah. A cat that shouldn't even be in his mountains.

Duncan tugged at the ropes around his wrists and watched as the hunter walked back to the cheetah. He paused and cautiously nosed the barrel of his rifle down to nudge the cat.

When he got no response, the hunter relaxed. After a quick look in Duncan's direction and apparently deciding he was no threat, the hunter shouldered his rifle, bent to the cheetah and reached for her nape.

The cheetah exploded up, knocking the man back and on his ass. She gave him no time to react. She was on him before he could get his gun up. She latched onto his hand, and his screams filled the air.

Duncan watched in fascinated horror as she treated the man like her own personal chew toy. At one point, the man rolled away, curling himself into a protective ball. The cheetah hissed and stalked a circle around him, prepared to pounce again.

The man scrambled to his feet, evidently deciding he was going to die running. To Duncan's surprise, the cheetah made no effort to pursue him. Instead, she turned her golden stare on Duncan.

Unease prickled up his spine. He was as vulnerable as a trussed up Thanksgiving turkey.

The cheetah circled behind him, and Duncan knew there was little point in trying to stagger up and run. In a foot race with the fastest land animal in the world? Yeah, he had a real shot at winning that one.

He tensed when he felt her teeth graze his hands. He waited, prepared for the pain, prepared to do anything to defend himself.

She began tugging and chewing. At the ropes. Not his hands. Un-fucking-believable. She was freeing him!

A few more tugs and the rope went slack. He pulled his hands to the front and rubbed at his wrists, unable to fathom that she hadn't bitten him.

Carefully, he got to his feet and slowly turned to face her. She regarded him with complacency, as if she hadn't just gone batshit on the hunter. As bizarre as it seemed, his ass had just been saved by a cheetah.

She slumped wearily to the ground, and he knew that the attack had cost her dearly. He felt a pang of guilt and sympathy for the creature.

He walked over to retrieve the jacket, and once again, he spread it beside her. She tried to lift her head, but her strength had fled.

The fear that had earlier taken hold of him vanished. For some strange reason, he knew this cat meant him no harm. She could have easily eaten him a dozen times over, and yet the only aggression she'd shown was toward the hunter.

He reached for her, pulling and turning her until he'd positioned her on the coat. Fatigue was taking its own hold over him, and if he didn't get them both back to his truck, they were going to be spending the night out here.

He trudged over to get his rifle, and this time, he would keep it up and ready.

Dusk was fast approaching by the time Duncan hauled the cheetah to his truck. The air had cooled around him as shadows fell, and the sweat that soaked his clothes covered him in a frigid cloak.

He dropped the jacket sleeves and dug for his cell phone. There was a weak signal but hopefully he could call Doc Robbins, the local vet, and have him come out with a cage and his truck.

He made the call and waited impatiently for an answer. He'd blown the entire day traipsing around the mountain, and now had a cheetah he had no idea what to do with.

When the answering machine picked up, Duncan hung up in irritation. He wasn't going to leave a message for Doc saying he had a damn cheetah he needed taking care of, nor was he going to hang around here until Doc called him back. Which only left taking the cheetah home with him.

He sighed and looked down at the cat, whose eyes were even droopier. Pain glittered in the golden orbs, and that worried him. An injured animal tended to be unreasonable.

Usually he'd unload his rifle, case it, and put it in the back of his truck. But if he was going to ride home with the cheetah in the cab, he was damn well going to keep the gun handy.

With a look at the cheetah and an unspoken "stay" he walked around to the passenger side and pointed the end of the rifle to the floorboard, leaving the stock in the air. He then pushed the passenger seat forward so there would be maximum room in the extra cab.

Leaving the door open, he walked back around to the driver's side where he'd left the cat on the ground. Her tail twitched, and she let out a low purr when she saw him. Sucking up his courage, he squatted down and gingerly extended his hand to her head.

She didn't flinch or draw away from his hand. She didn't move at all. He stroked her fur, and her eyes closed as the purring grew louder.

"Are you up for a ride home?" he murmured. "I need to get you into the truck. We need to get that arrow out of your leg. It has to hurt like hell."

She bumped against his hand then licked his palm. When she struggled to get up, he automatically reached to help her.

He tensed, wondering if he'd just made a huge blunder. But she didn't hiss or growl, nor did she try to make a meal of his arm.

He continued to soothe her, talking nonsense, hoping his tone would keep her calm as he urged her toward the truck door. Though nothing about this day should surprise him at this point, when she docilely crawled into the backseat of the truck, he shook his head and wondered if he'd somehow fallen into the twilight zone.

She settled onto the seat, her body stretched out, eyes closed, paws hanging over the edge. He quickly shut the door in case she changed her mind and decided she didn't like strange, enclosed spaces.

He didn't spare any speed getting home. On the way he called the dispatcher, gave her a description of the poacher and instructed her to put out an APB as well as call all the hospitals or clinics in the area. He really needed to be tracking down the fuckers himself, but there was a little matter of a cheetah in his possession.

After he hung up with dispatch, he called Doc Robbins again. He got no answer and decided to make a quick run by the vet's house just in case he was outside tending animals. Then Duncan could leave the cheetah, and she'd get the care she needed.

He pulled into the driveway of the clinic that doubled as Doc's residence. There was no sign of the beat-up old Suburban, and Duncan sighed. Any other time, Duncan would be tripping over the older man. But now that he needed him, he couldn't find hide nor hair of him.

"Guess you're stuck with me," Duncan muttered in the cheetah's direction as he backed out of the driveway.

A few minutes later, he pulled up to a rustic cabin about two miles out of town. He turned the truck off and got out, quickly shutting the door behind him.

The warm interior of the cabin was a welcome change from the brisk evening air, and his clothing was still damp with sweat. A long, hot shower was a high priority. Just as soon as he got his cheetah squared away.

The back mudroom made the most sense. It wasn't warm or inviting, but he could lock the cheetah in until Doc Robbins could come out.

Would she be hungry? And what did cheetahs eat? Red meat, obviously. He rummaged in the fridge and found a thawed steak he'd planned to eat for dinner. He filled up a bowl with water and set the food and the dish in the mudroom.

Satisfied with his arrangements, he walked back out to the truck and cautiously peered in the window. She was just how he'd left her. He eased open the door, and she picked up her head, pain still evident in her eyes.

She made a low chirping noise that sounded strangely vulnerable. He soothed a hand over her head in an effort to comfort. She closed her eyes and let out a purr.

"Come on, girl. You'll be more comfortable inside. And I have food. A nice, juicy steak."

He pulled slightly at her nape, and she hobbled out of the truck, favoring her leg as she jumped down. Would she follow him? She hadn't been resistant so far.

He started for the house and looked back to see her walking slowly, painfully behind him. He held the door open and felt a moment's relief when she padded inside.

He led her to the mudroom, and when she went inside, he shut the door, locking it behind her. As he walked back to the kitchen where his phone was, he shook his head. What a day. Just when he'd thought he'd seen it all, something always managed to crack that theory.

He called Doc and the answering machine picked up, but this time Duncan left a short message for Doc to call him back as soon as possible. He tossed the phone aside then headed back out to his truck to unload his rifle and bring it in. As he came back in, the phone was ringing, and thinking it could be Doc Robbins, he hurried over to answer.

"Hey Duncan, I hear you had trouble today," his close friend and fellow cop, Nick said.

"Yeah, I ran into some poachers," Duncan replied as he headed toward the bedroom.

"Get a bead on them?"

"Yeah, I already gave Mandy a description of one of the assholes. I'll follow up on the others when I come in tomorrow morning. They weren't from around here, not that I'm surprised by that."

"Figure out what they were hunting?"

Duncan paused. "Yeah, I did."

"And?"

"I'll talk to you about it tomorrow. I'm kind of beat. Long day."

"Everything okay, man?"

"Yeah, just tired. I'm gonna hit the shower and head to bed. I'll see you in the morning."

After hanging up, he trudged to the bathroom, already salivating over the idea of a hot shower.

For several long minutes, he stood under the hot spray, letting it wash over him. He cracked a grin as he soaped his big body. A cheetah. He had a fucking cheetah in his mudroom. It didn't get any more bizarre than that. He was going to take pictures because Nick would never believe him otherwise.

He took his time drying off and dressing. When he'd finished, he went into the living room to start a fire. His house was small, but it was his, and it was in his dream spot. He owned the acre of land the house sat on, and the view from his back deck was something you only found on postcards.

When the fire was crackling and a nice blaze had caught, he walked back to the kitchen, intent on fixing something to eat. The steak he'd planned was out, but he could make do with a sandwich.

Thoughts of the cheetah, and curiosity, niggled at him. Had she eaten? Was she in a lot of pain? Was she pacing the room, eager to be free?

Finally, he put the sandwich down and walked over to the door. A peek wouldn't hurt.

He cracked the door and eased it open. A single light bulb hung from the ceiling, bathing the small space in a harsh glow. But when he looked across the floor, it wasn't a cheetah that he saw.

All the air escaped his lungs in a gigantic what-the-fuck whoosh. He staggered against the door and had to grope for the doorknob to steady himself.

Lying on the floor curled into a protective ball, an arrow protruding from her thigh, was a naked *woman*.

Chapter Three

Duncan nearly shut the door, but the woman stirred, and the same golden eyes of the cheetah stared back at him. Fear flashed in her gaze, and she gathered her arms protectively around herself, feebly trying to shield her nudity. He could see her shiver, and blood trickled down her leg.

Her discomfort moved him to action, despite the argument he waged with his sanity.

"Holy Mother of God," he muttered as he knelt beside her.

She shrank away from him, and a sound of fright rushed past her lips.

"Shhh, I won't hurt you," he soothed. He reached for her, to touch her, to offer comfort in some way.

She tensed when his hand rested on her shoulder, but she didn't flinch away. Wide, frightened eyes regarded him questioningly.

"I won't hurt you," he said again. "I'm here to help you."

She relaxed the smallest fraction underneath his fingertips, and the fear in her expression turned to pain.

"Who are you?" he murmured. *What are you?*

Her mouth opened, and she licked her lips. A hoarse sound rose from her throat, and she frowned. Her hand gripped her neck and massaged. She seemed to have difficulty speaking.

He felt sudden guilt for having placed her in the mudroom. It was cold and uncomfortable, but Christ, he'd thought she was a cheetah. She *was* a cheetah. Cheetahs had fur. This woman was naked. Very naked. And very beautiful.

"Don't speak," he said firmly when she opened her mouth again. "Let me get you into the living room where you can warm up."

"The arrow," she whispered. "It has to come out."

Her low voice slid over him with a shock. He couldn't place the accent.

He curled his arms underneath her body and carefully lifted her, trying hard not to jar her wound. A small moan leaked from her lips as he shifted her against his chest.

"I'm sorry."

She didn't respond. Just let her head sag against his shoulder.

He carried her into the living room and marveled at the fact that she probably weighed more as a cat than she did as a human—was she human? Could you call someone who had been a cheetah just an hour ago a human?

"You can stretch out on the couch in front of the fire. I'll get you something to cover up with and take a look at that arrow."

"Thank you."

The two simple words sounded exceedingly heartfelt, and he could feel the ache behind them. With extreme care, he laid her on her side on the couch then reached for the afghan hanging over the back. Her skin was ice cold to the touch. Again he felt a pang of guilt for having stuffed her in the mudroom.

He arranged the blanket over the upper part of her body and over her behind to give her enough modesty while keeping the material a good six inches from the arrow. She clutched the ends of the afghan and pulled it tighter to her chin.

Without thought, he ran his hand through her hair, pushing it from her face to behind her ear. She was beautiful. Stunningly so.

And she was a cheetah.

He yanked his hand away and rocked back on his heels. There would be time to have his meltdown later. Maybe after he'd gotten the arrow out of her leg. Jesus. How was he going to get it out without filleting her leg? He needed a doctor, but how on earth was he going to explain how she had gotten an arrow in her leg? Not to mention if he took her to the hospital and they did blood work, wouldn't it come back all funky because she wasn't human?

He could just see the tabloid headlines.

"What are you?" he asked softly. "Where did you come from?"

The bronze-colored flecks in her eyes sharpened and glowed as she gazed at him. He could see the cheetah in her, knew it was there no matter how crazy it sounded.

She searched his face as if trying to decide whether she could trust him. Evidently she decided she couldn't because uncertainty flooded her eyes, and she looked down. Interesting. The cheetah trusted him. The woman did not.

"My name is Aliyah Carver," she said.

Well, that was something he supposed.

He glanced down at the wound in her leg. The broadhead was completely embedded in her thigh, probably resting against bone. No way for him to push it through, not that he would. Retracting it would be damn near impossible.

"Pull it out," she said calmly. "I will heal."

"Goddamn, do you have any idea how much that'll hurt?"

She nodded solemnly. "There is no other way. I can't go to a hospital. It isn't necessary. Once the arrow is removed, my wound will heal rapidly."

She relayed it so matter-of-factly. Clearly she had no idea how much a broadhead would make her bleed. And the pain. Jesus. He wasn't the only one having a serious issue with reality.

"I know you don't understand, but you have to trust me. The wound will heal. The arrow must be removed quickly."

"Like you trust me?" he asked pointedly.

She flushed. "I can't afford to trust anyone."

That was fair. If he were a cheetah, he guessed there wouldn't be a whole lot of people he could trust with that little tidbit.

He rubbed a hand through his hair. "Do you want a drink at least?" Hell, he could use one.

"Alcohol will impede the healing. I need my senses about me. It will require my full concentration."

He shook his head, a little sick at what he must do.

"Just do it," she begged. "Don't make me wait. The anticipation is the worst part."

He nodded grimly. If she could be so stoic, then he damn sure wasn't going to be a pussy. He got to his feet and stared down at the arrow. When he glanced back to her, he saw she'd closed her eyes, strain etched into her forehead.

He would do this quickly. There was no need for her to suffer the agony of waiting. He reached down and grasped the arrow just below the fletching. He sucked in a deep breath. His nerves screamed like a girl.

Not wanting to delay any longer, he yanked with all his strength.

Her cry ripped right through his gut as he stumbled backward, the arrow in his hand. Blood poured from the wound, spilling onto his hardwood floor.

He dropped the arrow and fell to his knees in front of her. He yanked the afghan down to press on the wound in an effort to staunch the flow of blood. Goddamn it, he'd known this was a bad idea. How the hell was he going to explain a woman bleeding to death in his living room?

A low sob reached his ears. He reached for her, dragging her into his arms. "God, I'm sorry."

She buried her face in his neck and held on tightly as pain quivered through her body. Then, as if remembering the blood, she rocketed from his arms and scrambled to a sitting position.

"I'm sorry. I'm getting blood everywhere. All over your floor."

He saw the paleness of her face, the evidence of shock in her eyes. Very gently, he put his hands on her shoulders and pushed her back down.

He gingerly pulled the blanket back so he could assess the damage. Amazingly, the blood had slowed to a small trickle. The flesh was open, raw and red. Angry. But the arrow should have caused a hell of a lot more injury. It was designed to inflict as much damage coming out as it did going in.

"Stay right here. I'll get some towels and something for you to wear," he said.

She looked down, as if just remembering her nudity. A bright blush worked across her smooth skin, and she reached self-consciously for the afghan that had fallen away and pulled it higher around her body.

It was a sight he wasn't likely to forget. A beautiful, vulnerable woman with tawny hair and golden eyes curled on his couch with a blood-soaked blanket wrapped around her like a shield. Hell of an image.

Duncan left the living room in need of a stiff drink. Maybe two. He prided himself on being a highly logical, no-bullshit law enforcement professional. He didn't believe in hocus-pocus woo-woo crap. But he knew two things. One, he'd locked a cheetah with an arrow in her haunch in his mudroom. Two, when he'd walked back in, a naked woman, also with an arrow in her thigh, had replaced the cheetah.

As much as he'd love to tell himself he was way overworked, in need of a break and that he was highly delusional, he knew it wasn't the case. He was as sane as the next person.

And if he wasn't insane, then he had to face the fact that the world as he knew it didn't exist.

He hurriedly collected a first-aid kit, towels and one of his T-shirts. When he returned, she was lying on the couch, eyes closed, her breaths coming in shallow bursts.

"Aliyah," he said softly.

Her eyes opened and once again, he was struck by the beauty of her gaze, how mesmerizing those golden eyes were.

He knelt in front of the couch and gently pulled the blanket away from her wound. Already it was smaller, but it still looked angry. Blood oozed at a much slower rate, but she was still losing too much.

He set to work bandaging the wound and did his best to ignore the curves of her body, tempting though they were. When he'd finished, he handed her the T-shirt. "Do you need help getting it on?" he asked.

She shook her head and pushed herself to a sitting position. He stood and discreetly turned his back, though he'd already gotten a view of her breasts.

Was he honest-to-God lusting over a cat? No, she wasn't just a cat. She was a woman. A breathtakingly gorgeous woman.

Who also happened to be a cat.

"I'm finished."

Her husky voice tingled over his ears, and he slowly turned back around. She sat on the couch, leaning away from her injured leg. Her hair was tousled, just the right amount of "messed up" to look incredibly sexy. Her eyes held an almost drugged look, a mixture of incredible fatigue and shock, he was sure. Wearing his T-shirt as she was, she looked just like a woman might after an afternoon of making love.

"Aliyah...we need to talk."

Worry flashed in her eyes. He didn't want her to be afraid of him, but he wasn't sure how to offer her reassurance that he had no intention of hurting her, or betraying her secret. It wasn't like he could go announcing to the world that he harbored a cheetah-woman. No one would believe him, and he could kiss his job as sheriff good-bye.

Her lips parted then closed again in agitation. "You deserve answers. I know."

He nodded.

She closed her eyes and pushed her hand through her long hair. "Ask then. I'll try to answer what I can."

He stuffed his hands in his jeans pocket and squared his shoulders. "Let's start with you telling me who you are—*what* you are."

Chapter Four

Aliyah felt at a distinct disadvantage, and she didn't like it. The man standing in front of her was intimidating. His gentleness didn't fool her a bit. He was what her people would call a warrior. A protector. If he were one of her people, only the fiercest of animals could be chosen by the spirit guide to accompany him on his life journey.

"You haven't told me your name," she said in an attempt to buy some time. She didn't feel comfortable revealing too much of herself to this man. Hers was a life of secrecy. She was very careful of whom she trusted. He hadn't tried to harm her, but she couldn't be sure of his intentions.

He eased down on one knee in front of her. "My name is Duncan Kennedy. I'm the sheriff here. I only want to help you, Aliyah. But in order to do that, you have to tell me what the hell is going on."

Law enforcement. She felt a shaft of fear invade her chest, and the cheetah inside her stirred. Her skin came alive, itchy, uncomfortable, and she fought the urge to change. She swallowed and tried to calm her nerves.

"What the hell just happened?" he demanded.

She looked at him in confusion.

"Your eyes. They changed. Just for a moment, but I'm not crazy."

Automatically, she closed them and turned her head away. He reached out, curled his fingers around her chin and tugged until she faced him again.

"Open your eyes," he said.

Reluctantly, she obeyed. His thumb stroked over her jaw as he stared intently at her. The chill she'd long fought waned, and she was unsure of whether it was because of his touch or his gaze. She felt warmed by both. The rough pad of his thumb scraped across her skin, sending a shiver racing down her neck that contrasted with the heat that bloomed under her flesh.

"It was the cheetah, wasn't it? You were about to change."

There was a bit of wonder in his voice, as if he were still coming to terms with what she was. Slowly, she nodded.

"When I feel frightened or threatened, the cheetah stirs within me. It's a protective instinct."

His brow furrowed. "What frightened you?"

"You're a cop," she said in a low voice. "You'll want to take me in. Turn me over to some government agency for testing."

He gave her a fierce frown. "That's not true. The only way I'd take you in is if you've broken the law. So far, all I know is that you were being hunted by poachers. That makes you the victim, not a perpetrator. Is there something you want to tell me?"

His eyes were expectant, piercing, like he could peel back her skin and see inside. It made her uneasy.

"They took me," she said simply. Her breath caught and hovered as she relived the terror of that day.

"Took you? How?"

She trembled, and his hand slid from her chin to her shoulder. Warm, comforting. Without thinking, she leaned further into his touch, wanting to be closer but afraid all at the same time.

"I won't let anyone hurt you," he said soothingly.

Sincerity reflected in his warm brown eyes. The hard lines of his face contrasted with the softness in his gaze. He was a man accustomed to harshness, to doing what it took to get the job done. While he was doing his best to put her at ease, she could well imagine how quickly he could turn, how unforgiving he could be with a criminal.

His other hand rasped over his short hair in a gesture of frustration. He was losing patience with her. Again, she felt the tingle of awareness as the cheetah rose and sought to take over. She shrank away from his touch, hoping to better control the urge to shift. She had been the cheetah for so long that her human form felt alien.

Duncan swore and snatched his hands away from her. He placed them on the edge of the couch and stared directly at her.

"Aliyah, I won't harm you. In your place I'd be scared too. I wouldn't trust anyone. You've been through hell. I want to help you. What can I do to make you believe that?"

The simple sincerity in his voice broke through the prickle of fear skirting down her spine. She took a deep breath and sagged. She hurt. She glanced down at her wound, frustrated to see that it was not yet completely healed. Staying in her cheetah form for so long had been physically demanding.

"It hurts," she said. "I'm unused to it. I don't normally take this long to heal. I'm not sure what to do to help it."

"Is there nothing you can take that will help? Do pain relievers not affect you?" he asked in a concerned voice.

She shrugged. "I do not know. I've never had to use them. We heal naturally and at a much faster rate than normal humans." She shivered again as another chill took over.

Duncan moved forward, his hands gently pushing her more upright. She glanced at him in confusion as he settled on the couch beside her. When he wrapped his arms around her, she panicked, not because she feared him, but because raw awareness gripped her as his warmth bled into her body.

"You're cold," he said.

He tucked the blanket carefully around her, making sure he didn't jostle her leg.

She relaxed against his body and let her head fall back against his chest. Weariness pulled at her. Her body ached.

Remembering she was supposed to be providing him answers, she opened her mouth to speak again. She was momentarily sidetracked as his arms tightened around her chest, and he rubbed his hands up and down her arms.

It felt good. So good. And she told him so.

His hands paused in their movement for a moment, and she could feel the slight catch in his breath. Could he feel it too? This pull between them?

"What were you going to say?" he murmured.

She searched her cloudy brain for what exactly she'd intended to tell him but came up blank.

"You said they took you. Who took you? And how?"

She shrank further into his arms, and he started sliding his hands up and down again in a soothing motion.

She searched her mind for what she could safely tell him without divulging too much.

"When I was younger, my parents moved us to Africa. As a child, I spent more time in my animal form than the other young of my kind. My parents feared I would be discovered. As I grew older, it became easier to control my shifts, and so we moved back to our home in Alaska.

"I had returned to Africa for a visit. It had been too long since I ran with the other cheetahs."

She closed her eyes as she conjured the memories of racing across the savannah, the wind in her face, the dry, parched earth pounding underneath her paws. There, she'd been free. Truly free. And ironically enough, it was where her freedom had ended.

"I was netted and then sedated by the poachers. They shipped me back to the U.S., and I was quartered with other exotic animals. For weeks I was kept in a cage, and then, finally, they turned me out to hunt."

A light shudder worked its way over her shoulders, and Duncan's hands tensed against her skin.

"So that's their set-up? They import animals to hunt here in the States?"

She nodded. "They charge exorbitant fees for trophy hunts. Instead of taking the hunter to Africa, they bring Africa to the hunter."

Duncan stiffened in anger. She could feel the rage radiating from his body.

"Son of a bitch," he swore. "God only knows how long they've been pulling this shit in my mountains. I fucking hate poachers."

Then as if fearing he'd frightened her, he relaxed his grip and turned her chin so she could see him in her periphery.

"I'm sorry."

She offered a faint smile. "They make me angry as well. What they do is not honorable."

"They could have killed you," he said hoarsely. "They *tried* to kill you."

"You saved me." She shifted in his arms so she could see him better. Then she reached up to touch his cheek with her hand. "Thank you."

Their gazes connected and locked.

"I don't understand what you are," he said. "If I hadn't seen it, I'd never believe it in a thousand years. And yet, you are a cheetah. How is that possible?"

She dropped her gaze then turned away once more, settling her back against his chest.

"I don't know the answers to your questions. I only know what I am. How is not so important, is it?"

He sighed in frustration, and she wilted just a little more. She was so tired, she physically ached. She needed rest. It would help in the healing.

"I need to sleep," she said. "I've not slept a full night since I was taken by the hunters." And for one night, she wanted to feel safe. Indulge in the soft comfort of a bed instead of a cold cage.

"You can have my bed," he said as he eased from behind her.

She was too tired to argue, and she wanted that bed badly enough that she wouldn't offer up any false protests about putting him out.

When she tried to get up herself, Duncan stopped her with a firm hand. Then he reached down and lifted her from the couch. She clung to his neck as he walked out of the living room and into a large bedroom.

He settled her down on his bed, and she sighed in sheer bliss when her head hit the pillow. She rolled to her side and pulled at the hem of the T-shirt. Not giving any thought to the fact he stood but a foot away, she lifted the T-shirt over her head and tossed it away.

The material irritated her skin. She'd gone so long with no clothing, the slightest touch set her nerve endings afire. Her eyes were already closing when he tried to pull the covers over her body.

She put her hand down. "No. Don't. I can't bear it."

"You'll freeze," he said.

"The material scrapes at my skin," she murmured.

He was silent for a moment, and then she heard him walk away. A few seconds later, he returned, and she felt the soft brush of fur over her body.

She clutched at it, holding it close.

"It's a bear skin," he said a little uncomfortably.

"Papa," she murmured as she snuggled deeper into the fur.

Duncan said something else, but she was sliding under.

Chapter Five

Duncan paced back and forth in front of the fireplace, his mind ablaze with the day's drama. A cheetah. She was a fucking cheetah. As mind-blowing events went, this one topped the list.

Apart from the fact that he had a beautiful, naked cheetah-woman camped out in his bed, he also had to deal with the fact that poachers were turning out animals to hunt in his mountains.

And to think he'd lamented the fact that nothing exciting ever happened in Elk Ridge.

His first priority... Hell, what was his first priority? He had an injured chee...woman. What was he supposed to do with her? And he had poachers to catch and make damn sure their days of importing exotic animals were over.

He spun around, took two steps toward the bedroom then stopped and walked back to the fireplace again. The bedroom was out. She was in his bed. Naked. There was only so much temptation a red-blooded man could take, and a voluptuous, golden-eyed goddess laid out like a Christmas present might well be construed a temptation.

He flexed his fingers then curled them until the skin stretched and whitened across his knuckles.

A sound from the bedroom had him yanking his head around.

He strode out of the living room and rounded the corner into his room. He caught the door frame with his hand as he came to a halt.

His breath stuck in his throat, swelled and rebounded into his chest.

The fur he had covered Aliyah with was bunched around her feet. She lay on her hip, but her upper body was twisted so that her back was pressed to the bed. Her left arm was thrown wide to the side, and her right hand was curled into a fist at her shoulder.

She was...quite beautiful, even in her state of distress. Apart from the inflamed-looking wound on her leg, her skin was unmarred by a single blemish. Slender legs led up to rounded hips, a tiny waist and two spectacularly formed breasts.

Jesus, they were perfect. She was perfect.

Gently rounded nipples, a soft peach color, so soft looking that he caught himself swallowing as he imagined tasting them.

He closed his eyes. He couldn't go there. He was turning to leave when she moaned again. As he looked back over at her, he could see a sheen of sweat glistening on her forehead. Her head twisted from side to side, and then her eyes blinked open.

They glittered gold, and the pupils elongated and shrank to a vertical sliver. Her muscles twitched and jumped, and he realized she was fighting against her instinct to shift.

Unsure of whether he should stay or whether he should get the hell out of the bedroom and lock the door, he stood there not knowing whether to shit or go blind.

Her distress decided things for him.

He hurried to the bed and knelt over her. "Aliyah," he whispered urgently. "Aliyah, wake up, honey." He reached down to touch her damp face. Tenderly, he pushed a tendril of golden hair behind her ear, and she nuzzled her cheek into his palm.

Her eyelids fluttered, and he breathed in relief when he saw her eyes were back to normal.

"Duncan?"

"I'm here," he said. Then he looked down and realized his hand still rested against her cheek. He started to pull it away, but she caught his fingers in his hand.

"No, don't go," she said. "Please."

To his utter astonishment, she reached over and wrapped her arms around his waist then proceeded to snuggle into his body as tightly as she could go. Oh hell.

He relaxed on the bed to alleviate the awkwardness of the position, which sent her seeking further into his arms.

"It's been so long," she whispered.

"Since what?" he asked as he smoothed her hair with his hand.

"Since I felt another's touch on my skin." She rubbed her cheek over his chest and then impatiently shoved at his shirt, raising it so she could press her face to his bare skin.

She ran her hands up his ribcage and over his chest as if she couldn't get enough. Her warm lips glanced over the hollow, and he groaned as his cock, which had jumped to attention the moment she touched him, swelled painfully in his jeans.

"Aliyah. *Aliyah*," he said louder when she ignored him. "Honey, you have to stop." He tried to pry her away, but he didn't want to hurt her. He grasped her wrists and pulled just as her lips met the column of his neck. "God." It came out more as a groan than an actual word.

"Touch me."

"Aliyah...we can't...don't do that...ah damn it."

Her lips whispered close to his ear, and she nibbled delicately at the lobe.

"Touch me," she whispered again. "Please." She captured her hands in his and raised them to her breasts.

He might have resisted even that, though the weight of the soft mounds resting against his palms made his fingers itch to rub over her nipples, but when she reached down and slid her hand between his legs to cup the discernible bulge there, he was lost.

"Slow down, sweetheart," he said. "I don't want to hurt you. We have to take it easy. Your wound isn't healed."

He groaned even as he said it. Surely this qualified him for sainthood. He had his arms full of a curvaceous hellcat intent on rubbing herself over every inch of his body and he was saying shit like *let's slow down.*

He might as well cut off his dick and throw it out the window.

With a delicious-sounding purr, she arched her body and slid along his chest until her breasts bumped him right in the mouth. Unable to resist such a sweet offering, he nipped at the swell then lapped at the nipple with his tongue.

She threaded her fingers into the hair at his nape and pulled him closer until he sucked the tender bud into his mouth.

"Yes," she whimpered.

No longer able to fool himself into thinking they'd be taking anything slow, he wrapped his arms around her and lowered her to the bed. He was tugging at his jeans while she yanked at his shirt. And then he had an awful thought.

Oh Jesus, let him have something. He shot off the bed and hurried into the bathroom to yank open the drawer. Hallelujah. One half-empty box of condoms. He hoped like hell the damn things didn't expire because it had been a while since he'd used them.

When he returned, Aliyah was spread out all over his bed, her lips parted, hair splayed out on his pillow, and those delectable nipples were puckered and just waiting for his mouth.

Her gaze wandered down his body, and he felt himself harden further when her eyes glittered in appreciation. He wasn't a vain son of a bitch, but when a beautiful woman looked at you and liked what they saw, it definitely added two inches to your dick.

He tossed the condoms onto the nightstand and then crawled onto the bed beside her. The wound on her thigh was still red and angry, so he bent down and kissed the area just above it.

Her hand tangled in his hair and coaxed him away to the rest of her body. He was hard and impatient, and he was positively itching to get between her legs. But he figured the quickest way to fall out of grace with a woman who practically threw herself at you was to make it all end in three minutes flat.

As he lowered his body carefully to hers, she moaned in pleasure.

"You feel so good," she murmured as her hands ran over his back. "Hard, strong. My people would call you a warrior."

"I'm hard all right, sweetheart, and it has nothing to do with being a warrior."

She giggled, and then he lost his breath when she reached between them and curled her hand around his cock.

"Honey, if you have any desire to make this last, if you want me to touch you as you so very prettily asked, you need to move your hand."

With a sensual smile, she complied. "I do want you to touch me. Everywhere. With your hands. Your mouth. And then I want you to take me. Hard. Fast. I use to lie in the cage at night and dream of being human again. Of having a man's hands on my skin. Touching me. Loving me. Of having him fill me again and again."

Dear God, he wasn't going to survive this.

"I guess I better be damn glad another man didn't find you then," he gritted out.

She pulled him down so that their mouths met. Hot, wet and lusty, their tongues met, and he tasted her. Golden. Like she looked. Warm like sunshine.

"Not any other man," she gasped between kisses. "Only a warrior. Like you."

He wasn't sure he really believed that any man wouldn't have done in a pinch, but her words were a salve to his ego. No man liked to believe he could be substituted on a whim. Even if it were true.

Impatiently, she pulled his head down to her breasts. He smiled and lazily ran his tongue around one of the taut little buds. She shivered, and he glanced up at her face.

"You like that, sweetheart?"

She nodded.

He liked it too.

He toyed with the nipples, enjoying the velvety texture against his work-roughened skin. Soft, like her. The plump mound of her breast moved with each stroke.

No longer able to keep from tasting, he bent and sucked the nipple into his mouth. She arched into him with a gasp. He sucked and nibbled, alternating gentle sweeps of his tongue with a sharp nip of his teeth.

His little kitten enjoyed the pain.

When he released her breast, her nipple was red and erect, a direct contrast to the other that still lay untouched. It was a matter he'd quickly rectify.

As he captured the second nipple in his mouth, he slid his hand down her belly and into the soft curls between her legs. She opened to him immediately, and his fingers delved into her damp core.

"Duncan," she murmured, and he felt a keen sense of satisfaction as his name spilled from her lips.

His fingers slid easily through her folds, gliding over her clit and to the opening below. One finger eased inside, and he damn near came as he imagined what it would feel like as it closed over his cock. Hot. Silky. Wet. The ultimate paradise.

She sucked at his finger, wrapping tightly around the tip. Sweat broke out over his body. God, she was small. He couldn't wait to dive in.

But first he wanted to give her what she wanted.

Willing himself to maintain control, he eased down the bed and began at her feet. He rubbed the soles while he took each tiny toe into his mouth, sucking lightly in turn. She twitched every time he hit a sensitive spot but he held firm, forcing her to let him have his way.

When he'd finished with her feet, he kissed a line up the inside of each leg. He took special care around her injury and pressed his lips in a circular pattern around it.

He bypassed her pussy, which incited a protest from her. He just grinned and ran his tongue around the shallow indention of her navel.

"I'm saving the best for last," he murmured.

He played with her breasts, nibbling and licking, and enjoying every sound of pleasure that she made. He loved the contrast between the tightness of her nipples and the lush softness of her breasts. Then he imagined sleeping with his head pillowed on them. Wasn't that every guy's fantasy?

He followed the curve of her shoulder to the column of her neck and to the tender skin below her ear. For a moment, he toyed with the lobe and grinned when he felt little chill bumps race across her skin.

When he finally made it back to her lips, she kissed him ravenously, her arms circling his neck and locking him into place. She fed from him; there was no other way to put it.

He returned her kisses, enjoying her passion and her excitement. He couldn't remember ever making love to a woman who was so responsive, so eager for everything he could give her. It was damn addicting.

With reluctance, he pulled away from the sweetness of her lips and slowly moved down her body again. She trembled, and he smiled because he knew she knew what he would do next.

He lay there at her side, stroking the golden curls between her legs with gentle fingers. Light and teasing, he petted, gradually growing bolder, going deeper.

The plump flesh there enticed him, made him want to explore further. He wanted to taste her, feed from her. With two fingers, he parted the layers and sent a third finger seeking within.

Whisper soft, he touched, stroked and touched again, enjoying how her clit grew erect and taut, how she shook every time he rubbed her just right.

With his free hand, he reached down and circled his cock with his fingers. As he continued to stroke her, he stroked himself, enjoying the pleasure and imagining how it would feel when her pussy was doing the stroking.

He glanced up at her to see her watching him through half-lidded, passion-glazed eyes.

"Do you see what you do to me?" he asked huskily.

She licked her lips, and he damn near came in his hand. He yanked his hand away, but his cock remained painfully erect, bobbing away from his body.

"I want to taste you," she said.

He groaned. "Honey, there isn't much I'd like better, but if you're going to wrap that sweet mouth of yours around my dick, I want to be in a state where I can enjoy it. If you go anywhere near me with that tongue, I'll be done for."

She pouted, sticking that luscious bottom lip out. Damn if he didn't want to go nibble on it again. But there were other parts of her body he wanted to feast on first.

Ignoring the ache between his legs and the fact that he was so damn hard he feared splitting his cock at the seams, he rotated over her hips so that his face was just inches above the wispy blonde curls at the apex of her thighs.

"Spread those legs for me, beautiful. Careful, and don't hurt your wound."

Slowly she shifted, lifting her uninjured leg so that her glistening pink flesh was bared to his view. He lowered his head, pressed his tongue to her opening and licked upward in one motion, sliding over her clit, then pausing there.

She cried out and fisted her hands in his hair. He chuckled between her legs. "Let up on the hair, sweetheart. You're going to yank me bald."

She eased her grip, and he ran his tongue in tight circles around the straining little nub of flesh. It had always amazed him how much of a woman's passion was wrapped up in one tiny bundle of nerves.

You could bring a woman to orgasm in thirty seconds flat with just the right amount of stimulation.

Or you could take it nice and slow, just like he planned to, and build and back off, build and back off until she was begging. There wasn't much to be said about getting off in thirty seconds, anyway.

He sucked gently at her clit until she whimpered and squirmed beneath him. Then he wandered down to the tight little opening and rimmed it with his tongue. He spread her wider with his fingers and slid his tongue inside, tasting her warm honey.

"Duncan! Oh please," she gasped.

He smiled.

He eased one finger inside her pussy while his tongue lapped upward again. Like velvet, her pussy clung to his finger, cradled it as he worked deeper. Then he found the area he was seeking, slightly rougher and different in texture than the slick walls of her vagina.

He crooked his finger upward, and she cried out, her head coming up.

"Duncan!"

He sucked at her quivering button and worked his finger in a slow back and forth motion until she writhed beneath him. He knew she was close to coming when every single part of her pussy convulsed and tightened around his finger.

Only the knowledge that he wanted her to come with him, wanted her exploding around his cock, had him pulling away.

She whimpered her disappointment, but he grinned and worked his way back up her body with tender kisses.

When he got to her mouth, she fastened greedily on him then paused for a slight second as she tasted herself on his tongue. He deepened the kiss, the idea that they were sharing her essence between them sending spasms of desire coursing through his body.

"I want you."

Those were beautiful words coming from deliciously swollen lips.

He glanced down their bodies and grimaced. There just wasn't an easy way to do this. He sure as hell didn't want her screaming in agony when he bumped her leg. He wanted her screaming for a completely different reason.

"What's wrong?" she asked with a frown. "You don't want me?"

He laughed. God, what else could he do? Not want her? He was going to fucking implode if he didn't have her, and soon.

"I don't know how we're going to pull this off, sweetheart. That leg is going to hurt no matter how I go about it."

She put a hand on his chest and pushed at him. With a frown, he let her move him away as she slowly worked her body until she was lying on her stomach.

With a deep breath, her fingers curled tightly around the sheets, she heaved her body upward until she was on her knees.

"Oh honey, no, don't," he said, not wanting to cause her any pain.

She turned to stare at him over her shoulder, her eyes glittering bright gold. "Take me."

Those two words sent an edgy need crawling over his skin until it was tight and uncomfortable. She leaned forward, her ass stuck in the air, her legs parted so that her pussy was open to his gaze, his hands, his cock...

With the wound facing outward, and the need to spread her wide gone, it just might work. His cock was screaming at him to mount up, but he didn't want to hurt her. So he eased behind her, grasping her hips in his hands. And then he remembered the condom.

"Give me just a second, honey." He rolled off the bed and grabbed one of the condoms, ripping the package open with his teeth and fumbling with the wrapper. In another two seconds, he had the condom rolled on, and he repositioned himself behind her.

As he guided himself toward her opening, he briefly wondered if this would work. She was small. He wasn't. While he worried he'd hurt her, he also looked forward to how she'd feel all wrapped around his cock like a vise.

His hands smoothed over her ass, kneading and fondling as he spread her wider. When the tip of his dick touched her wetness, he had to close his eyes and pray for control.

Inch by inch he moved forward. He clenched his teeth as he worked inside her. She moaned and convulsed around him. She tried to move back, wanting more of him, but he staved her off with his hands.

"I don't want to hurt you, sweetheart," he managed to rasp out.

Her head came up, and she looked back at him, her bottom lip sucked between her teeth. "Fuck me, Duncan."

Oh hell. Her words acted like a whip and spurred him to action. He surged forward, burying himself deep inside her. When he looked down, he saw he still had two inches to go. He'd get there. He just had to coax her into accepting more of him.

He pulled back and thrust again then looked down to make sure he wasn't jarring her wound too badly. She didn't seem to care, though. She moved back to meet his thrust and strained against him.

"I want you to take all of me," he gritted out. "Can you do that, Aliyah? Can you take all of my cock?"

She shuddered at the erotic words and lowered her head so that his angle of penetration was better.

He withdrew and thrust again. This time harder. She took another inch.

He closed his eyes and held her there for a moment, simply enjoying the sensation of so much silky, wet flesh surrounding his dick. When she stirred impatiently underneath him, he began thrusting. Lightly at first and then harder with each thrust.

With a soft cry, she opened more for him. He could feel her pussy gently give way and accept him, and the globes of her ass met his abdomen. God almighty, there wasn't another feeling like this in the world.

His body took over. He began hammering forward, his mind wrapped in a cloud of euphoric pleasure. She tightened around him, her body shook, and he could hear her whimpers and the sweet little sighs escape her mouth.

He cursed the condom. He wanted to feel her skin on skin. He wanted to erupt inside her, wanted to see his seed trickle out of her pussy when he was done.

He felt her let go, heard her scream, and then felt a burst of wetness surround him as she orgasmed. It spurred his own. His balls tightened painfully. He swelled as his orgasm rose, raced up his cock. With one more hard lunge and a shout, he buried himself deep in her body and felt himself turn inside out.

He rested there on his knees, slumped against her ass as his cock jerked and spasmed with the last of his release. He hoped to hell he hadn't reopened her wound or hurt her.

He glanced down and ran a gentle hand over the injury to make sure she wasn't bleeding. Then he carefully eased out of her body.

Her legs trembling, she turned on her good side and collapsed onto the bed. He yanked the condom off and aimed it at a nearby trash can. Then he crawled up beside her and gathered her in his arms.

"That was..." She seemed to struggle over just the right words. He could understand her difficulty, because damn if he could put words to what had just happened between them. "Duncan, that was so wonderful," she whispered.

She nestled into him, her body limp and warm. She made contented little sounds against his neck, and he thought maybe he had truly died and gone to heaven. This...this was perfection.

"Rest now, honey," he murmured against her ear.

He smoothed back her hair, stroking the strands with his fingers as she closed her eyes and melted against him. When he was certain she was asleep, he carefully reached behind him to turn off the lamp and then wrapped himself back around her.

This wasn't exactly how he envisioned the night going, but he damn sure wasn't going to complain. He still hadn't figured out what the hell he was going to do with her, but he guessed there would be plenty of time to figure that out tomorrow.

Chapter Six

Duncan awoke before dawn as was his usual habit, only this morning he wasn't in any hurry to get out of bed. Aliyah lay in the crook of his arm, her arm thrown across his chest. Strands of her hair tickled his nose, and he reached up to brush them away.

She was the calmest he'd seen her since discovering her in the mudroom. Her breaths came deep and even, and there was no muscle twitching to signal an impending shift. Apparently sex and good sleep cured all things.

He lay there enjoying the feel of a woman in his arms. The darkness in the room began to fade as dawn crept through the window. He had to get up soon. There were reports to file, poachers to catch, and there was the matter of Aliyah.

There was still little he knew about her other than the fact she was only half human. She'd mentioned family and that she'd lived in Alaska. And that she'd been in Africa when she'd been taken by the hunters.

He frowned when the thought occurred to him that she hadn't asked to contact her family. If she had been a captive for six months, wouldn't she want to be reunited with her family? Wouldn't she want them not to worry any longer?

The idea that she'd been so reticent bothered him. Not that she owed him anything, but he wanted her to trust him.

His mood turned thoughtful, and he inched his way out of bed and headed for the shower. As the warm water sluiced over his body, he wracked his brain for a solution to the predicament he and Aliyah faced.

Aliyah would have to stay here, and that made him nervous. His work would take a few hours at the least, and leaving her alone that long didn't sit well. But he couldn't take her with him. He could just see it. Something would set her off, she'd freak out and *poof*. Cheetah unleashed in the sheriff's department.

He finished scrubbing and stepped out, grabbed a towel and walked naked into the bedroom, wiping at his hair. When he pulled the towel away from his head, he glanced over to see Aliyah staring at him with sleepy eyes.

Neither spoke. He quickly wrapped the towel around his waist then crossed the room and sat down on the edge of the bed.

"I have to go into work," he said, breaking the silence. "Will you be okay here...alone?"

She studied him for a moment, her head cocked, her golden eyes lighting over his skin. "You're really asking if I'll still be here when you get back."

He stared at her for a moment then slowly nodded.

She stared back, nodding as well.

He reached for the sheet and pulled it down to bare her leg. The wound didn't look as angry, but it was far from healed.

"There's food in the fridge. Help yourself to whatever you need. The number to the station is by the phone. If anything happens or you need me, just call. I'll try not to be too long."

"Are you going after the poachers?"

He nodded grimly. "I'm going to try."

"I could probably help."

"No," he said, then realized he'd barked at her. "No," he said in a lower voice. "I won't put you at risk. I need you to stay here and inside the house. Don't go out for any reason."

"Okay."

He leaned down and ran his finger down her cheek. "Take care of yourself while I'm gone."

He stood and went to dress. He could feel her gaze as he pulled on his clothing, and the warm hum of arousal heated his veins.

He turned to her one more time as he prepared to leave the bedroom. "I'll start a fire and stack some wood on the hearth so all you'll have to do is add logs throughout the day."

She smiled, and he gave her one last stare before he walked out.

Aliyah watched him go then laid her head back on the pillow with a confused sigh. She was free after six months in captivity. She should be going home as fast as she could, and yet here she was, making promises to stay that she couldn't keep.

For the first time in several long months, she felt at peace. Calm. Her reprieve from the stress and edginess was hard fought but welcome.

During the night she'd twitched and spasmed as she'd fought the urge to shift. Several times he'd come awake, his hands gliding over her body as he murmured comforting words. She'd loved the way his voice glided over her skin, a much-needed balm. She wanted more. She needed this man, and it frightened her.

She threw back the covers and slid her legs over the side of the bed. She stood, testing the strength of her injured leg. Shaky and a little wobbly, but otherwise she could walk on it. It gave her a twinge as she made her way toward the door, but in another day or two, she should be well enough to travel.

And that was the excuse she fed herself for staying. She needed to regain her strength before she attempted to return to her family.

They probably thought she was dead, and that saddened her. In the six long months of her captivity, what had tortured her most wasn't her fear or the terrible conditions she'd been forced to endure. It was the thought of her mother's tears and her father's grief.

She wasn't sure they could endure it again after losing one child so long ago.

As she looked down at her naked body, it occurred to her that she had absolutely nothing to wear. With a frown, she went to Duncan's closet and thumbed through the hangers until she found a flannel shirt. It would be warm and soft and hopefully wouldn't irritate her skin. The more time she spent in human form, the more she'd adapt.

She pulled it on and gathered it close, inhaling Duncan's scent as it surrounded her. Spicy, a little like wood. Warm and masculine. Strong. Like him. It made her feel safe.

She buttoned the shirt but left her legs bare, not wanting to aggravate her wound. It felt a little odd to be walking bare-assed through Duncan's house, not because the immodesty bothered her, but because she was in a strange man's house, bare-assed naked.

Then she laughed, because it wasn't as though she hadn't stuck that bare ass in the air in a clear invitation for him to ride her hard. Her cheeks warmed, and she closed her eyes against the embarrassment tightening her skin.

He'd felt so good, though. So incredibly right. She'd never felt that way with a man. They could make her feel good. Any man with a modicum of know-how could make a woman get off, but Duncan...he knew how to love a woman. Knew just how to touch her, to kiss her. Sex with him had been... She shook her head. She couldn't even come up with a descriptor that did it justice.

She padded into the living room and stopped at the small French doors leading to the wooden deck at the back of the cabin. A light frost had kissed the earth, and when she touched the glass, it felt cold.

Winter was coming. Her parents would be safely ensconced in their Alaskan cabin on one of the small islands off the coast of Kodiak. She closed her eyes and imagined herself there, gazing out over the emerald green waters of the inlet where the cabin was nestled.

Eagles flew regularly overheard, and often her mother would join them. Kodiak bears roamed freely over the island. She'd watched her father amble through the forest then stand to his magnificent twelve-foot height, his brown fur glistening in the sun.

They had made a great sacrifice in leaving their haven to take Aliyah to Africa. But after Kaya's discovery and disappearance, they hadn't wanted to risk the same happening to Aliyah.

Kaya. Even now, so many years later, sadness gripped Aliyah when she thought of her sister.

Kaya had also been a great cat. A North American mountain lion. The majestic cougar. Aliyah, though young when Kaya disappeared, could vividly remember staring into the beautiful amber eyes of her sister.

Chilled from standing so close to the door, she stepped away and moved toward the fireplace. She allowed the heat to warm her front before turning her back to the flames.

Her gaze flickered as it fell on the telephone sitting on the coffee table. She ached to call her mother, to let her know she was alive. She waged an inner war with herself over the need to talk to her parents and the desire to keep them and herself safe.

She continued to stare at the phone, her gut churning, her eyes burning. She closed them as her mother's face shimmered in her mind. Soft, gentle, so warm. There was nothing like a mother's hugs, and Aliyah had gone so long without them.

She walked to the couch and sat down, staring at the phone. Should she do it? Call her parents and at least let them know she was alive and that she'd tell them more when she could? She didn't even know where she was. Colorado. She knew that much. But it was a big state, and she had no idea how to tell her parents her location.

Duncan could tell them. Her breath caught in her chest as indecision held her in its grip.

Could she trust Duncan? Was he even now contacting the state or even the federal authorities? Who would you even call if you found a cheetah that happened to turn into a woman? If her secret was discovered, her people would be at a big risk. The government wouldn't believe she was a freak occurrence. Surely where there was one there were others.

She covered her eyes with one hand and massaged her temples. She should go. Leave now before he returned. She glanced down at her leg and knew she'd never make it in either human or cheetah form, not that she'd put the cheetah at risk. She had no money, no clothes, no identification. She was at the mercy of Duncan's hospitality until her parents could come for her.

When she took that into consideration, she didn't have much choice but to wait for Duncan, bide her time and heal. A good meal would be a great starting point. She was ravenous and looked forward to human food again instead of the raw scraps thrown to her by her captors.

Even as she rummaged around the small kitchen, she found herself watching the clock and hoping Duncan would return soon.

Chapter Seven

Duncan sat in his office ready to bellow in frustration. It would figure that on a day where he needed to finish and get the hell out of the office, everyone and their mama decided they needed something.

He hung up the phone and shoved back from his desk, prepared to bolt when Mrs. Humphreys stuck her head in the door.

"Sheriff?"

He managed to keep from sighing. Barely.

"Mrs. Humphreys, come in. What can I do for you?"

She offered a smile and gripped her purse in front of her as she walked in and sat down in the chair in front of his desk.

"I wondered if you'd found out anything about those hunters out behind my house."

Duncan twisted his lips and mulled over how to best proceed. Bureaucratic B.S. usually seemed to work. "I'm working on it. I have a few leads I'm following up on. As soon as I know anything I'll let you know."

She gifted him with another smile and reached up to smooth a few silvery strands of hair that had escaped the bun. "Oh well, that's good. I hate to think of those poor animals being shot at. I have to tell you, I was rooting for that cheetah, and I never heard shots so I'm hoping it escaped."

Duncan lunged forward in his seat, his hands flat on the desk. "What cheetah, Mrs. Humphreys? You never said anything about a cheetah."

A puzzled frown creased her face. "Oh but I'm sure I did."

Duncan shook his head. "No ma'am. You said *lion*. Not a mountain lion, but a lion."

"Well, there was a lion too. Before the cheetah. Oh dear, maybe I forgot to mention the cheetah."

Fuck. Now he had someone else who had seen Aliyah. Could it get any worse?

"Tell me about the cheetah," he said, directing her back to the matter at hand.

"Well, it was early, and I'm always up early. I went out back to feed Riley, and I saw two SUVs driving across the back boundary of my property. They stopped at the bottom of the first switchback and started unloading a bunch of stuff. So I went inside to get the binoculars.

"I saw that they carried rifles and bows. And then, one of them opened the back, and they lifted out a cage. I couldn't really see what kind of animal it was until they turned it loose. Now I wouldn't swear in court, mind you, but it certainly looked like a cheetah. I'd just watched a documentary the night before on Animal Planet."

Duncan blew out his breath and dragged a hand through his hair. "Did you get a good enough look at the men to be able to give a detailed description? And would you know them again if you saw them?"

"Oh my, I just don't know. Maybe?"

He smiled kindly at her. "It's all right, Mrs. Humphreys. You've been very helpful. I think you should keep this information to yourself, though. We don't want people to get the idea that a bunch of wild animals are roaming around our mountains."

The last thing he needed was a bunch of hot-to-trot good ol' boys armed with high-powered rifles mounting a search for dangerous animals. It would be more fun than the town of Elk Ridge had had since old man Hildebrandt swore he saw Bigfoot.

"Of course," she said.

They were interrupted when Nick stuck his head in the door. "Duncan, I need a minute when you get time."

Mrs. Humphreys rose from her seat and turned to smile at Nick. "That's all right, young man. I was just going."

Duncan rose. "Thanks for coming by, Mrs. Humphreys. I appreciate the information, and I want you to know, we're doing all we can to make sure those poachers are found and arrested. In the meantime, if you see anything else, you call me immediately."

She nodded and headed out the door as Nick walked in to plop in the chair she'd just vacated.

Duncan stared at Nick and tried not to let his impatience show.

"So what's going on?" Nick asked.

Duncan blinked. "Going to give me an idea of what you want to know? Or do you want a detailed accounting of my entire morning?"

Nick's brow arched. "Someone piss in your cereal? I'm talking about yesterday. You going looking for hunters, then calling dispatch and telling them to contact local hospitals to see if anyone showed up with injuries. Yet you come out alone, don't file a report other than you have suspicions of illegal hunting. It doesn't take a rocket scientist to figure out something's fishy as hell."

Damn. He hadn't even stopped to think about what asking dispatch to notify the local hospitals would imply. He took a deep breath and quelled his agitation. Nick was his friend and a damn good cop. He didn't deserve Duncan's impatience.

"I think one of them was injured," he said slowly. "They were tracking a kill."

"So you saw blood. What made you think it wasn't the animal's blood?"

"It was an idea," Duncan said shortly. "I'm covering all the bases."

Nick stared suspiciously at him. "You're holding back on me, man. What's that shit?"

Duncan nearly groaned. He and Nick went way back. Both had grown up here and felt a deep loyalty to the town and to the mountains. No, he hadn't ever held out on Nick. There had never been a need. But he wasn't ready to share Aliyah with anyone. And who the hell would believe him anyway?

Duncan grabbed for the phone in relief when it rang. After a few moments, he hung up and looked back up at Nick. At least now he could do something besides sit here while Nick stared him down like a bug under a microscope.

"Looks like their kill has been found. Locals out scouting found a dead lion about a mile up the mountain at the Turner Creek crossing."

"A mountain lion?"

"No. A lion," Duncan said evenly.

"You mean a lion as in fucking *Lion King?*"

Duncan nodded.

"Holy fuck. So maybe Mrs. Humphreys wasn't off her rocker when she said she saw a cheetah."

Alarm prickled up Duncan's spine. "You heard that?"

"Yeah, came in on the tail end of the conversation. What the hell is going on, Duncan?"

Duncan sat back in his chair and put his hands behind his head. He trusted Nick. There was no doubt about that. No, he didn't want to tell him about Aliyah, but that had more to do with the possessive need crawling through his veins. The need to keep her to himself, sheltered from the rest of the world.

But the rest he could trust Nick with. "It would appear that our poachers are importing exotic animals into the states and turning them out to hunt here in Elk Ridge. Why don't you head out with me, and I'll catch you up to speed on what I know."

Duncan got up, collected his jacket and walked out of the office, Nick on his heels. They climbed into Duncan's truck and headed for Turner Creek.

They rode in silence for a long time. Frustration edged up Duncan's neck and gripped his jaw. The longer it took him to run down leads, the longer Aliyah was left alone in his house. He was in a hell of a fix. He couldn't have her with him while he worked to try and track down the men who'd hunted her, but he felt uneasy about leaving her alone and without protection for such a long period of time.

"You okay?" Nick asked.

Duncan glanced over at his friend. "Yeah, I'm good. Just tired. Wagged my ass all over the damn mountain yesterday looking for those damn poachers."

Nick's expression darkened. "I want them out of our mountains, Duncan."

Duncan nodded. "You and me both. Last thing we need is a bunch of outsiders shooting up the damn woods and loosing animals like lions. The locals get wind of this and they'll posse up and go after the poachers themselves."

As they neared the Turner Creek crossing, they saw two trucks parked a quarter-mile up the road. Duncan pulled in behind them and hopped out.

He and Nick walked over to where Heath Barnes and his son, Michael, stood with Sam Crenshaw. They looked up.

"Sheriff," Heath said with a nod.

Duncan looked down at the dead lion. Large adult male. Gunshot wound behind the left shoulder. Rigor had set in and the body temperature was cool, no warmth when Duncan touched the stiff body. Probably shot late yesterday or possibly early this morning.

He looked up at the three men who gathered round the fallen lion. "You fellows see anyone around?"

They shook their heads.

"What's going on, sheriff?" Sam asked. "What's a lion doing around here?"

Duncan rose and rubbed a hand through his hair. "I wish I knew. Looks like we have a poaching ring."

The men's faces twisted in anger.

"It's bad enough we have to put up with so many damn out-of-state hunters every fall," Heath muttered. "Now they're running illegal animals?"

Duncan sighed and pulled out his cell phone to check his signal. One bar. A call might go through. He dialed Doc's number, hoping this time he'd actually get a hold of the man.

After the fourth ring, Doc's gravelly voice bled through the line.

"What can I do for you, Duncan?" Doc asked. "Sorry I didn't get back to you last night. It was damn near two a.m. before I got in. Had a difficult delivery out at the Bransons."

"No problem. Look Doc, if you aren't busy, I could use you."

"Sure, what's up?"

"I need you to do an autopsy...on a lion."

"A mountain lion? Whatever for?"

"No, Doc, a lion. African lion. I've got a dead one at Turner Creek. I need you to preserve what evidence you find, recover any bullet fragments and give me a detailed report of your findings."

"You bringing it in or do you want me to come get it?"

"I'll have my deputies bring it to you," Duncan said.

"I'll be waiting. Oh, and Duncan, what was it you needed last night? You sounded distracted."

Duncan paused. "Nothing. It wasn't important."

Doc grunted. "Whatever. I'll be at the clinic."

"Thanks, Doc."

Duncan hung up and glanced over at Nick. "Can you handle things here?"

Nick nodded. "Where are you off to?"

"I need to go back to the office and run over some maps. If I can get a chopper out tomorrow morning we can do an aerial recon of the area. See if we get lucky."

"Good idea. If nothing else, we can rule out a lot of ground to cover on foot. I'll radio dispatch and have them send an off-duty deputy. I'll catch a ride back to town with him when we take the lion out to Doc's."

"Thanks, Nick. I appreciate it."

Nick eyed him curiously. "It's my job."

"Yeah, I know, but thanks anyway."

"Duncan, are you sure everything's okay? You're taking this awfully hard."

Concern and curiosity flickered in Nick's eyes, and Duncan felt a surge of guilt. He wasn't one to keep secrets. Aliyah, though? One secret well worth keeping. Especially if it kept her in his arms a little longer.

"I'm good, man. Keep me posted."

Duncan started back to his truck. He tried to view the lion's death as he would any other animal's demise, but he kept imagining a golden-eyed cheetah lifeless on the ground.

It could have been Aliyah. It *would* have been Aliyah if he hadn't found her when he did.

The idea of her running for her life, helpless against the hunters pursuing her, sent a cold chill down his spine. As long as he lived, he'd never forget the sight of a cold, shivering Aliyah lying naked on the floor of his mudroom, an arrow protruding from her thigh.

He wanted to get back to her. Make sure she was safe. Not hurting. But first he had to do what he could to ensure the hunters were no longer a threat to her.

He was eager as hell to see Aliyah again, and he knew it had little to do with police procedure, his investigation or anything else. He wanted to touch her. Run his hands over her body.

His groin grew heavy, and an ache began as his cock stiffened.

He climbed into his truck and stared down in disgust at the bulge in his crotch. Then he shifted in an effort to alleviate the discomfort. All the way home, he thought about the coming snow. Ice. Frost. Cold showers. Anything that would make it less likely that he'd walk into his cabin with a hard-on from hell.

On the other hand, he could think of better ways to ease the ache than thinking of icebergs and penguins. Like diving into a warm pussy.

Chapter Eight

It was late when Duncan turned into his drive. He pulled up to his house and sat there for a moment, his hands gripped tight around the steering wheel. Fatigue worked deep into his muscles, but at the same time anticipation licked up his skin. He realized, as he walked toward the front door, that he wanted her to be here. He didn't want to walk into an empty house like he did every other day.

He inserted the key into the lock, turned then paused as he slid his hand down to grab the handle. Quietly, he eased the door open and stepped inside.

Relief lightened his chest.

Curled up on the couch in front of the fire was Aliyah. Lying on her side, her knees drawn up and one arm dangling over the side of the sofa, she was sound asleep.

It looked frighteningly domestic. Like a man returning home after a long day at work to find his woman waiting. Soft. Beautiful.

He walked forward, drawn to the alluring image she presented. As he moved closer, he frowned. Her skin rippled with tiny quivers. Her muscles twitched and jumped, and her brow was creased, her lips drawn into a tight line.

He knelt in front of the couch and laid his hand on her shoulder. She was wearing one of his flannel shirts. He slid his hand down her arm then over her hip and to the bare skin of her leg. His fingers tracked back up to the hem of the shirt, and he pushed until it revealed her wound.

It still looked painful, though he couldn't imagine anyone else healing this rapidly. And she seemed to think it was taking much too long.

He pressed his lips an inch below the jagged seam of the closed wound and kissed. Beneath his mouth, she stirred. He glanced over to see her looking at him. A smile curved her full lips.

"Hey," she murmured.

"Hey yourself."

She put her hand down to push herself into a sitting position. He clasped her shoulder and helped her up.

"You doing okay?" he asked.

She rubbed her hands over her arms and expelled a shaky breath. "Yeah, I'm good."

He touched her cheek, outlined her lips with his fingers. Her eyes simmered liquid gold as she nuzzled her face into his palm.

"I'm starving," he said. "Come keep me company while I whip up something to eat?"

She smiled and nodded.

"You want something?" he asked as he helped her to her feet.

"If you're offering to cook." She grinned. "I snacked on some of the stuff in your fridge, but I'm a disaster in the kitchen. Opening a can is about the extent of my culinary expertise."

She glanced down at her bare legs then back up at Duncan. "I don't have anything to wear. Your shirt was all I could find. I hope you don't mind me borrowing it."

He reached out to finger the lapel and ran the tip inside over the strip of flesh bared by the V. "That shirt never looked that good on me."

She smiled again and started for the kitchen.

"I should have thought about getting you some clothes," he said as he followed behind her. "Everything will be closed now, but I can go out tomorrow morning first thing and pick you up a few things."

She gingerly perched atop one of the barstools, her bare legs dangling down. "That's sweet of you. I'd appreciate it." She cocked her head to the side and studied him. "You look tired. Long day?"

Warm pleasure surged through his veins at her concern. He set a skillet on the countertop and reached over to touch her hand.

"We found a dead lion."

Sorrow filled her eyes and then she looked down. He raised his hand to her cheek.

"I'm sorry."

She looked back at him, her eyes shining with a sheen of tears. "He was taken from the same game preserve that I was. He was a beautiful animal."

"Aliyah, I'll find the people who did this to you, to the other animals. I promise. They won't hurt you again."

She nodded, sadness still etched into her features. He pulled away and began preparations for a quick dinner.

A few minutes later, he dished up omelets for both of them. She dug in with enthusiasm and sighed in pleasure as she put a bite into her mouth.

"Real food. I'm in heaven."

He looked up from his own plate. "Yeah, I guess you haven't exactly had decent food lately." Then he remembered his own offering of the raw steak and grimaced.

She ate quickly and with great enjoyment. When she pushed back her plate with a yawn, he felt the prickle of fatigue skate up his neck as well.

"We should probably get to bed," he said as he picked up their plates and headed for the sink. "I'll, uhm, take the couch." He didn't want to assume anything even though they'd had sex the night before. Maybe she already regretted it.

He turned around to see her staring intently at him, those golden eyes glowing in the light.

"I don't want to sleep alone," she said softly.

His chest tightened. He didn't want to sleep on the couch. He'd much prefer having her in his arms again.

She walked forward, stopping mere inches in front of him. Their bodies were so close they were nearly touching. Her warmth reached out, curling around him, soft and feminine like her.

She put her hand on his chest and gazed up at him, her eyes beseeching.

"What are you asking?" he said hoarsely.

"For you to hold me. And maybe..."

"Maybe what?"

He cupped his hand over hers, sliding his fingers over her wrist and to her fingertips.

"And maybe you could touch me," she whispered.

"Do you *know* what you're asking?"

She touched his cheek. "I know what I'm asking for, Duncan. The question is, can you give it to me?"

Chapter Nine

Duncan stood in the doorway of his bedroom, arm resting against the frame. Aliyah was lying on the bed. Naked. The flannel shirt she'd worn a few minutes ago was carelessly strewn on the floor.

She stretched on her side and stared up at him, eyes glowing a golden, iridescent glitter. There was clear invitation in her gaze, and he quickly unbuttoned his shirt then peeled his pants off. As the material gathered around his ankles, he hastily kicked off his boots then stepped out of the jeans.

He moved forward, drawn to the enticing figure she posed. As he put a knee on the bed and crawled forward, she rose up on her elbow. Her long hair fell forward, sliding over her shoulder.

She wasn't shy at all. He liked that about her. She reached out and cupped his erection, boldly stroking over the length, up and then down again, her fingers curling around his sac.

He loved the way he filled her tiny hand, how she could barely get her fingers wrapped around the thick base of his dick. Each caress sent a sharp bolt of pleasure ricocheting up his spine.

Finally he pried her hand away and pulled it high over her head. He moved over her body, straddling her waist. Arousal flared deep in her eyes at his dominant position. Muscles he didn't even know he had tightened and spasmed as he stared down at her submissive pose.

Hell, he didn't even know he possessed caveman tendencies, but damn if she didn't bring them screaming to the surface. He wanted her. Wanted to own her, possess her. Brand her until there was no question that she belonged to him.

Something dark and primitive flared to life within him. Edgy need crawled over his skin, burning and restless.

He glanced down, just behind where he straddled her body,

checking her wound. Though it was better than the previous day, he knew he still had to take care with her.

A growl erupted from his throat as the uncivilized part of him demanded he just take her. Ride her hard. Then he remembered the night before. Taking her from behind alleviated the need to spread her so wide, to put more pressure on the wound by pushing her legs up and apart.

He rolled off her and made a grab for the condoms still sitting on the nightstand. Then he flipped her over on her stomach. He circled her small waist with his hands and pulled her down until her pelvis cupped the edge of the bed and her feet dangled just inches from the floor.

The tempting swell of her ass beckoned him. Sweat broke out on his forehead as he tried to control his raging need.

He feathered his fingertips down her spine, touching, lightly stroking. She shivered and moaned, and he felt the prickle of little chill bumps dance over her skin.

Her hands splayed out over the sheets on either side of her head. Her fingers curled, gripping the material so tightly her knuckles turned white.

A smile curving his lips, he lowered his head to run his tongue from the small of her back up her spine. When he reached the base of her neck, he stopped and nibbled at the soft skin, making the baby-soft hairs at her nape stand on end.

A light groan filtered through the room, and he honestly couldn't tell if it was her or him. Light and teasing, he ran his mouth over the contours of her neck, down the slight curve to her shoulder. Then he sank his teeth into the column, and she went rigid beneath him.

Her frantic movements stirred the primitive male lurking just under the surface. He let out a snarl and pinned her body against the mattress, holding her still as he continued his sensual exploration of her body.

His chest pressed into her back, and he gripped her wrists with his hands, holding them tightly against the bed.

His cock lay in the seam of her ass, and he rubbed up and down, reaching down into the wetness of her pussy. Her scent floated up, curling through his nostrils until they flared and his breaths came harder.

It was as though he turned into a beast himself. No woman had ever made him feel this way, so possessive, so raw. The need to take her overwhelmed him. *Mine.* Every instinct screamed that she was his.

He was thick and rigid between her legs. He easily found her entrance, his hands never leaving her wrists. Then he closed his eyes and groaned. Condom. Fuck.

Letting go of one of her hands, he grabbed the packet from the bed and ripped it open. He reached down between her legs and rolled it on. His body shook with impatience. He could hardly contain the overwhelming desire to bury himself deep.

Aliyah reached back with her free hand to touch him, to feel the coiled muscles in his chest. He let out another growl as he clamped down over her hand, pressing it back to the mattress and preventing her movement. With one surge of his hips, he was balls-deep in her pussy.

She cried out at his sudden possession. Her body rippled and seized around him, delicious waves of pleasure rolling over her like thunder.

He lay against her for a long moment as she simply enjoyed the sensation of being filled by him. Then his body took over, demanding more, moving, thrusting frantically against her.

There was no finesse to his actions, just the urgent need of a male to dominate his woman. His woman. The thought echoed sharply through her mind. *His.* The sound of the slap of his hips against her ass rose sharply.

She pushed back against him, taking more of him, swallowing him into her body. She whispered his name and closed her eyes as he owned her.

Her body tensed around him, and a flood of moisture burst around his cock. She was close, so close. She wanted more. She wanted it all. Wanted to be completely and truly his. Then he stopped his movements, holding himself deep inside her pussy.

She whimpered her protest and squirmed against him, trying to get him to thrust again. His hands tightened around her wrists, a warning for her to be still. Power emanated from him as he pressed his lips to the center of her back.

It was an exquisitely sensual gesture, not soft. No, he marked her, pressed his mouth to her spine then licked her. His teeth grazed over the ridges and sank into her quivering flesh.

"Duncan, please!"

He chuckled lightly as he kissed a small pattern up her spine.

"I need to come," she begged.

"So do I, sweetheart. So do I."

He slowly dragged his cock over her clenching flesh until the head of his dick just rimmed her entrance. He held there until she writhed underneath him, arching her ass, trying to take him again.

"Greedy wench," he murmured.

His fingers slid over the tops of her hands. She curled her hand around his just as he lunged forward. He rode her hard and unrelenting.

She gasped then yelled his name as he pounded deeper. His groin met the fleshy globes of her ass, flattening them with each thrust. Harder and harder, faster and faster.

"Aliyah!"

His cry sent her over the edge, and he tumbled after her. She screamed, he yelled, and he came completely apart as his orgasm splintered and broke like a perfect wave.

He lay over her, gasping for breath, struggling to process just how completely he'd lost control. Then he realized he had her pinned to the bed, his much larger frame flattening her.

He let out a curse and eased off her, pulling out of her moist heat. She made a sound of protest, and he smoothed his hands over her back, cupping her buttocks in a gentle caress.

"Just lay there, honey. I'll be right back to take care of you."

She made a sound of contentment then, one that seared right through his chest and lodged in the vicinity of his heart. He tore the condom off and disposed of it before crawling back onto the bed.

Tenderly, he rolled her on her side then coaxed her into his arms, careful not to bump her wound.

"Am I alive?" she mumbled.

"Was I too rough?" he asked anxiously. God, now that the moment was over, he cringed at just *how* caveman he'd acted. He was just waiting for her to kick his ass out of bed.

"Oh no," she said breathlessly. "You were absolutely perfect. So perfect that if you'll give me a bit to recover, I want to do it all over again."

Oh hell. His dick stood up and waved. He didn't think he'd ever recovered that fast.

"How much time you need?"

She laughed, low and husky. "A couple minutes. Maybe one?"

He rolled until he was over her. "I like that answer."

He stared down at her, the warm, happy glow in her eyes sending a surge of satisfaction through his body.

"Did I hurt you?" he asked.

She smiled and reached up to touch his face. "No. I won't break, Duncan."

"It's a good damn thing," he growled. "Because I plan to fuck your brains out."

She giggled.

"What, not romantic enough for you?"

"Romance is highly overrated," she said dryly. "I like raw. Hot. Unrestrained."

His entire body tightened. How had he been so damn lucky to find a woman like her? Okay, so he wasn't going to dwell on how he'd found her. Definite mood killer.

When she tried to part her thighs, he clamped his legs around her, holding her in place.

"You just let me do all the work, honey. I don't want you hurting yourself."

She purred in contentment. "I could get used to this kind of treatment." She stretched sensuously and arched her chest, pushing her breasts outward. It was more temptation than Duncan could withstand.

He lowered his mouth to one peak. The nipple melted in his mouth, conforming to the shape of his tongue. Sweet, so sweet. Delicious.

He sucked at her like a man starved. With each pull of her breast, she became more restless, twisting and whimpering with need.

His teeth grazed the point then nipped sharply, and she gripped his head with strong fingers, calling out his name.

He loved that she was so responsive. How could his caveman instincts not be riled when she made him feel like he was the only man in the world? Like no other man had ever fired her blood as he had.

Reluctantly, he released her nipple and kissed his way to her navel. Her supple skin gave way, molding to his lips, sliding like silk over his tongue.

"You taste so damn good," he rasped. "I've never tasted sweeter."

He settled between her legs, parting the golden curls at the apex of her legs. Trailing a finger between the plump folds, he enjoyed the slick wetness. Then he lowered his head and swept his tongue from her small opening upward to her straining clit.

They both groaned, and she jumped. He gripped her waist to hold her in place then licked her again. Her scent wafted through his nose, flowing deep, surrounding him and pulling him in.

He couldn't get enough of her. He wanted more. He wanted everything.

He nuzzled deeper, devouring her, lapping hungrily at her essence. Her limbs shook around his face then clamped tight, holding him in place.

Lazily he tongued her, in no hurry to bring her to completion. He wanted her wild, frantic for him. As desperate for him as he was for her.

Gently he pried her legs apart, careful not to stress her injury. He raised his head to look at her. Her eyes glowed gold. Rich and vibrant. There was a peace about her that lulled him deeper, ensnared him like a fly in a spider's web.

"Turn over, honey," he urged as he rotated her onto her uninjured side. His fingers feathered over the wound then he lowered his head to kiss the raw spot.

"Right there," he said in approval, preventing her from going all the way onto her stomach.

Her pussy was directly in line with his straining dick. Perfect. Again, he reached for a condom, but this time, he wasn't as hurried. Calmly, he tore it from the wrapper and slowly rolled it over his engorged cock.

His fingers found her moist center and slid inside, testing her readiness. She was slick and hot, quivering around his fingers as he stretched her, pressed inward, gliding against her velvet heat.

She looked beautiful, curled on her side, her hair strewn against the pillow. Wild and exotic, her eyes glowing with need, her face flushed and pink. Her lips parted in a gasp as he carefully pulled his fingers from her pussy.

Soft and swollen, inviting his kiss. He ached to taste her mouth again, to explore those plump lips.

He reached down and grasped his cock, guiding it into the small opening. She convulsed around him, gripped him like a vise, sucked and grasped at his dick as he slid in with agonizing precision.

He breached her carefully, mindful of the different position and the angle of his entry. His palm covered the cheek of her ass, cupped it and caressed the soft, supple flesh. With his other hand, he touched her wound, soothing the hurt.

Deeper he stroked, his chest tightening as she made little sounds of approval. He shouldn't have feared hurting her. She was more than accepting of his advances.

Her hand rose high in the air, reaching blindly back toward him. He lifted his hand and twined their fingers together, bringing them to rest against her hip.

Back and forth, absent the urgency of earlier, he thrust. Long, easy slides, enjoying the tingle each time his cock dragged across the clutching tissues of her pussy.

He loosened his hold on her hand long enough to raise his other hand. He switched her hand into his other then reached between her thighs, sliding up until his fingers found her clit.

A jolt skittered through her body, and she tightened around his cock. He let out a moan, knowing he wouldn't last much longer. He fingered her taut nub, lightly at first, then harder, rotating in tight circles.

She moved restlessly, squirming and writhing against him. He squeezed her hand harder, holding on as he sank into her again and again.

"Harder," she gasped. "Please, Duncan, I need..."

"I know, honey," he said in a low voice. "I know what you need. Give it to me. Let go."

He picked up the pace, driving into her with more force. He pinched her clit between his fingers just as he rammed as deep as he could go.

Her body went rigid. Her eyes flew open where a moment before she'd had them tightly closed. Then she screamed. The sound was an electric shock to his system. Blowing over him, igniting every single sensory receptor.

Tension coiled like a snake in his balls, twisting then rising, shooting up his cock, pausing an infinitesimal second before billowing out. He exploded inside her even as he cursed the condom. He wanted to mark her, to come all inside her.

He ground himself against her, his agonized cry matching her scream of pleasure. He started to fall forward but caught himself before he landed against her leg. Moving to the side, he slumped onto the bed, pulling her body into the curve of his.

They both heaved, their harsh breaths echoing through the room. He reached down to yank off the condom then turned back and threw it toward the trash can. Not even looking to see if he'd hit his mark, he turned back to Aliyah and wrapped his arm over her trembling form.

His lips nuzzled her shoulder, and he absorbed her sweet sound of satisfaction.

"I'd like to sleep this way," she murmured. "You feel so good, Duncan."

"You just try and move away from me," he growled.

She laughed lightly and burrowed her ass further into his groin. A deep sigh escaped her, and he felt her go limp against him.

He was dead tired, but he was unable to resist the temptation to run his hand down her curves. He let his hand rest possessively on her hip and then moved it back up to cup her breast. He thumbed her nipple once then tightened his hold.

"Duncan?"

"Yes, honey?"

There was a slight hesitation. "Thank you. That was wonderful."

He smiled. "You're more than welcome, sweetheart."

Chapter Ten

Aliyah woke with a sense of loss. The bed felt cold. Empty. She reached a hand to rest in the slight indention left when Duncan had gotten up to go to work.

She shivered and pulled the covers higher but quickly discarded them again when the material scraped over her skin like needles. Her body crawled with the need to shift. The cheetah rolled within her, protesting its captivity.

She got out of bed and paced in an effort to work off the nervous tension. A shower. She'd take a hot shower and hopefully it would soothe the savagery welling within her.

The water scorched her skin when she stepped under the spray a few minutes later. Still, she stood underneath the heat and turned her face up as the water ran over her body.

Duncan. She missed him already, as absurd as it sounded. She didn't look forward to an entire day without him again. She wasn't even sure she could maintain her human form until he returned. And when he did, she was going to have to go out and give the cheetah free rein.

She tensed and fought against the images of the cheetah. Control. She could do this. It was imperative that she regain dominance.

Her chest heaving with exertion, she stepped out of the shower and quickly toweled off, wincing as the material abraded her skin. She walked naked into the living room, unable to stand the thought of anything touching her.

Coals glowed in the fireplace, and the charred remains of wood lay at various angles. She hastened to add more logs to the fire and watched as the flames licked over the dry wood.

The warmth reached out and wrapped around her body,

caressing, soothing.

The cordless phone lay on the coffee table, and she stared at it as she eased onto the couch. Her mouth went dry, and her pulse pounded a little harder. *Mama.*

She lay her head down on the couch, and a hot tear slipped down her cheek and soaked into the cushion. She missed her family. Missed being with people who she didn't have to hide her true nature from.

Even as well as Duncan had taken the fact she was a cheetah, she still caught him staring at her when he thought she wasn't looking. There was a mixture of awe and disbelief in his dark eyes.

She reached out with a shaking hand, slid the phone off the coffee table and drew it against her chest. Her thumb trembled over the on button and finally she pressed.

The dial tone sounded, loud in the silence. She stared for a long moment before punching the first number. The others followed in sequence. By the time she was finished, tears streaked silently down her cheeks.

She put the phone to her ear and listened as it rang. Four. Five. Six times. Her heart sank as it continued to ring. They weren't home.

The lodge answering machine clicked on and gave the standard greeting in her mother's cheerful voice.

Aliyah pulled the phone away from her ear and gently pushed the off button. Then she turned her face into the sofa as her tears soaked into the material.

Duncan folded the maps and stuffed them into his glove compartment before getting out of his truck. The helicopter landed fifty yards away, and a state wildlife officer hopped out and hurried in Duncan's direction.

Duncan met him halfway and shook his hand.

"You ready?" Cal Stevens shouted over the noise.

Duncan nodded and followed him back to the helicopter. They climbed in, and Cal handed him a set of headphones. When Duncan slid them over his ears, Cal's voice sounded.

"What are we looking at, Duncan?"

Duncan quickly explained his suspicions about the illegal poaching ring as well as his run-in with the hunters and the dead lion.

Cal's frown deepened with every word. Cal had worked with the Colorado Division of Wildlife ever since Duncan had been old enough to hunt. He'd been a good friend of Duncan's father and had often joined them during hunting season. The poaching ring would piss Cal off, and he'd be damn eager to break it up.

"Let's see what we can find from the air," Cal said. "If we can narrow the search area, we'll have a much easier time of it when we go in on foot."

Duncan nodded his agreement.

After several hours of sweeping the area surrounding Elk Ridge and the region where Duncan had first run across the hunters, they turned up nothing.

The pilot indicated that they were low on fuel and would have to head back in. Duncan stared down at the terrain in frustration. He'd hoped the air search would turn up something. Instead he'd wasted an entire afternoon with nothing to show for his efforts. He was no closer to finding the hunters now than he had been two days ago.

They landed, and Cal got out and walked with Duncan over to his truck.

"What's your next move?" Cal asked. "What can I do to help?"

Duncan shook his head grimly. "I'm not sure yet. I'm going to have to get with Nick and my other deputies. Put our heads together and come up with a search plan. Those sons of bitches are out there."

"You know you can count on me to help. I can get some of my guys together. I know you probably don't want the feds crawling all over your mountains but whether you call them in to help apprehend your poachers or call them in after you've taken them down, one way or another, they're going to be involved. Those sons of bitches have broken all sorts of federal laws with the shit they're pulling."

"Yeah, I know." Duncan sighed. "I'd rather hold off as long as possible. If we can't come up with anything by tomorrow, we'll have to call them in. I don't want to risk these assholes escaping, or worse, continuing to turn these animals out to hunt."

Cal clapped a hand over his shoulder. "I've got to go. Pilot's waiting on me. Call me if you need me."

"Thanks, Cal. Will do."

Duncan watched as the older man returned to the helicopter. As it lifted off, Duncan climbed into his truck to begin the drive back into town.

His mind was abuzz with what his next plan of action would be. It was getting dark, which prevented any further search today, but tomorrow he would resume. He could gather Nick, his deputies, call up Cal and some of his men and launch a ground search in the denser areas not able to be viewed from the air.

For now...he was going back to his cabin...and Aliyah.

First he stopped off at the small supply store on Main Street and chose sweats, a few shirts, and a pair of boots for her. The shopkeeper raised a brow but didn't question Duncan's purchases, a fact he was grateful for.

When the clothes were bagged and paid for, Duncan headed back out to his truck, ready to be home after another long day.

The eagerness with which he drove to his cabin was alien. It had been a while since he'd felt such intensity toward a woman, and never quite this way.

Tonight, there was no hesitation when he walked into the door. He looked for her and found her pacing the kitchen, naked, agitation radiating from her.

"Aliyah," he said softly.

She whirled around, her eyes flickering, the pupils fluttering and changing shape. She rubbed her hands up and down her bare arms in a clear sign of distress, and then with a small cry, she launched herself at him, wrapping her arms around his waist and burying her face in his chest.

He caught her against him and hugged her as he stroked his hand through her hair.

"Aliyah, honey, what's wrong? Are you in pain?"

Unease prickled his neck. He pulled her away from him so he could look at her more closely.

She rubbed her hands up her arms again and shivered lightly. Tiny little goose bumps dotted her skin. "I need...I need to shift for a while. I can't control it for much longer."

He was shaking his head before she ever finished. "No way. Aliyah, that's crazy and you know it. There is no way we can risk it. There are poachers after you, not to mention you could be seen by a number of other people. Everyone around here is already uneasy because of the strange animals being spotted."

She closed her eyes then reopened them and locked her gaze to his. "I know it's insane but if I don't get out soon, I won't be able to

71

control when and how I shift. I was hoping you'd know somewhere we could go where the chance of me being spotted was small if we went late, after dark, and I'd be careful. It's just that I've spent so long in shifted form that the cheetah is dominant. I'm growing weaker, and I need the rejuvenation that being in my cheetah form will bring."

"Aliyah—" He was still shaking his head. He couldn't even get his protest out fast enough.

"I don't need your permission, Duncan," she said softly. "But I would like your support. And your protection. But if you refuse me both, I have no choice but to seek out a place on my own. It's not smart. I know that. I could place myself in a lot of danger. I know that too. But I cannot prevent a shift for much longer."

"Can't you do it here?" he asked, sweeping his hand across the interior of the cabin.

"I need to run. I need to be free in a manner I haven't been free in six months. I need to regain my strength. I grow more unstable by the minute."

Fuck. He didn't like this. Even while she made sense, he didn't like it one bit.

"I'll be careful."

He blew out his breath in a long whoosh. "You'll stay in the truck out of sight until we get out of town. I don't want you anywhere near here when you do your cheetah thing. We'll go south an hour or so."

She wrapped her arms around him again as she nestled back into his embrace.

"Thank you," she said as she squeezed.

He let his hands fall down her back, and he rubbed up and down before he placed one hand behind her neck, the other arm around her waist and held her close.

"First you're going to get dressed. I picked up some clothes for you from town. Then we're going to make this quick," he grumbled. "This whole thing seriously freaks me out."

Chapter Eleven

Duncan drove slowly down the bumpy, winding ATV trail off one of the closed national forest roads. He'd picked the most obscure spot he could think of, but that didn't guarantee they wouldn't come across campers seeking a remote place to pitch their tents.

Every one of his instincts told him this was a bad idea. Not just a bad one, a stupid risk that Aliyah had no business taking. But he couldn't let her go off alone without any form of protection.

He glanced over at her, and even in the darkness, he could see her tense with anticipation. She was edgy, almost wild, and he knew that she was hanging on by a thread.

"It's not far now," he said as they forded a small creek and rounded a sharp bend.

The road had narrowed considerably, and they wouldn't get much further with his truck, four-wheel drive or not.

She didn't reply but kept her gaze fixed ahead, as if waiting the opportunity to bolt from the truck. When he finally pulled to a halt, she gripped the door handle then finally looked over at him.

"Aliyah, how much of yourself do you retain when you...uhm...shift?"

She cocked her head in confusion. "I'm not sure I understand."

"A wild animal has instincts. You're free now."

"Ohhh. You want to know if I'll run and keep on running."

He nodded slowly. "I guess I'm asking if you'll be back."

She stared at him, her gaze steady. "I'll return, Duncan."

"Okay." He shrugged away his relief and opened his door. "Then let's get this over with."

They both got out and walked around to the front of the truck. To his surprise, she kicked off her boots then began to pull off her socks and then her pants, both of which he'd just purchased. She held them out to him even has her other hand began fumbling with the buttons on her shirt.

He took them from her, and in another minute she was standing naked in front of him, moonlight bathing her pale skin.

"I don't want to ruin them," she said with a grin. "Plus, I'll need something to wear when I shift back."

"You're going to freeze your ass off," he grumbled.

He watched in a mixture of horror and fascination as a shudder rippled over her body. She fell to her knees then braced her hands on the ground as her back arched.

Tawny fur prickled across her skin. Black spots shimmered into view. Her fingers that dug into the dirt and rock became paws, and her legs buckled then bolted upward as she rose on all fours.

Her long, golden hair raced upward to her scalp, disappearing and then falling lightly over her nape in a scruffy mane. When she turned her head to him, he found himself staring into the golden eyes of the cheetah.

She continued to regard him for a long moment, and then she simply loped away, disappearing into the surrounding forest.

Her paws pounded the earth, and her heart rejoiced in her freedom. She kept to the shadows, leaping behind rocks and keeping under the cover of the trees. She was whole.

Power pulsed through her veins. She was the guardian, charged with keeping her human safe. With each leap, each push forward, she could feel her strength returning. Just as transforming to human had rejuvenated the cheetah, shifting to cheetah was healing the human. Two halves that made up the whole. Each dependent on the other for survival.

The human part of her mind cautioned against going too far, warning her to return soon and shift back as soon as possible. The cheetah only wanted to run free, to exhaust herself and later succumb to a healing sleep.

Her lithe body stretched and coiled as she pushed herself harder. Her soul sang and rejoiced as she embraced the wind.

As she began to tire, her human mind regained more control, and she remembered that Duncan waited for her.

Reluctantly, she turned back, returning slower than she'd come.

Fatigue rippled through her muscles, and she slowed to a walk. Her breath escaped in a light fog as she panted. Her energy was spent, but she felt lighter than she had in many months. Since she'd run along the African savannah with her cheetah kin.

By the time she neared the truck, the change was already working its way over her body. She fell to the ground, shivering with cold and exhaustion as the human regained control.

Mustering her strength, she pushed herself to her feet and made her way unsteadily back to where Duncan waited. When she stumbled onto the road, Duncan looked up and started for her. She collapsed into his arms as he gathered her shivering body close.

"Dear God, Aliyah, you're like a freaking icicle."

She burrowed into his warmth, absorbing his heat and his scent. He scooped her up and carried her back to the truck where the clothes still lay on the hood.

"I should have kept the truck running so it would stay heated," he murmured as he began dressing her. "I just didn't want to draw any attention to our location."

"Duncan, I'm fine," she said around chattering teeth. "I'm just tired."

She sagged against him when he finished buttoning her shirt. Again, he simply plucked her up and deposited her into the passenger seat.

He retrieved her socks and boots and put them on her feet as she lay against the still-warm leather. He quickly shut her door and walked around to his side.

A brief burst of cold air blew in when he opened his door, but he got in quickly and started the engine. He flipped the heater on high and then reached over to touch her cheek.

"Are you all right?"

She nodded and closed her eyes, leaning further into his hand. She loved his touch. Found much comfort in his tender gestures.

"Come here," he said and pulled her against him.

She curled her legs into the seat and snuggled into his side. He put his arm around her and pressed a kiss to the top of her head.

"Let's go home."

He turned the truck around and headed back down the narrow road as she lay against him.

Home.

She was suddenly filled with a fierce longing. Not for her own home and her parents whom she hadn't seen in so long. No, she was imagining what home would be like with Duncan. With this untamed warrior. Someone who knew what she was and accepted her. Who understood her and protected her. It was something she'd never dared hope for outside her own race.

She liked Duncan, and, she decided, she trusted him. Her time with him was limited, but she wanted to enjoy the attraction between them, wanted to share her body with him, and, she knew, a part of her soul. A part that would remain with him when she left. A part she wouldn't want back, just as she would take a part of him to keep forever.

"Duncan?"

"Yes, honey."

"In a few days..." She let her hand slide down his leg. "In a few days, I'll have to go."

He stiffened against her. "Why do you have to go?" he asked, surprising her with his bluntness. Was he asking her to stay?

But she couldn't stay, even if he wanted her to. Her parents thought her dead, and they'd already lost one daughter. She risked discovery here with the poachers crawling over the mountains like vicious, hungry ants.

She couldn't do that to her parents or to her people. Sadness clogged her throat. How telling was it that on the eve of her freedom she was reluctant to take it?

With a sigh, she turned her face up to Duncan.

"I like you. And I think you like me. I'd like...I'd like to make the most of our remaining time together."

His hand tightened on her arm then relaxed, and he stroked his fingers up and down the flannel of her shirt.

"I'd like that too," he finally said.

"I want you to make love to me again. All night long. I want to spend what time we have in your arms."

"Then that's where you'll spend it," he said simply.

Chapter Twelve

It was well past midnight when Duncan pulled up to his cabin. He glanced down at the sleeping Aliyah and gently shook her awake.

She opened her eyes and gave him that warm, sleepy look that made him want to take her straight to bed. She sat up then reached for her door, but he put a hand out to her arm.

"I'll come around."

He hurried out and walked around to her side to open the door. When he held out his arms, she climbed down into them and buried her face in his neck.

This was something he could get used to, he thought, as he walked toward the house, his arms full of a vibrant, beautiful woman. The fact that she was a cheetah would take a little more getting used to. But she was leaving soon, and he couldn't give her a single reason to stay. And why should he?

She didn't fit into his world any more than he fit into hers. But he wanted to, and that was the rub.

He set her down on the couch then knelt down to pull off her shoes and socks. When he was done, he ran a hand up her leg until his palm rested over her injury.

"How is your leg?" he asked. It had healed at a remarkable rate, and he wondered if by now it was even visible.

"Only a twinge now and then. By tomorrow, I won't even know it was there. At any rate, it's nothing you need to worry about tonight," she said lightly.

He reached up and pulled a blanket over her. She'd made no secret of what she wanted, and he wasn't going to dance around the issue.

"How do you feel about making love in front of the fire?"

She smiled and stretched sensuously. "Build it, but I doubt we'll need the warmth."

He kissed her, long and hot, until they were both breathing hard. Then he placed his finger over her lips. "Hold that thought. I'll be right back."

Aliyah watched as he went to the fireplace and stacked logs over kindling. Soon flames flickered over the dry wood, and the snap and pop echoed across the quiet cabin.

When he would have turned and come back to her, she stopped him. "Undress for me," she said. "Right there. I want to watch."

Something dark and arousing flickered in his eyes. He shrugged off his jacket and tossed it toward a nearby chair. Next he kicked off his boots and peeled away his socks. He stood there, staring at her, his gaze never wavering as he reached for the button of his fly.

He undid his pants, leaving them open as he worked the buttons free on his shirt. His broad chest came into view, and the muscles in his arms coiled and rippled as he slowly let his shirt fall to the floor.

He was beautiful. All male. Powerful.

Her breath caught in her throat when he began to pull his jeans downward, his underwear coming with them. He paused, giving her the barest glimpse of the dark hair at the top of his pelvis. Then he continued downward, and his cock, freed from constriction, bobbed upward.

Thick, hard. Her mouth watered with the need to taste him. She wanted to lick every inch, suck him deep into her throat, hear him moan with pleasure.

His jeans pooled at his feet, and he stepped out of them. He posed an impressive figure standing in front of the fireplace, naked, lean, power radiating from him in waves.

Her protector. She wanted to explore all her fantasies. Discover his and make them reality. She wanted to fit a lifetime into the few days they had, and she didn't want to waste a minute.

She crooked her finger, and he gave her a cocky grin before he sauntered over to the couch, seemingly unabashed by his nudity. But with a body like his, he certainly had no reason to be ashamed.

He straddled her lap and eased down, careful to keep his full weight off her. Unable to resist a moment longer, she ran her hands over his chest, exploring each dip and curve, every outline of each muscle with her fingertips.

"I'm here, now what are you going to do with me?"

His seductive voice slid over her skin like suede. Her nipples beaded against her shirt, and her groin ached with need.

"What are your fantasies?" she asked huskily. "What are your deep, dark secrets?"

He laughed. "Now that's a loaded question to ask a guy with a raging hard-on."

Her hands slid lower, into the crisp hair surrounding his cock. She circled him with her fingers, testing his thickness, stroking the hard length with light caresses.

"I'll be more specific," she purred. "What are some things you've always wanted to try...but haven't?"

He arched a brow, indecision flickering in his eyes. It was her turn to laugh.

"That juicy, huh? Come on, you won't scare me away."

She captured a single drop of moisture from the slit at the tip of his cock and slowly raised her finger to her lips. She sucked it into her mouth and watched his entire body tighten, his pupils dilate.

"I'd love those lips wrapped around my dick," he said in a strained voice. "What guy wouldn't love that?"

She gave him a patient stare. "I'm not interested in what every guy wants. I want to know what you like. What you've never tried but wanted to. If you could do anything you wanted to me, what would you do?"

"You really want to hear this?"

She continued to caress him intimately, cupping and massaging his balls, alternating it with firm strokes to his cock.

"I don't want to just hear it," she whispered. "I want to do it. All of it."

"Christ." He put his hand down to stop hers. "Let me catch up, baby. I'm so turned on right now that I'm not going to last for thirty more seconds, and if you're offering yourself to me on a silver platter, I damn sure want to be capable of devouring you."

She smiled but moved her hands up over his hips, behind to rest against his firm buttocks.

"I want to fuck your mouth. Hard, fast, down your throat. I want to come and for you to swallow every drop."

"Mmmm, I'd like that too. What else?"

He shook his head. "Oh no, it's your turn. I share, you share."

She grinned. "Okay, that's fair. I want you to fuck my ass. Hard, deep, relentless. I want you to own me. I want to feel you in every inch of my body."

His eyes widened in shock. "You're kidding right? Chicks don't like anal sex."

She shrugged. "Well, if you aren't interested..."

He growled. "Honey, you bring that sweet little ass and I'll fuck it. That'll mark off fantasy number two on my list."

"You've never?" she asked.

He let out a grunt. "I think most guys get off on the idea of trying it at least once. But if we value our balls, we don't go around advertising that fact."

She almost laughed at the hope in his voice.

"You like it?" he asked. "Really?"

She smoothed her hands up his back and gave him a lazy smile. "It's exciting. Edgy. Forbidden. It's downright naughty. I love that first thrust, the sudden pain, when my body tightens and bucks, like it doesn't know how to react, and then the overwhelming pleasure that mixes with the bite. I like it hard while I touch myself. I can control my orgasm, taking as long as I want or as little time as I want. I like to come when the guy does, when he pours himself into me."

His cock nudged her belly, and despite his earlier protest, she reached for it again, wanting her hands wrapped around that steel.

"Your turn," she said sweetly.

"Fuck. How am I supposed to top that?" A disgusted look crossed his face. "Damn."

She looked up at him. "What?"

"I uhm don't have any lube, you know, for us to have anal sex."

He looked so disappointed that she had to stifle her laughter.

"Have any good olive oil? Body lotion? Either will do."

He gave her a look that was a cross between surprise and admiration. "You're one kinky girl."

"I prefer to think of myself as adventurous," she said with a wink. "Now, what's next on your list?"

He lowered his head and angled to kiss her. Lightly at first, just a touch. Then he curved his hand behind her neck and tilted her head up to meet his mouth. Deeper, his tongue swept across her lips, coaxing them open, then moving inside, over her tongue, tasting, exploring.

As he drew away, his eyes smoldered with desire, melting the brown into a pool of chocolate.

"Next on my list is getting you naked."

"Funny, that was next on my list," she said as he slid off her lap.

He pulled her up to stand in front of him, his hands going to her shirt to unbutton it. With each inch of flesh he bared on his way down, he pressed his lips to it until she was shivering.

When the last button was undone, he pushed the material over her shoulders and let it fall to the floor.

"You have such perfect breasts," he murmured.

Instead of touching them like she thought, *hoped*, he would, he merely bent down and licked one of the taut nipples. Her knees buckled, and she had to grasp his shoulders to keep her balance.

"Sweet. You taste so good."

He ran his tongue over the valley between her breasts and over the swell of the next and finally to her other nipple. He sucked it between his teeth and tugged gently.

She murmured a protest when he pulled away and reached for the band of her sweats.

He didn't hurry. Instead, he eased them down, inch by inch until she squirmed with impatience. Finally she kicked the pants away, and they stood naked before each other.

She pressed her body to his, delighting in the feel of skin on skin. His hardness against her much softer body. He ran his hands down her back and over the swell of her bottom. His fingers tightened as he cupped and squeezed, and she tingled all over as she imagined him sliding his big cock deep into her ass.

But first she was going to give him number one on his list.

She stepped away until the backs of her knees met the edge of the couch, and she sat, eye level with his very large, very erect penis.

She glanced up at him and uttered the invitation. "Fuck my mouth."

Raw desire sparked in his eyes. He moved forward and cupped the back of her neck with one hand. With the other, he grasped his cock and guided it toward her mouth.

"Open," he said in a guttural voice.

She licked her lips, brushing the tip as he thrust into her open mouth. He was tentative at first, sliding gently to the back of her throat and retreating, but she wanted more. She wanted his passion, the power she felt simmering just below the surface.

She pulled away and stared up at him. "Don't hold back. I want all of you. I won't break, Duncan. Fuck me."

With a predatory growl, his grip on the back of her neck tightened, and he thrust forward, burying himself in her mouth. Her lips stretched to accommodate his width, and her tongue glided over the smooth hardness, tasting, absorbing the rugged maleness.

She inhaled deeply, surrounding herself with his scent, the smell of sex and power heightening every one of her senses.

His hand twisted in her hair, pulling her to meet his thrusts. She closed her eyes and surrendered to him completely. His moans filled the air, and she sucked greedily at him, wanting more, wanting to give him the same pleasure she was taking.

A light burst of fluid spilled onto her tongue as he pulled back. She swallowed even as he rode forward again.

"Deeper," he growled. "I want you to take all of me. That's it. Swallow me whole. God, baby, I'm going to come. Down your throat. Swallow it all."

His movements became more urgent, and both hands grasped her head, tangled in her hair. He slid all the way in. Her nose pressed against the springy hair at his groin just as she felt the first jet of his release slide down her throat.

He strained against her, pumping harder as more hot liquid filled her mouth. She savored it, holding it for a moment before swallowing it as he'd demanded.

He continued with shorter, gentler thrusts as she licked and sucked every drop from his skin. His grip on her head eased, and finally he pulled away from her.

She looked up to see him staring down at her, desire and deep satisfaction mirrored in his gaze.

"Do you have any idea how sexy you look with your lips all red and puffy, wet with my come?"

She ran her tongue over her top lip in a slow, deliberate motion, and he groaned.

"That was fantastic," he breathed. "You're fantastic. I think I need to sit down."

She grinned as he sank onto the couch beside her. He reached up and pulled her back against him, and she went willingly, cuddling against his chest.

His heart thudded against her ear, and his chest dipped with shallow breaths. She slid her hand down to his softening erection and touched and petted, enjoying the contrast to the iron hardness of just a few minutes ago.

"Not so impressive now, is it?" he said with a grunt.

She laughed. "You men are so hung up on your appendages. It's still quite impressive," she consoled.

His chest shook with laughter. "Still want it up your ass?"

A light shiver raced over her skin as she stroked and caressed his balls. She glanced up at him. "Imagine how tight I'll feel. Like you can't even get inside me. For just that moment when my body resists your invasion and then when it gives way and you're balls-deep in my ass. So tell me, do you still want up my ass?"

Already she could feel him stir against her fingers.

"Oh, I'm going to fuck that sweet little ass," he murmured. "I can't wait to see you bent over, ass high in the air. I'm going to ride you long and hard just like you asked me to."

She rotated over him and settled astride his lap as he had done to her earlier. "I suppose this is the point where we need to discuss sexual history, whether or not you have crotch rot and the fact that I'd rather not use a condom for anal sex."

He cocked one eyebrow at her. "I hate to tell you this, honey, but determining whether or not I have crotch rot would have been a good idea before I fucked that pretty mouth of yours."

His eyes twinkled devilishly, and she smacked him on the chest.

"I've always practiced safe sex, with the exception of one guy two years ago when we had anal sex. I trusted him. Maybe I shouldn't have, but I've had check-ups. Now it's your turn," she said.

"Straightforward. I like that. You manage not to make this sort of conversation awkward," he said with a grin. "If you must know my dark, dirty secrets, then I haven't had sex in a little over a year. I used condoms. Before that I was in a committed relationship with a girl for two years. We did have unprotected sex, but I was faithful to her and vice versa."

"What happened?" Aliyah asked.

He shrugged. "She wanted more than I could offer her. It was a civil break-up. She moved to Denver. Last I heard she was engaged to some lawyer."

"You don't sound too terribly torn up about that," she said dryly.

He wrapped his arms around her waist and pulled her breasts to his mouth. "We weren't right for each other," he said simply, just as he began nibbling on one of her nipples. "Now, not that I don't love discussing past girlfriends," he said, "but I'd much rather discuss how fast you can take that ass into the bedroom so I can fuck it."

Chapter Thirteen

Aliyah scampered ahead of Duncan into the bedroom. He followed behind a few moments later with a bottle of extra virgin olive oil in one hand and a bottle of baby oil in the other. She cracked up at the devilish glint in his eye.

"I'm not even going to ask why a manly man such as yourself has a bottle of baby oil." She even managed to say it without snickering.

"Just think of how sweet your ass will smell," he teased.

He tossed aside the olive oil then dropped the baby oil on the bed. She sashayed over to him and ran a finger down the midline of his chest, lower until she traced his semi-erect cock to the tip.

"The secret to getting a woman to offer you her ass? Make her so crazy with desire, get her so worked up that she'll do anything to get off. The more turned on I get, the naughtier I get," she said with a wink.

"In that case." He wrapped his arms around her and fell onto the bed, his body over hers. He held her arms high above her head and set about tormenting her with that sinful mouth of his.

He licked her. Bit her. Sucked her. Kissed her.

He rolled the taut peaks of her breasts between his teeth and laved his tongue over the nipples. All the while he murmured to her in great detail precisely what he was going to do when he turned her over and mounted her. How he was going to force himself as deeply as he could go and ride her ass long and hard.

Her breaths were coming so short that she felt light-headed. God, she wanted to roll over and let him mount her now. She wanted it. Needed it. But he seemed perfectly content to torture her with words and deeds.

He blazed a sensual trail down her belly where he swirled his tongue around the shallow indention of her navel. He played there awhile as he edged her thighs further apart with one shoulder.

His fingers brushed through the light hairs between her legs, delving into the soft folds, spreading and exposing the tender bud above her pussy opening.

Warm and soft, his breath blew over the sensitive flesh. Goose bumps raced down her legs, over her body, urging her nipples to puckered little nubs.

He licked lightly. The rasp of his taste buds over the tender skin sent shivers of delight through her pussy. He tasted her like candy, sucking, lapping, like he couldn't get enough of her sweetness.

When she was sure she couldn't possibly take any more, he spread her legs in a sudden move and lunged up her body. His cock slid into her waiting pussy, taking the breath from her in a forceful lurch.

"Duncan!"

"Tell me what you want," he demanded as he rose above her, buried deeply inside her body. He placed his hands on either side of her head and rolled his hips, rocking them forward and then back again.

"I want you to fuck my ass," she gasped. "Please. I want it. Take me, Duncan. Make me yours."

He ripped himself out of her and rolled her over. He gripped her hips and yanked her to her knees. She heard the squeezing sound as he squirted baby oil, and then his hand found the cleft of her ass.

He slid one well-oiled finger inside. No preliminary. She groaned in delight as her body spasmed and protested the invasion. God, it was nothing next to what she would feel when he got his cock inside her.

"Touch yourself, sweetheart," he rasped. "Get yourself ready. I can't hold out much longer."

She laid her cheek on the bed, arching her ass higher, giving him better access. She braced herself with her right hand and slid her left hand between her body and the bed, reaching up to stroke her clit.

He slid another finger into her tight hole, and she stroked her clit harder, moaning with pleasure. His fingers left her, and then his hands gripped her hips as he came up on his knees behind her.

"I want it hard," she said. "Don't hold back, Duncan."

He hesitated. "I don't want to hurt you, honey."

"The pain is part of the pleasure. I want it. You know you want to thrust into my ass. Don't make me wait."

She closed her eyes and gently worked her finger over her clit as her body tensed with anticipation. She felt the broad tip of his cock settle between her ass cheeks, and then he spread her impossibly wide. She caught her breath just as he rammed forward.

Her eyes flew open in shock, and her body tightened like a bowstring. She shook and spasmed and bucked against him, her first instinct to reject his advances. He growled and yanked her back to him, and oh God, she loved that sound. That possessive cry. *Mine.*

She moved her finger harder, seeking to make the burn subside and the pleasure seep into her body. He grunted above her and demanded that she take it all.

She closed her eyes once again and raised her ass submissively higher in the air. His hands splayed over her buttocks as he thrust again. Her body gave way, surrendered to him as his balls slapped against her pussy.

"Dear God, you're so tight. So fucking incredible."

She was incapable of speech. She could feel every ridge, every vein, every inch of his massive cock as he worked it back and forth through the tight little muscle guarding the entrance to her ass.

She stretched to accommodate him and clamped down when he tried to retreat. His fingers dug into her hips, his hands tight around her body, demonstrating his claim, his brand. For tonight he owned her and she gloried in it.

Her release hovered, so close, so tempting, but she wasn't ready. She slowed the stroke of her fingers and for a moment simply enjoyed the steady slap of his abdomen against her rounded cheeks.

He withdrew in one long, slow motion. The head slid out with a light pop, and she moaned her protest. His thumbs smoothed over her ass, spreading the cheeks as her opening slowly closed. Then she felt him position himself again. He waited a moment and then he rippled through her opening in one long shove.

She nearly orgasmed then. She fought for control as raw, edgy desire coursed through her veins.

"You're not going to give it to me," he said. "I'm going to take it."

He reached under to push her hand away. He pulled it around her back and held it with one hand while he rode her relentlessly.

Her orgasm built. The fire raged, but she knew she wouldn't succumb until he touched her. Until he did what he was preventing her from doing. She was in his power, helpless to receive only the pleasure he was willing to give her. And he gave her everything.

"Tell me you want to come," he uttered in a harsh whisper. "Tell me to touch you, Aliyah. Tell me how to make you scream."

"Oh God. Touch me, Duncan. My clit. Please. I need to come. But with you. Only with you."

"Then get ready, sweetheart, because I'm going to come all over your ass."

He slid his other hand beneath her, to her clit. When his finger ran lightly over the swollen bud, the first waves of her orgasm hit. Still, he took her higher.

Deep, he was so deep, forcing her to accommodate him, to take him all.

He applied more pressure to her clit, rotating, and she screamed as her body exploded. Mindless ecstasy rocked her. She lost all sense of time and place. She felt the first hot spurt of his release deep in her body, and she pushed back against him, wanting more.

He pulled back. He guided her hand downward and once again told her to touch herself. Then he gripped her buttocks with his palms and spread as he pulled out. She felt him grip his cock and jerk, and then she felt the hot splatter against her opening. It slithered inside, some seeping inward while more ran down the cleft of her ass.

As she worked her finger over her clit, she felt the sharp edge of another orgasm blow up and explode in a matter of seconds as warm trails of his seed trickled down the insides of her thighs and the backs of her legs.

Then he slid into her once again, easier this time. Slower, gentler as he worked back and forth. He rocked against her as his cock softened, and he emptied the remnants of his come inside her body.

She let her hand fall, her pussy too sensitive to take any further stimulation. She lay there, content to let him finish with gentle strokes until finally her body released him with a soft sigh.

He leaned over and pressed a kiss between her shoulders. "I'll be right back," he whispered.

A moment later, she felt a warm washcloth work gently over her skin.

"I've started a shower for us."

She tried to turn over, but her muscles were jelly. Slack, sated, she couldn't have moved if she wanted.

He reached down, gathered her in his arms and picked her up to carry her into the bathroom. He set her down in the shower under the warm spray, and she leaned against him, too weak to stand on her own.

He wrapped his arms around her and held her tight. For the longest time they stood there, under the hot water, neither moving.

"The sex was mind-blowing," he finally said. "But it was more. Goddamn it, it was more, and I can't even grasp it. What happened, Aliyah? Because I damn sure can't explain it. It should have just been hot, kinky sex, but I've never felt like that before."

She didn't have an answer for him, because she knew exactly what he was struggling with. Theirs was more than a physical connection, more than two bodies lusting, sweating, fucking.

She clung to him as he washed her and then himself. They stepped from the shower, and he wrapped a towel around her, still holding her close as if he couldn't bear the separation.

When they were dry, she leaned weakly against him. "Anything else on your list?" she cracked.

He kissed the top of her head and threaded his fingers through her still-damp hair. "All I want is to take you back to bed and hold you. And later I want to make love to you. Again and again."

She sighed because it was exactly what she wanted. To be held and cherished by this man.

He swung her into his arms and carried her back to the bed. He glanced at the sheets with a grimace then set her down in a standing position.

With hurried movements, he stripped the top sheet and tossed it toward the corner. "Don't move. I'll be right back."

His footsteps retreated, and in moment, he returned with another sheet that he hastily arranged on the bed. He yanked the down comforter from the pile on the floor and pulled it up in a semblance of an arranged bed.

She crawled under the covers and turned to face him as he got in beside her.

"Come here," he said huskily as he opened his arms.

She snuggled in tight against him, letting his body heat envelop her. He pulled the covers over them and then wrapped his arms around her, molding her to his body, and she marveled that they fit so perfectly. Her softness to his hardness, her curves aligning with the muscular planes of his form.

Her head tucked beneath his chin, and she threaded her legs through his until there wasn't an inch of space separating them.

This, she thought...this was perfect.

Chapter Fourteen

A rifle shot shattered the morning stillness and jerked Duncan from a sound sleep. His eyes flew open as he registered the proximity of the gunfire. He automatically reached for Aliyah only to feel an empty space beside him.

His blood ran cold.

He scrambled off the bed and yanked on the first pair of shorts he came across. He ran for the front door and flung it open, stumbling into the brisk air.

Nick stood by his truck, rifle up and trained on a distant object. When Duncan followed the direction of the barrel and saw a cheetah huddled on the ground, he roared and charged for Nick.

Duncan tackled him as Nick squeezed off another shot. The rifle went flying as the two men landed in a heap on the ground.

"What the fuck? Duncan, what the hell are you doing?" Nick shouted.

"Stand down," Duncan barked even as he bolted up. He ran toward the spot where the cheetah had lain, praying that Nick had missed.

As he drew closer, he saw that Aliyah now lay naked on the ground, shivering, curled into a protective ball. Duncan fell to his knees, shouting her name. He ran his hands over her body searching for a wound, blood, anything.

When she opened her eyes and stared up at him, he sagged in relief. His hands shook so badly he couldn't even do more than touch her.

Nick could have killed her.

Finally managing to compose himself, he gathered her naked body in his arms and strode back toward the cabin. He spared a glance at

Nick who stood staring at the woman in Duncan's arms in abject horror.

Ignoring him, Duncan went into the cabin and laid Aliyah on the couch. He wrapped a blanket around her then crushed her to his chest.

"I'm okay," she murmured.

But still, he couldn't let her go. He was reliving that horrible moment when he knew that Nick was going to shoot, and there wasn't a damn thing he could do about it.

"Why were you out there?" he asked hoarsely. "Damn it, Aliyah, what you did was stupid. Are you just trying to get yourself killed?"

He pressed his lips to her hair and closed his eyes. She stirred against him and pulled away.

"I went out to get a shirt out of the truck. I didn't *intend* to shift."

"What happened?" he asked. God, he couldn't get his heartbeat under control. He'd never been so scared in his life.

"I heard the truck pull up, and I hid behind the door, but then he got out, and he had a gun, and I got scared. I couldn't control it," she said softly. "The cheetah took over."

"What the hell is going on?" Nick bit out.

Duncan looked up to see Nick standing in the doorway of the cabin, rifle in hand, a fierce expression on his face.

"Put the gun away, Nick. Now."

"I'm not putting shit away until you explain what the fuck happened out there." He stared at Aliyah with blatant disbelief and deep suspicion. His gaze shot back and forth between her and Duncan, including Duncan in the flickering distrust in his eyes.

Duncan sighed but turned so that he shielded Aliyah from Nick. She slid her hand up his back, and he could feel her tremble. It angered him that she was afraid in the one place she should feel safe. His house.

"Back off, Nick. You put the goddamn gun away and sit your ass down. Then we'll talk."

Nick stood for a long moment before finally relaxing slightly and lowering the rifle. He still kept his hand curled around the stock, but he sat down on the hearth, never taking his eyes off Aliyah.

"I shot at a cheetah. I did not fucking imagine it. There was no woman. I don't shoot unarmed women." Nick shook his head adamantly as he spoke, his words terse.

Duncan looked back at Aliyah, his lips drawn in regret. "I have to tell him," he said in a low voice. "He has to know so that he doesn't tell anyone else. I trust him, Aliyah. I wouldn't put you in danger. But if we don't explain and this gets out, things will get bad for you here."

She nodded slowly, but he hated the fear in her eyes. He put his hand out to cup her cheek. With his other hand, he smoothed the hair from her face in a tender gesture.

"I'll protect you, honey. I won't let anyone hurt you."

"Tell him then," she said.

Duncan turned and drew in a deep breath. It had been hard enough for him to accept the truth about Aliyah. It wouldn't be any easier for Nick.

"First of all, Nick, what you saw today, what I'm about to tell you, goes no further than this room." He pinned Nick with a forceful stare. "I'm asking this as your friend."

Confusion flickered in Nick's eyes, and he leaned forward, concern creasing his forehead. "Okay, man. You know...you know you can count on me. Whatever it is, I'm with you."

Duncan nodded and relaxed. Nick was solid. He was someone Duncan could count on when the stakes were high. They'd been through a lot together, and he was one of the few people Duncan trusted implicitly.

He looked back at Aliyah, moved over to the side so that she could see Nick, but he was careful to arrange the blanket around her to shield her nudity. He curled his hand around hers and squeezed reassuringly.

Taking a breath, he turned his attention back to Nick who had laid the rifle aside. "Nick, this is Aliyah Carver. She has the ability...to change into a cheetah."

To Nick's credit, he didn't say a word, but then his expression said it all. He looked as though Duncan had just announced he was having a sex change.

"You saw it, Nick. You saw the cheetah. You shot at her. You saw the woman lying where the cheetah had been just moments before."

Nick grayed as the realization struck him that he'd shot at a living, breathing woman.

"Jesus," he breathed. He scrubbed his hand over his face. "Holy fuck. Duncan, you're telling me... What the hell are you saying?"

Duncan didn't answer. He just allowed it to sink in and watched as Nick battled against logic and what Duncan was telling him.

Nick shook his head. "No way. No fucking way. It's crazy. People don't just become animals."

Aliyah let out a sound of impatience and moved against Duncan. He put out a hand to soothe her, but she shoved it away and struggled out of the blanket to stand in front of the couch. As the rest of the blanket fell away and she stood naked in front of both men, Duncan growled his protest and reached for the blanket.

Nick's gaze was riveted to Aliyah, and while Duncan couldn't blame him, he was ready to knock Nick on his ass. Shock and confusion blazed across Nick's face as he stared in astonishment at Aliyah's naked body.

As a shudder worked up her spine, Duncan realized what she was doing.

"Aliyah, don't!"

She turned, her eyes already glittering with the change. Vertical slits of the cat's eyes stared back at him. "It's the only way," she whispered. "We don't have time to convince him."

With that, she fell to the floor, and Nick started forward as if to help her. Duncan stopped him with the force of his glare.

"Stay the fuck away from her," he said menacingly.

Duncan watched helplessly as Aliyah writhed and contorted. Nick's eyes widened in horror, and his mouth fell open in a wordless exclamation as he watched the golden cat rise where a woman had lain.

The cheetah rose unsteadily at first, and then she gained her footing and padded slowly toward Nick.

"Do not make any threatening moves," Duncan warned. "She won't hurt you. She's cognizant of her actions."

"Fuck," Nick whispered. "Fuck!"

The cheetah stopped in front of Nick and stared up at him. When she moved her head to rub against his leg, he flinched away and raised his hands in a protective gesture.

The cat continued to rub her head against his leg, and slowly, Nick lowered his hand, lightly touching the tuft of hair on her head. She bobbed her head upward and licked his hand then turned and walked back to where Duncan sat on the edge of the couch.

She leaped onto the sofa next to him and rubbed against him affectionately. A purr rippled from her throat and vibrated against

Duncan's shoulder as she continued to nudge at him.

He stroked her fur, and she ducked under his hand and licked his cheek, and then she simply lay across his lap, her contented purrs filling the room.

"Un-fucking-believable." Nick stared at Duncan in stupefaction. He edged forward, cautiously, his movements slow and calculated. "Can I...can I touch her?"

Duncan looked down as he continued to stroke behind the ears of the cheetah. When she continued to regard him with lazy, contented eyes and purrs rumbled from her throat, he nodded at Nick.

Nick put his hand on the cat's shoulder and snatched his hand back when the cheetah turned her head to stare at him. She sniffed the air in Nick's direction but made no effort to move.

Nick emitted a nervous laugh and put his hand back to touch her fur. He stroked hesitantly, but when she made no aggressive moves, he grew bolder, petting her neck and down her body.

Duncan's lips grew tight. How fucked in the head was he that he didn't want Nick touching the damn cat? Aliyah was his, whether in cheetah form or human, he didn't give a damn. He didn't want another man's hands on her.

When he felt the shudder roll over her body, he glared up at Nick. "Back off."

Nick scrambled back, and Duncan slid out from underneath the cat and turned protectively to shield her from Nick's view as she began the transformation back to human.

Soon she lay on the couch, her eyes closed, her breaths coming in weary spurts. Duncan quickly covered her with a blanket and gathered her in his arms. Uncaring of Nick's presence, he picked her up and turned so he could sit on the couch and hold her in his lap.

For several minutes, he held her, rocking slightly, his lips pressed to her hair as she regained control. He glanced up to see Nick staring at both of them in astonishment.

Nick's mouth rounded to an O as understanding dawned. Duncan hesitated only a moment and gave a short nod. His acknowledgement that Nick's observation was correct. Duncan was staking his claim.

"I'm sorry," Nick croaked. "God, I'm sorry. I could have killed you."

Aliyah stirred in his arms and fixed her gaze on Nick. "You didn't know," she said simply. "I got scared and freaked. I usually have better control. The last six months have been difficult for me."

Duncan's arms tightened around her. She riled every one of his protective instincts. He wanted to tuck her away where she was safe, where he could protect and cherish her.

His chest tightened uncomfortably, and a seed of panic grew when he thought of her leaving as soon as she was able.

Where would she go? Would she be safe? Who would protect her? Look after her? Keep her warm and clothed after her shifts?

He frowned again as he remembered once more that she'd made no attempt to call her family. It was a matter he intended to take up with her as soon as they were alone again.

"Why did you come out so early?" he asked Nick.

Nick looked momentarily surprised by the question, as though he'd forgotten entirely his reason for coming. Then his lips turned down into a frown, and a fierce light entered his eyes.

"I got a hit on the men you put out an APB on. They were spotted at a pharmacy in Hollis last night. One of them sported a rather interesting injury to his hand. The clerk said it looked like he got it caught in a meat grinder."

"That's him," Duncan said. "He's the one who pulled a rifle on me."

Nick jerked his head up in surprise. "You didn't say anything about that, Duncan."

Duncan sighed. "I didn't because at the time I had a cheetah in my truck with an arrow in her haunch. The hunter tried to collect the cheetah hide while I was trying to haul her out of the woods, and she attacked him."

"I'm guessing you didn't know she was human at this point," Nick said dryly.

Duncan cleared his throat in discomfort. "No, that didn't come until later."

Aliyah still lay quietly in his arms. Too quietly. He glanced down to see a troubled look set deeply into her features.

"What's wrong, honey?"

"It's not safe for me here," she said in a quiet voice.

No, it wasn't, but the alternative was her leaving, and he didn't want to think about that. He hated the fact that he couldn't guarantee her safety.

"Hell, it's not safe for you anywhere," Nick muttered. "How could it be?"

Duncan quickly relayed how Aliyah had come to be in the Colorado mountains, but even he knew the details were sparse, lacking a whole lot of history, like how Aliyah came to be in the first place, and if there were others like her.

Nick shook his head in amazement. "What do we do, Duncan? We can't let those bastards keep getting away with what they're doing. And fuck, if Aliyah is a cheetah, then what about all those other animals they're hunting? Are they humans too?"

Aliyah shook her head somewhat sadly. "There are very few of us left."

Duncan suddenly wished they were alone, because he wanted to know all there was to know about her, and he felt for the first time that she trusted him enough to confide in him.

He turned his attention reluctantly back to Nick. "I went up with Cal in the chopper yesterday. Didn't see anything. We're going to have to go in on foot." He hesitated for a moment. "I need to keep this as quiet as possible because of Aliyah. If we can gather the men needed to take down the ring ourselves then that's my preference. However, if we can't find it ourselves or it becomes too risky, I won't have a choice but to call in federal law enforcement."

He glanced at Aliyah as he spoke. "I won't let this compromise you. You have my word."

"I could help," she said in a quiet voice.

"No," Duncan said firmly. "Absolutely not."

She gathered the blanket tighter around her and leaned away from him so she could look into his eyes. "The cheetah could help, Duncan. I couldn't lead you back to where I was held, but she could. She knows their scent. I'm fast and I'm careful. I would only remain in cheetah form long enough to guide you to the hunters, and I could stay back, wherever you put me. I don't have any more desire to put myself in danger than you have to put me there, but this is something I could do with minimal risk."

"She's right, Duncan," Nick said thoughtfully. "If I headed up the team of our men with Cal's, you and Aliyah could go ahead, lock onto the location and radio back. That way she stays out of sight."

Aliyah touched her hand to Duncan's face and stared up at him, her golden eyes seething with emotion. "I want to do this, Duncan. They stole from me. They stole my freedom. They stole those other animals from their rightful homes. Some of them are *dead*. If it can be done safely, I'd like to help you put them away."

He captured her hand in his and turned his head so that his lips came into contact with her fingers.

"I want you here," he said hoarsely. "Where I know you'll be safe."

She stroked her fingers lightly over his lips then cupped his cheek in her hand. She nestled her body closer to his, cuddling into his chest. "But I'll be with you, Duncan. And that's the place I feel the safest. With you. You know what I am. You won't allow anyone to hurt me. I have faith in that."

The stalwart belief in her voice shook him, humbled him.

"I won't let the others get close to you, Duncan," Nick said. "You'll radio your location to me. I'll radio that we're coming in. That should give you plenty of time to make sure Aliyah is in a safe place."

The plan made sense, and it could work. The thought of Aliyah in danger made him ill. As long as the hunters were out there, she wasn't safe.

"All right. We'll do it. I don't like it, but we'll do it."

He glanced down at Aliyah and kissed her tenderly, not caring that Nick was sitting a few feet away. "You'll do as I say. You won't place yourself in danger nor will you take any unnecessary risks. If anything, and I mean *anything*, happens to me or things go wrong, you're to get your ass out of there."

She wrapped her arms around his neck and kissed him fiercely. "Nothing will happen to you. I'll make sure of it."

Chapter Fifteen

"Tell me about your people," Duncan said as he returned to the couch after seeing Nick off.

He sat down next to her, and she automatically curled into his body, not caring that she was still naked beneath the blanket. His arms came around her, and she laid her cheek against his chest, feeling the strong beat of his heart.

"Why haven't you contacted your parents? They must be so worried."

She inhaled a deep breath and pulled slightly away so she could look at him, though his arms remained wrapped around her.

"I did try to call them while you were at work. I wasn't sure I could trust you at first," she said simply.

"And now?"

His brown eyes bore into her, a flicker of hope warming the dark orbs.

"I trust you."

Satisfaction glinted, though he showed no other outward reaction to her statement.

"Then tell me," he said.

She did trust him. Unwavering determination reflected in his every action, his every word. She knew he'd protect her and wouldn't betray her. And that had an unnerving effect on her. She wanted this man. She wanted him with a painful longing. One that had built and swelled within her since the moment he'd gathered her in his arms.

She licked her lips, knowing she would tell him all. Tell him things she'd never told another soul.

"My father is the great Kodiak bear. My mother, a majestic eagle. It's why we lived in Alaska at first. They could move in relative obscurity because the island we inhabited had a healthy population of both.

"Then my sister was born, and the spirit guide gifted her with the cougar. And then I was born and was given the cheetah. As a child, I spent more time in animal form than other children of my race. I was playful and mischievous, and my parents feared that I would be discovered, even as remotely as we lived.

"And then..." A surge of pain threaded through her chest. It had been so many years, but the loss still felt fresh and vibrant in her mind.

"Then what?" Duncan asked gently.

"My sister was taken. We believe she was taken. She simply disappeared, and we never found her. My parents were distraught. It nearly destroyed them. And then there was me, spending more time in cheetah form than human. The cheetah has always been strong within me, and I was too young to learn dominance.

"We spent a year searching, hoping, but then my parents had to face the fact that she was gone, and they were so afraid the same would happen to me. So we moved to Africa.

"One of our kind manages a game preserve. He's a lion shifter. We went there so I would be safer, so I could be with more of my own kind. It was hard on my parents because now they were the ones forced to be so careful. They spent much time in human form, but our animal self has to be nurtured or the relationship suffers. There is trust between human and animal. A bond that cannot be broken.

"When I was old enough and mature enough to better control the divide between human and cheetah, we moved back to Alaska. My parents and I operate a lodge for travelers. It was during a visit back to Africa that I was captured by the hunters.

"Ironic, isn't it?" She laughed but it cracked and came out feebly. "The one place I felt truly safe...free...was the place I was captured. I was stupid and careless."

Duncan smoothed her hair from her face and pulled her back against his chest. "You have such an amazing life. Such an incredible story. I can't even fathom that there are people out there just like me only they're animals."

He stopped for a moment, and she could feel another question brewing.

"How is it you're all so different? I would have thought it was genetic, and yet your parents, you, your sister, you're all completely different. Entirely different species."

She smiled. He was logical, and she'd just shattered his understanding of the world he lived in.

"We aren't born a certain animal. It is a gift bestowed to us. What the parents are has no bearing on what a child becomes. When a woman becomes pregnant, she is visited by the spirit guide. I suppose you could call him God. Is he your God? That I can't answer. Maybe they're one and the same.

"There is a scripture in the Bible, though, that I've always carried with me. *Before I formed you in the womb I knew you.* Because when a woman is pregnant, she is given a vision of what gift will be bestowed on her child. That scripture has always resonated with me. The spirit guide knew me before I was placed in my mother's womb. He knew what gift I would carry with me. I find that comforting."

"And when you have children? Will they carry those gifts as well? Are you required to marry within your race for it to be passed down to your children?"

"There are no rules, Duncan. We are few. Fewer now than ever. I don't know why. Not every child is gifted with the ability to shift. Some parents who are both shifters give birth to fully human children while some of the very few who have partnered outside our people have borne children who were given the ability."

"So it's random?" Duncan frowned. "That doesn't seem very logical."

She shook her head. "I don't believe it's random. I don't think anything is. I firmly believe there is a reason why some are gifted with the ability and others aren't. Some things are beyond the scope of human understanding. Some things just *are*."

"But where did you come from? You speak of people of your kind, and yet you're scattered."

She sighed. "We are an old race. We arrived in America before the first Native Americans. I suppose you could say *we're* the original Native Americans. We were small and secretive. Instead of engaging when others encroached on our land, our territory, we would simply move on, seeking out other places where we could be free."

"You speak as though you were there," he murmured.

She smiled. "No. But stories have been passed down from generation to generation. Carefully safeguarded, meticulously retold. We fear putting anything in writing.

"It was that same fear that eventually caused us to disperse and go our separate ways, no longer living as a community. Many of us have lost touch. Our numbers aren't known. Smaller groups of us keep touch and help each other when we can. We fear…" She swallowed against the knot growing in her throat. Duncan's hand continued to soothe down her hair, over her shoulder and down her arm.

"What do you fear?" he asked.

"Extinction," she whispered.

He kissed the top of her head, and she lay there for a long moment, resting her cheek against his chest. His heartbeat thudded comfortingly next to her ear. Strong. Steady. Like him.

Slowly, she pulled away and stared up at him, her heart in her throat. "I'd like to call my parents now if that's okay with you."

He nodded. "Of course, honey. You stay here. I'll get you the phone."

Butterflies winged their way through her stomach and into her chest. Tears stung her eyes. She wasn't even sure she'd be able to form a coherent sentence. *Let them be there this time.*

When Duncan returned, he settled beside her and touched her gently on the cheek. "Tell me the number, and I'll dial it for you."

She related the number in a shaky voice then looked up at him fearfully as he handed her the phone. She waited anxiously as the phone rang, and her breath caught and held when her mother's voice came over the line.

"Mama?" she whispered. "Mama, it's Aliyah."

There was a moment of stunned silence before her mother began babbling in her ear. They were both sobbing as Aliyah poured her story out, and then her father picked up, his gruff, deep voice shaken with emotion.

"Where are you, baby? We'll come get you."

Aliyah frowned. She didn't even know where she was. Colorado. She knew that much. She couldn't even tell her parents how to come get her. She looked to Duncan for help and then told her mother to hold on for a moment.

She held the phone out to him. "They need to know where I am so they can come get me. I-I don't know how to tell them."

Duncan's hand closed over hers as he took the phone. "Don't worry, honey, I'll tell them what they need to know."

Aliyah listened as Duncan politely introduced himself to her parents and then assured them that she was okay and that she was safe with him. There was a moment of uncomfortable silence when Duncan told them that he was well aware of what Aliyah was and that it didn't make a damn bit of difference to him because no one was going to hurt her.

Finally, he gave them the information they needed before he handed the phone back to her.

"We'll be there as soon as we can," her mother said. "We're leaving now. Your father is calling the pilot to get us to Kodiak, and from there we'll book a flight into Denver. We'll see you soon."

"I love you, Mama," she whispered.

"Oh, I love you too, my baby. I'm so glad you're alive."

Aliyah hung up and closed her eyes. Tears slipped from underneath her eyelids and trickled down her cheeks. Warm lips sipped them from her skin and kissed a path up her face until he pressed his mouth to one closed eyelid and then the other.

She reached blindly for him, wrapping her arms around his neck. "Love me," she whispered.

They only had another day. Tomorrow she would lead Duncan to the hunters, and her parents would arrive soon after.

He gathered her in his arms, letting the blanket fall away. He carried her into the bedroom and laid her gently on the bed. He followed her down, pressing his body to hers, kissing her, nibbling delicately at her neck and jawline.

"I need you so much."

He swallowed her words into his mouth, and he ravished her lips. He pulled at his clothes, never leaving her but for the briefest of seconds as he tossed his shirt and pants across the room.

She was waiting with open arms when he returned, lowering his body to hers. Skin on skin. Warm. Soft against hard. Loving. So tender. So gentle it made her heart ache. For all their erotic romping of the night before, this was, in effect, their good-bye.

She ran her fingertips up his sides then over his back until they dug into his shoulders. Her head fell back as she bared her neck to his seeking lips.

They traced downward, over the column of her shoulder then down to her breasts. Warm, liquid desire, like a cup of hot chocolate on a cold winter night seeped into her veins, heating her body. Her breasts swelled and ached, the nipples tightening to rigid points.

He licked at one then the other, alternating the swipes of his tongue with sharp little nips of his teeth. She wiggled and squirmed, but he held her fast, her body laid out like a feast.

"I want inside you so bad," he murmured. "Give me a minute to get the condom."

"No," she protested, wrapping her legs around his waist. His cock brushed against the damp flesh between her thighs, and she quivered. "Please. I want you now."

His gaze focused on her. "Aliyah, honey, are you sure?"

"Please. Let me have all of you tonight."

He pushed into her wetness with a groan. She cried out at the fullness, in shock at the exquisite feel of his flesh against hers, no barrier between them.

He slid his hands underneath to cup her buttocks. He squeezed and spread her wider as he planted himself deeper and deeper still with each thrust.

"Open for me, sweetheart. Take all of me, just like before. Relax and let me have you just as you have me."

His words sent a shockwave of desire soaring through her belly. She arched into him, opening, surrendering, letting him take everything she could give him.

"Give me more," he growled.

And she felt herself open for him, accept all of him as he thrust deep, touching the deepest part of her soul. Her body cradled his as he took her over and over, possessing her, owning her.

I love you.

At first she thought she'd said it aloud, but it welled up from the depths of her heart. Her mind screamed it, her heart accepted it.

"Take me," she whispered. "I'll always be yours."

He shuddered above her and poured himself into her welcoming body. Her world fractured. Splintered as tiny fragments of pleasure burst around her. She felt his warmth fill her and found peace as she slowly fell back to earth.

She held him tightly against her, refusing to let go. Not wanting their time together to end.

Chapter Sixteen

They gathered at dawn. Nick, Duncan and Aliyah stood in the cold morning air, their breaths coming in puffs in the pale light.

"You go meet with your team, Nick. I'll take Aliyah, and we'll see if we can find their trail. When I have a location, I'll holler. You'll move in, and I'll make sure Aliyah is safe before I join you."

Nick nodded and started to climb into his truck. He paused with one leg inside and turned to Aliyah. He started to speak but shook his head.

"I don't even know what to say. I guess good luck will have to do. I hope we meet again someday."

She smiled. "Thank you, Nick. It was very nice meeting you. Even if you did scare the living daylights out of me."

He winced and then got into his truck and drove away.

Duncan wrapped his arm around her shoulders, and she gazed up at him. "Are you ready?" she asked.

He stared at her for a long moment. "If I'm honest, no. I'm not ready. I don't want you involved. I want you here where I know you're safe."

She reached up on tiptoe and kissed him. Then she crawled into the truck on his side and scooted over to let him in.

They drove back out to where Duncan had first found her. They parked as close as he could, and they hiked the rest of the way. When he thought they were far enough to avoid being seen, he turned to Aliyah. And he nearly called the whole thing off.

He didn't want this. Didn't want her to do this. The whole thing had a very bad feel to it.

She put small hand on his arm. "Duncan, it'll be all right. You'll be with me."

Him and his damn arsenal. He'd brought his rifle, two pistols, and a compound bow, just in case. He wasn't taking any chances with her safety.

Without any hesitation, she peeled off the layers of her clothing and handed them to him so he could stuff them into his bag.

Her golden eyes, so beautiful, stared unblinking at him, and then they flickered as the change came over her. She seemed to embrace it with more ease this time, as if she had more control. She fell gracefully to the ground as her skin rippled and was replaced by tawny fur.

When she was fully cheetah, she rose and padded over to him to rub against his leg. Her throat rumbled with purrs as she nuzzled closer.

He knelt and dug his fingers into her fur, and she licked his face before rubbing her jowls against his cheek.

"Let's go find our hunters, girl," he murmured as he rose once more.

She picked up the trail quickly, but she seemed to be locked on the memory of where she had been rather than relying solely on scent. She was tense, wary and on alert as she guided him further into the mountains.

Three hours later, she stopped and growled, her face lifting into the wind as she sniffed. Duncan put his hand on her, a command for her to get down. She readily complied, lowering her body until she was lying on her stomach.

He got out his binoculars and focused on the cabin in the distance. It was in a good location, sheltered on three sides by natural cover. He frowned when he got a glimpse of several empty cages on the porch. A moving truck with the back opened was parked close to the front door. A moment later, three men carrying a cage with what looked to be a tiger inside, came out and hoisted the cat into the back of the truck.

Bingo.

He took out his radio and GPS and quietly relayed the coordinates to Nick. Nick radioed back that they were at most an hour away and would close in rapidly. They set up a rendezvous point and signed off.

Duncan put his hand on the cheetah, and she looked lazily up at him before shifting her head so she could lick his hand. He reached for his pack and pulled out her clothing, hoping she'd get the hint that it was time to shift back.

A few seconds later, she lay on the ground, naked and shivering.

Duncan quickly helped her get dressed then urged her away. He had to find a place to shelter her. A place he could stash her so she'd be safe until he could return.

They hiked back about half a mile in silence until he found an area surrounded by thick brush with several boulders she could huddle behind. He pulled a blanket out of his pack and wrapped it around her as he settled her as comfortably as he could.

He squatted beside her and left the pack beside her then handed her his radio. "If you have any trouble, you call for me or Nick. Hopefully this will all be over soon, and I'll be back for you."

He leaned in and kissed her forcefully. She reached up to cup his face and kissed him back just as hard. His hands trailed down her body, touching her, reasserting his claim. Her lips trembled under his, and she pulled away.

"Be careful, Duncan. Please."

"You bet."

He stood and gave her another long look before finally turning away. With each step, he felt more dread creep over him. But he had a job to do. He had to keep Aliyah safe and make sure this sort of thing didn't happen to her again. Those bastards would pay.

Aliyah tried to relax. She knew she was in for a long wait, and she was determined that she wouldn't give Duncan any cause for concern. He had enough to do with taking down the poaching ring.

She dozed for a while, though it was an uneasy sleep. As the sun rose higher overheard, warmth filtered through the trees and provided more heat. She checked the time on the GPS unit and saw that a few hours had elapsed.

She stretched, shifting her position then froze when a light sound carried to her on the wind. The cheetah within her stirred, her instincts riled. Aliyah sat unmoving, listening to the disturbance she felt more than heard.

There, again. A sound, a human sound moving through the brush. It wasn't Duncan; he would have called to her.

Fear took hold, and the cheetah protested, immediately rising, wanting to protect. Aliyah forced her back and tried to control her panic. It could be nothing.

She edged around one of the boulders so she could get a view downhill.

A hunter.

She recognized him as the one she'd attacked. He was moving stealthily, looking back as if someone were pursuing him. Then she heard a voice, heard someone call out to him.

Shit.

There were two of them, and they were headed directly for her. No way they wouldn't see her.

She reached for the radio and eased it up. She raised it to her mouth and whispered into the receiver.

"Duncan, Nick, it's Aliyah. Don't answer. There are two hunters. They're close. I don't want them to hear."

Her heart pounded viciously against her breastbone, and her breathing ratcheted up. The cheetah within howled, wanting to break free, to flee. Aliyah tried to push down the urge to shift, but she knew she fought a losing battle. The cheetah rose up, forcing its will on the human, the need to protect all consuming.

The change crawled over her body with amazing speed. Adrenaline surged through her veins as her limbs reshaped and her back arched.

She shot from her hiding spot, knowing she'd have the element of surprise. Hopefully she would be away before the hunters could react.

A shout of surprise sounded behind her, and she knew she'd been spotted.

One rifle shot cracked the air, and then another. She leaped forward, pushing her body to its limits. Another shot echoed and pain exploded in her shoulder. She fell hard.

She struggled to get up, but she was losing blood fast. Still, she crawled forward, trying to reach the ravine she and Duncan had passed. She could slide down and into the river and let the current sweep her away.

As she reached the edge, she looked back to see the two hunters staring at her down the sights of their rifles. Despair washed through her. She didn't want to die.

"That's the cat that mangled my hand," one of them bit out. "I want her hide. No, I want her stuffed and mounted."

She only had one chance. The river. With the last bit of her strength, she vaulted to her feet. Pain lanced through her body, nearly causing her to collapse. She held on by sheer force of will. The will to live.

Another rifle shot exploded as she hurled herself over the edge of the ravine.

Chapter Seventeen

Duncan handcuffed another suspect and unceremoniously stuffed him into the back of one of the SUVs. He was seething with impatience to get back to Aliyah.

He looked up to see Nick hurrying toward him, a grim expression on his face. Duncan held up a hand. "I don't have time for whatever it is, Nick. I've got to get back to Aliyah."

"Aliyah radioed, Duncan. She's in trouble."

Duncan slammed the door and rounded on Nick. "What happened?"

"She radioed and said there were two men, two of the hunters closing in on her location. She didn't want me to answer so they must have been close."

A distant rifle shot sounded. Then another. Then silence and a third shot. From the sound, it had to be at least a mile away. Maybe two. But it was undeniably the sound of a high-powered rifle.

Fear nearly paralyzed him. He grabbed Nick's shirt. "You're with me."

He shouted a quick explanation to one of the other deputies, and he and Nick jumped on two of the ATVs confiscated in the raid. Duncan tore off in the direction he'd left Aliyah with Nick following close behind.

It took an eternity to backtrack to the area he'd left her. When they finally reached the spot, Duncan leaped from the four-wheeler and scrambled over the rocks to where he'd left Aliyah.

His blood became ice when he saw the tattered remnants of her clothing lying on the ground. The radio and GPS unit were on the ground next to the blanket and his bag, but there was no sign of Aliyah.

"Duncan," Nick called. "You need to see this."

Duncan looked up to see Nick fifty yards up the incline staring down at the ground. He didn't like the sound of Nick's voice at all.

He ran.

When he saw the blood on the ground, his heart nearly stopped. "No. Oh God, *no*."

"There's fur, Duncan." Nick's voice was grim. "She was in cheetah form when they shot her. I have fur and blood. A lot of it, and it heads toward the ravine."

Nausea welled in Duncan's stomach as he stumbled after Nick. There was a distinct blood trail, and he could see the paw prints, and then an indention where she obviously fell.

She'd been trying to make it over the edge.

"The blood stops here, and there's a lot. It pooled here," Nick said. "She stopped here, probably fell."

Duncan stared at the ground, searching for more evidence, something to tell them what else had happened. Boot prints. Humans. Blood mixed in. They'd followed her up here. Then what?

He spotted another splotch of blood closer to the edge of the ravine, and panic squeezed his chest. He bolted the remaining steps to the edge, looking down at the distinct blood spatters.

The trail led right to the edge. There were scuff marks in the dirt, paw prints right to the very last. As he glanced down the incline, he could see more blood smeared on the rocks. She'd gone into the river.

"They headed south, Duncan," Nick called.

Duncan tore his gaze from the river and hurried over to where Nick stood.

"She went into the river," he said hoarsely.

"You go after her," Nick said. "I can call for backup, and we'll head after the hunters."

Duncan hesitated. "Don't go after them alone," he ordered. "Call Cal. Have him meet you here with at least two deputies. I'll have the radio. If I find her...if I find her alive, I'll take her back to the cabin, and then I'll double back to help finish up."

Nick eyed him levelly. "Go, Duncan. We can handle this without you. She's hurt, and she needs you. You can't leave her." He thrust his pack at Duncan that held medical supplies and survival gear.

Duncan grabbed it and ran back to the ravine. When he reached the edge, he got down on his knees, rotated around and dropped his feet down.

The pressure in his chest was unbearable. He felt a sense of dread he hadn't felt since the day he'd been told his parents were gone. Aliyah had to be alive. He couldn't lose her this way.

He scrambled down the rocky incline, the sound of the water growing louder in his ears. It would be dark soon, and it was growing colder. If she'd taken a dive into the river, and if she shifted back to human, she could be hypothermic in short order.

When he reached the bottom, he scanned the bank, looking for any indication she had merely run along the side. No blood. No fur.

He closed his eyes and swallowed the panic back. Aliyah was counting on him. He'd already failed her, broken his promise to keep her safe.

He unclipped his flashlight from his pants and started down the rocky bank, a fervent prayer spilling from his lips. He followed the winding path as it curved through the small valley. At one point it narrowed as it cut through a gorge and then plunged outward again as the terrain flattened. In another quarter-mile the river shallowed to a point where the current couldn't possibly carry a body, cheetah or human.

His breathing ratcheted up until his vision blurred. Would he find her lying in the calmer pools? He charged ahead, nearly running now. His chest burned as he pushed himself harder.

As he rounded the bend of the last series of rapids, his gaze locked onto the smoother waters only ankle deep. He didn't know whether to be relieved or scared to death when he saw no sign of her anywhere. The water rippled along as though no disturbance had ever occurred.

And then he saw it. Blood. Just a small splatter on the rocks in front of his feet. He shined the flashlight on the ground. Adrenaline rocketed through his veins when he saw another small splotch on the rocks heading into the woods.

She'd survived the river.

Resisting the urge to charge into the trees after her, he forced himself to follow the blood trail. He hands shook as he saw the blood increase the further from the river he went. She was still bleeding heavily.

He stopped when he came to a large blood smear, heavier than the prior trail. His heart began pounding furiously. She'd stopped here.

He swung the flashlight in a tight radius, and then he saw it. A

112

human footprint in the bloody soil. She'd shifted.

"Aliyah," he called. "Aliyah!"

He narrowed all his focus to following her footprints, relying on blood when the terrain was too rocky to register the indention of her feet.

"Aliyah!" he called again as he navigated the next rise. He swung his light downward and across the area in front of him. He froze, his hand stopping the sweep when the pale light of human flesh reflected in the glow of the flashlight.

He scrambled down the hill and dropped to his knees in front of Aliyah's still form. He reached for her neck, feeling for a pulse. Her skin was still warm to his touch even amidst the chill of the air. He nearly wilted in relief when he felt the faint tremor against his fingers.

He turned her body over, looking for a wound. As he gently rolled her and shined the light across her torso, he saw the jagged wound in her shoulder. Blood still oozed from the wound, but at a much slower rate than the earlier trail had suggested.

"Aliyah," he whispered as he trailed a hand across her cheek. "Aliyah, honey, wake up."

Knowing he had to move fast if he had any prayer of getting her back to the cabin, he tucked the flashlight into the waistband of his pants and hoisted her gently into his arms. When she was high against his chest, he moved her up and over his shoulder in a fireman's carry.

He reached first for his radio with his free hand.

"Nick, do you read me?"

There was a long silence, and then the radio crackled.

"Duncan, yeah, I'm here. What's going on?"

"Target acquired. I'm proceeding with the plan as I outlined."

Again there was a pause.

"Roger that. We've apprehended two suspects. I'll be down at the station processing them. I'll see you when I see you. And Duncan? Good luck," he finished softly.

Duncan shoved his radio back onto his clip then snagged the flashlight from his pants. He shifted Aliyah's weight and started back to the river. If he followed the bank another mile, it would lead him to an old national forest road that would take him just a quarter-mile from his cabin.

He curled his arm over her legs and focused on each step. One foot in front of the other. Aliyah depended on him. He wouldn't let her down again.

An hour later, he staggered from the national forest road onto the county road that would lead him to his cabin. His shoulder ached. Pain splintered down his spine, but still he continued on.

Aliyah's head bumped against his back, and he slowed his walk so he didn't jostle her more than he had to. Sweat rolled down the back of his neck even as the cold evening air made him shiver.

He caught the lights of his cabin ahead, and he redoubled his efforts, lengthening his stride. When he turned into the gravel drive and saw the silver Ford Expedition parked close to the door, he stopped cold.

A multitude of expletives bubbled in his throat. He tossed the flashlight and reached for his gun. Ducking as low as he could while still carrying Aliyah, he crept closer to the house. He had no choice but to stash her outside and go in to secure the cabin.

He laid her gently on the ground behind a clump of bushes, shrugged out of his jacket and laid it over her. He reached for his radio again.

"Nick, I may need backup. I have an unknown vehicle parked in front of my cabin. I had to leave Aliyah on the ground out front. I'm going in."

"I'm on my way," Nick said shortly.

Duncan pocketed his radio again and crept toward the cabin. He stopped near the front window, pressed himself against the wall and peered around the edge. Through the sliver the curtain bared, he saw a middle-aged couple standing in the living room.

He relaxed a fraction. Aliyah's parents? Whatever the case, they didn't appear to be armed. He pulled his radio out.

"Nick, stand down. I've got it from here."

"You sure?"

"Yeah. I'll check in later."

Duncan raised his gun and hurried for the door. He put his free hand on the knob, twisted and burst in, weapon pointed at the couple.

The man shoved the woman behind him and immediately raised his hands.

"Who are you?" Duncan demanded.

"Lawrence Carver," he replied. "We're here for Aliyah."

Duncan lowered his weapon. "Stay here. I'll get her."

The woman darted from behind Lawrence. "Where is she? Is she all right?"

Duncan held up his hand. "Stay here, Mrs. Carver. I have to go back for Aliyah."

He turned and hurried back to where Aliyah lay. He holstered his gun and quickly picked her up. As he strode back to the cabin, he heard Mrs. Carver's anguished cry.

They stood back so Duncan could pass through the door. He walked over to the couch and laid Aliyah down. Her mother flew to her side and knelt on the floor beside her. Her hands fluttered over Aliyah's face.

"What happened?" she asked.

"Merry, she's alive," Lawrence said as he sank to his knees beside his wife. He touched Aliyah's wound with trembling hands then turned his gaze to Duncan.

"What happened?"

"Hunters," Duncan said grimly.

"But why was she out there?" Merry asked desperately.

Duncan scrubbed a hand over his face as he faced her parents. "She helped us locate them," he said quietly.

"You were supposed to protect her. You were supposed to keep her safe until we got here."

The accusation in her voice made Duncan flinch.

"You have to take her away," Duncan said. "She's not safe here." His gaze swept over her wound, and he took in the worried stares of her parents. "Will she heal?" His voice cracked, and he swallowed the knot building in his throat at the idea that this would be the last time he saw her.

"It will take time," Lawrence said in a quiet voice. "She will need to once again find the balance between herself and the cheetah. It will aid her in her recovery. We'll take her home at once. You have our undying gratitude not only for saving our daughter but for keeping her...our secret."

"I have to go," Duncan said. "We made several arrests. I brought her back here to shield her from scrutiny, to keep her out of the case. It would be better if she weren't here. I don't know what all the hunters saw."

Lawrence nodded, and the ache in Duncan's chest grew. He moved hesitantly toward Aliyah. Her mother stood and moved back a step as if sensing his need.

He knelt by the couch and put his hand gently over her forehead. He smoothed his fingers through her hair and pressed his lips to her brow.

"Good-bye," he whispered. "Be safe. I—" He broke off and turned away, rising to his feet. He cast a quick glance at Aliyah's parents. "Tell her...tell her I'm sorry."

He turned and walked out of the house to get into his truck. For a long moment he sat behind the steering wheel, watching as Lawrence Carver carried his daughter from the cabin and put her inside his vehicle.

Duncan's fingers curled around the steering wheel, and he felt the quiet rise of despair. He keyed the ignition, put it in reverse and backed out of the drive.

Chapter Eighteen

He missed her. No two ways about it.

Duncan shed his coat and tossed it on the couch then followed it down with a weary sigh. The last few weeks had been a pisser. Elk Ridge had made national news, and as a result, the media had been swarming over the small town, interviewing the locals and everyone who'd ever claimed to visit the region.

Arrangements had been made for the animals recovered in the sting operation. Arrests had been made, and the poachers awaited trial on a host of federal charges. It had been a circus, but now things were finally quiet again.

And here he was, home, alone, thinking about a golden-eyed temptress and missing her with his every breath. It was pretty pathetic, and he was fairly certain it made him a pussy.

He hadn't heard from Aliyah or her parents, a fact that made him crazy. He didn't know how she was doing, if she was hurting, healing, but then he hadn't tried to call them either. He didn't want any link discovered between him and Aliyah and the possible questions that could arise were it found out that she had been here when the raid went down.

You love her, fool.

Yeah, as crazy as it sounded, he'd fallen and fallen hard in the few days they'd been together. He'd even managed to get around the fact that she spent part of her time as a cheetah. Yep, he'd lost his mind. Or more accurately, his heart.

He rubbed tiredly at his neck and briefly contemplated hitting the sack early, but going to the empty bed that awaited him in his bedroom wasn't remotely appealing.

A light scratching noise interrupted his self-absorbed malaise. He cocked his head, thinking maybe he'd imagined it, but then he heard it again. Coming from his front door.

With a frown, he got up and walked cautiously to the door, his hand reaching for his sidearm that he hadn't yet taken off.

There it was again. Definitely something outside his door and getting louder and more persistent.

He cracked open the door but before he could even look out to assess the potential danger, he was flattened by a flying fur ball.

He fell back as a cheetah pounced on him. His back hit the floor with a resounding thump as a golden-eyed cat licked him and nuzzled his face.

Aliyah.

His surprise turned to complete and utter joy. Relief.

And then suddenly he found himself holding a gorgeous, naked woman in his arms.

"You've really got to stop doing that shit," he grumbled. "It's disconcerting, and it looks painful."

"Aren't you glad to see me?" she asked as her lips met his.

"Oh, honey," he groaned. "If you only had any idea how much I've missed you."

He stretched his leg out to kick the door shut then wrapped his arms around his woman and proceeded to kiss her senseless. Her lips were cold against his, and she'd never tasted sweeter.

Her hair fell over his face, and her breasts pressed against his shirt. He smoothed his hands over her body, wanting to touch her, absorb her, make sure he wasn't in the midst of a dream. One he'd had many times since she'd left.

And then it hit him. She was here. And she shouldn't be here. She should be safe in Alaska. With her parents. Not here where she risked discovery.

"What are you doing here?" he asked even as he stroked her skin, touched her face, twined his fingers through her hair and stole another kiss. "You shouldn't be here, honey. It's dangerous."

"I love you," she said simply, and his heart nearly stopped. He actually felt light-headed, which he was sure made him even more of a pussy than all the mooning he'd done.

And yet she said it as though it answered the mysteries of the universe, as if those three simple words held the answer to all things and by virtue, her appearance made total sense.

It didn't.

"As much as I love lying here on the floor on my back, on the *hard* floor on my back with my arms full of a gorgeous..." He stopped to kiss her again. He simply couldn't help himself. "Could we move this conversation to the couch?"

She grinned and crawled off of him then extended her hand down to help him up. As soon as he was standing, he pulled her into his arms and held her tightly even as he maneuvered toward the couch.

He sat down, pulling her down on his lap so he could hold her. God, he just couldn't stop touching her. And of course he was going to have to open his mouth and say something stupid. Something he didn't want to say but needed saying nonetheless.

"You shouldn't be here. It's dangerous. Aliyah, what if you're discovered? How do your parents feel about this? They must be freaking out."

She put a finger over her lips then nuzzled closer to him and kissed him, long and hot. Her tongue swept over his lips and then inside, rippling over his, teasing, taunting. And he promptly forgot what he'd been trying to tell her.

When she pulled away, her eyes sparkled with laughter, with *happiness.*

He put his hand to her shoulder as it suddenly occurred to him that she might not yet be fully healed.

"I'm fine," she said huskily. "See?" She turned her arm so he could see that not a single mark marred her sun-kissed skin.

He kissed the area where he'd last seen the angry, bloody wound. "You scared me," he admitted. "I was afraid I'd lost you. I did lose you. You shouldn't be here."

She laughed. "You aren't going to lose me any more than I'm going to lose you. You're mine, Duncan. And I keep what's mine. I'm very possessive that way."

"But honey—"

"Do you love me?" she asked, her gaze earnestly searching his face.

"Yes, but—"

"No buts. Do you love me? Do you want me?"

He crushed her to him. "God yes, I love you. I want you so damn much. I don't want you to ever leave. I want you here with me always. I love you. I love you so damn much it hurts."

Her arms crept around his neck, and he could feel her tremble against him. Her soft lips kissed the pulse at his neck and then she pulled away.

"Then that's all that matters."

"It matters if I can't keep you safe," he said.

She smiled, her eyes shining bright with such faith that it humbled him. "You'll keep me safe, Duncan. And I'll be careful. We'll be careful. It will take sacrifice. I know that I won't be able to shift when I want and where I want. I know that there will always be a risk if we're together, but I can't live without you. I don't want to be without you. I'm willing to risk anything to be with you. Always."

When she put it that way, how could he argue? She was willing to risk everything. She was willing to sacrifice her freedom to be with him. He didn't feel worthy of her, but damn if he was going to let that get in the way.

"I love you," he said hoarsely. "I don't want you to go. Stay. With me. We'll make it work. I'll protect you with my life."

She cupped his face in her hands. Tears shone in her eyes, making the gold liquid and glistening. "I love you too," she whispered. "I'll stay. Always."

Amber Eyes

Dedication

To Fuh-teen and Natalie, for always coming through in my time of need!

Chapter One

"She's back," Jericho said from his position by the window. Behind him Hunter got up and came to look out at the snow-covered ground.

A storm had blown all day, dumping a foot of snow on the high country cabin Jericho and Hunter shared between assignments. Now, just as dusk was falling, the wind had died down, leaving a pristine layer of heavy, wet snow. Thankfully they'd stocked up on supplies because they weren't getting down the mountain unless they were up for a long walk in snowshoes.

"She's hurt," Hunter murmured over his cup of coffee.

Jericho nodded as he watched the mountain lion limp through the snow. Every once in a while, she fell heavily, encumbered by the high drifts. Then she'd struggle up and continue her slow trek toward the cabin.

It had been several months since they'd seen the mountain lion Hunter viewed as a pet. Not since the end of summer when they'd stumbled wearily into their cabin, washed out from another assignment.

The cat had been there, watching from a distance, as though she'd waited on them. But as always, after a day she'd disappeared back into the mountains.

Hunter set his cup down on the small end table by the couch and walked to the door.

"She won't come in," Jericho said. "She never does."

She'd stand outside watching them, her nose quivering delicately as she inhaled their scent as though trying to decipher whether or not they could be trusted. They often left food for her just outside the front door. Though they never saw her eat it, it was always gone. Whether she ate it or another scavenger did, he couldn't say, but he liked to think the cougar received their gift.

Hunter opened the door, and Jericho frowned as a blast of cold air shoved its way inside the warm interior. But Jericho kept his gaze trained out the window to where the cat pulled up as she scented Hunter.

Her ears flattened against her head, and she raised her nose, her nostrils flaring. Then, to Jericho's surprise, she started forward again. Her limp became more pronounced as she waded from the heavier snow banks onto the freshly shoveled stone walkway leading up to the cabin.

Patiently, Hunter waited inside the open door as the cougar drew closer.

"Hunter, I'm not sure this is such a good idea," Jericho began.

"She's hurting," Hunter said quietly, pain evident in his own voice.

Jericho shrugged. That the cougar was in pain wasn't in doubt. Hunter had a soft spot for animals that didn't extend to most people. Instead of ribbing his friend over his weakness, he gave thanks that Hunter could still feel anything.

Hunter backed away a few steps when the cougar stopped a few feet from the open doorway. Jericho moved so he could see better and also where his rifle was in grabbing distance. Hunter may trust the damn thing, but it was still a wild creature, and he had no desire to be lunch for a feline.

She sniffed delicately at the air, leaning forward and rearing her head up and down as her amber gaze swept between Hunter and Jericho. Then tentatively, she crept forward, her body low to the ground.

Jericho reached for the rifle hanging on the wall, lifted it and brought it down to his side. The cougar froze and began backing away.

"Put the goddamn gun away," Hunter said harshly.

Jericho frowned and started to argue, but Hunter strode across the room and snatched the rifle from Jericho's grasp. With a snarl, Hunter tossed the gun onto the couch then turned back to where the cougar was hunkered down in the walkway.

"Close the door," Jericho grumbled. "It's fucking cold in here."

"I'll close it when she comes in and not before," Hunter said in a voice as cold as the air surrounding them.

Before Jericho could ask him if he'd lost the few remaining

marbles he had, Hunter turned back to the doorway and began crooning to the cat in a soft tone Jericho hadn't heard him use since Rebeccah.

He murmured soft words, nonsensical, but the soothing tone couldn't be mistaken. There was a call to trust the man behind it, and Jericho, despite his initial misgivings, found himself keenly interested in whether Hunter would lull the wild beast.

Keeping a mistrustful eye on Jericho, the cat inched forward again, her ears twitching. When she got to the doorway, unease skittered along her spine, raising the fur as she jerked her head back and forth between Jericho and Hunter.

Hunter reached down, his movements slow and measured, and touched the top of her head. The cat's eyes closed in pleasure, and she rubbed her head roughly against Hunter's palm.

"I'll be damned," Jericho murmured.

"Open the door to the back porch," Hunter said in his quiet, even voice, never raising it above the low pitch he used to calm the cat. "I'll see if I can get her there."

Jericho did as Hunter asked even as he wondered what the hell Hunter was going to do when he got her confined to the screened-in patio.

Hunter backed toward the porch, his hand extended, still talking nonsense. If Hunter weren't so utterly serious, Jericho would give him hell about talking shit to a cat, but Hunter...well, he had his priorities. Animals and children were held high in his regard. Everyone else? Not so much.

"I know it hurts, girl," Hunter said as he coaxed her through the kitchen. "Just a little further and I'll look at that paw. Got it caught in a trap, did you?"

Jericho looked at the left front paw she wasn't putting much weight on and saw dried blood, but couldn't make much more of the wound. Could be anything from an embedded thorn to her getting caught in some trapper's steel jaws.

Hunter was a damn fool if thought he was going to doctor a wounded cougar. Cat would take his head off. Jericho shook his head. Well, someone had to look after the moron. Jericho grabbed the rifle from the couch where Hunter had thrown it and followed the limping cat through the kitchen.

Hunter looked up from his crouched position on the floor of the porch, his eyes glittering with anger.

"I told you to get rid of the gun."

Jericho shrugged. "I never took orders worth a shit. Besides, if she tries to have you for lunch, I'm going to take a chunk out of her hide."

The mountain lion turned her amber gaze on Jericho. There was sadness to her expression, almost as though she understood the men's conversation.

Jericho shook his head and muttered under his breath. He was losing his damn mind. He gripped the rifle a bit tighter, refusing to feel guilty for trying to save his friend's ass. Even if the idiot didn't want saving.

"Okay, shut the door," Hunter ordered.

Jericho reached back and gave the door a shove. For a moment the cat went on alert. She looked wildly around, her eyes glittering with a mixture of fear and pain. Hunter held out his hand, words of comfort tripping over his lips in their haste to get out.

The cougar fell to the floor, slumping as though the last of her strength had left her. Hunter touched her head, petting and then rubbing behind her ears. His eyes were bright with sympathy.

"Are you going to let me see your paw, girl?" Hunter said in a quiet voice. "I won't hurt you. I just want to see what you've done to yourself."

He moved with great care, inching his hand closer to the injured paw. When he finally touched the blood-matted fur, the cougar merely raised her head and sniffed experimentally in Hunter's direction. Then she settled down again, laying her head on the floor.

"Get me the first-aid kit," Hunter said.

"Tell me you aren't going to play vet with a friggin' wild animal," Jericho said, even though he knew arguing with Hunter was like pissing in the wind. Stupid any way you looked at it.

"I can at least put some antibiotic ointment on it and hope it prevents infection," Hunter said impatiently. "She trusts us. I want to help her."

Jericho went back into the house grumbling about hardheaded do-gooders, and then he had to laugh at the idea of labeling Hunter a do-gooder. Hard-assed bastard? Yes. Granola do-gooder? Uh, no.

He came back out a few moments later, first-aid kit in hand. Not wanting to get close enough to upset the cat, he tossed it to Hunter from the doorway.

The cougar rolled, a lazy-looking move that implied a level of comfort and trust. She gazed up at Jericho, her amber eyes glittering warmly. There was invitation there. Jericho frowned hard and shook himself. Now he was psychoanalyzing the body language of a damn cougar?

"Pet her," Hunter said firmly. "She wants you to."

"And you know this, how?" Jericho asked dryly.

"She's perfectly relaxed. She enjoys my touch. You could pet her while I clean her wound."

"Oh sure, let me be the sacrificial kitty meal," Jericho grumbled even as he started forward.

Gingerly, and with more than a little caution, he knelt close to the cat's head. She sniffed curiously at him as he lowered his hand. Then to his surprise, she licked his palm and bumped her head against him.

An unexpected smile softened his irritation. She continued to rub against his hand, and he allowed his fingers to dig into her soft fur.

A low growl rumbled from her throat when Hunter swabbed at her paw, but she didn't make any aggressive moves. Her body tensed under Jericho's fingers, but she remained still.

"Hurts, doesn't it, girl?" Jericho murmured.

Hunter gave him an amused look, and Jericho returned it with a sour gaze. Yeah, he'd given Hunter hell, but here he sat talking like a damn pussy to the animal.

While Hunter meticulously cleaned and applied the ointment to the inflamed wound, Jericho continued stroking her head. After a while, her eyes closed, and she went limp. She looked to be exhausted, and who knew how far she'd come through the snow to their cabin.

Hunter rocked back and stood from his crouch in front of the cat. "That's about all I can do for her."

"What was it?" Jericho asked.

Hunter shrugged. "Looks like she got it caught in a trap. Or could be she got into a fight with another animal. Hard to tell. Her paw is pretty mangled, though."

Jericho watched through narrowed eyes as Hunter started for the door. "You're not going to leave her locked up in here, are you?" Jericho didn't like the idea of locking her in the porch. She might go nuts trying to get out once she figured out there wasn't a way to escape.

"If I don't, she'll leave," Hunter said with a shrug. "She doesn't need to leave yet. She's hungry and injured. We can help her."

"Yeah, well, you're cleaning up the mess when she goes ballistic," Jericho said as he followed Hunter inside.

Chapter Two

The cougar waited patiently until the cabin went dark and all sounds within were silenced. Hunger gnawed at her belly, and pain was her constant companion. She needed food. She needed to shift.

Her eyes glowed in the dark as she stared, alert and listening for movement. It was time.

There on the floor, the golden brown fur rippled and blurred. Pink skin replaced animal hide. Long, honey colored hair, feminine tresses, flowed down her neck as the eyes of the cat became human.

Fingers curled and dug into the hard floor, and a human gasp of pain hovered in the room as her injured hand protested the change.

Never before had she attempted to shift when she was so close to humans. But she needed food, and she needed the rejuvenation her human form would bring. It had been too long since the cat had made a kill. Game had been scarce.

Now that she was human again, the raw meat of her prey was no longer enticing. Her mouth watered and her stomach growled at the thought of cooked food. She couldn't remember the last time she'd enjoyed such a luxury.

She picked herself up and stood, wavering on unsteady legs. Chills chased up and down her naked skin, causing an uncontrolled shiver to quake her spine.

"I am Kaya," she whispered as she stared down at her human form. It was a reminder, one she gave herself on the few occasions she embraced her humanity. Over the years, her memories had become fuzzy, and it was hard to separate what was real from what was fantasy.

She had been forgotten by the humans, but she wouldn't let herself forget her past or her heritage.

On silent feet, she crept toward the cabin door, testing the lock. To her relief, it opened easily, and she slid inside the much warmer interior. After so long spent seeking what warmth she could in dens and small caves, the heated interior of the cabin was as close to heaven as she would ever come.

For a moment she simply stood there, soaking in the warmth, allowing her insides a slow melt. Then, remembering that she was no longer the cat, she hurried forward. It wouldn't do for the two men to discover her.

Jericho and Hunter.

She didn't know why she'd been drawn to them or what possessed her to seek them out each time they returned to their cabin. Maybe it was her own loneliness and a desire to be around other humans even when she herself was not in human form.

A large shirt lay carelessly over a chair as if thrown there without thought. She reached out and caressed the soft material. She inhaled, scenting the male who'd worn it last. The one called Jericho.

She loved his smell. His and Hunter's. It was what had first drawn the cougar to the isolated cabin high in the Rocky Mountains.

She knew from their conversations that they were as mistrustful of other humans as she was. Had they been cast aside like her? Forgotten?

They liked her and looked forward to her visits. The idea that her company brought them pleasure gave her an inexplicable thrill.

The material of the shirt felt good against her fingertips, and without thought, she picked it up and wrapped it around her body. It enveloped her, brushing across her skin like the warm spring sun after a harsh winter.

She quickly buttoned it even though she'd have to remove it before she shifted back. It was a temporary pleasure she wouldn't deny herself. She enjoyed so few that she clung tenaciously to this one.

Irritated that such a simple treat could sidetrack her from her goal, she hurried into the kitchen, the smell of fresh food guiding her. Her mouth watered as she found a pot of a wonderful-smelling concoction on the stove and next to it a half-eaten round of cornbread.

She stared impatiently at the meat mixture in the pot and sniffed, trying to ascertain the contents. It didn't matter. She was so hungry, she could eat anything.

Grabbing the large spoon from the counter, she dipped it into the pot and brought it to her mouth. She slurped hungrily at the food even as her injured hand reached for the cornbread. When she lowered the spoon to get more, she stuffed a piece of the cornbread in her mouth, chewing rapidly.

She worked at it indelicately, shoveling food into her mouth in an attempt to soothe the desperate hunger beating at her.

"What the hell?"

She froze and then jerked around, her heart pounding viciously. Jericho stood in the doorway to the kitchen, his eyes dark and his expression hard. The light was on behind him in the living room. She hadn't even registered it or him coming into the kitchen, so absorbed was she in eating.

She dropped the spoon with a clatter and immediately sidestepped to try and get around him.

"Whoa now," he said in a soothing voice. He held out his hands in a placating manner even as he circled toward her. "I'm not going to hurt you, lady. I just want some questions answered. Like what the hell you're doing in my kitchen wearing nothing but my shirt."

"Jericho?" Hunter's sleepy voice, laced with grumpiness, reached her ears. "Who the hell are you talking to?"

Kaya used that moment of inattention, when Hunter rounded the corner of the kitchen and laid shocked, angry eyes on her, to her advantage. When Jericho turned to Hunter, she launched herself across the kitchen and past Jericho.

She heard his curse and then the pounding of feet as he took off after her, but she was out already. She burst onto the porch and flew to the door, her last barrier to freedom.

Fumbling only for a split second with the hook, she flung it open and leaped into the snow. The cold was a shock to her bare skin, but she didn't stop. Finding the harder, packed snow, she flew across the ice and headed for higher ground. The safety of her den.

She couldn't be certain whether they followed, so she didn't shift. Her footprints would lay heavy in the snow, and she couldn't very well leave a trail that showed human prints turning to animal. And there was the shredded shirt she'd leave behind.

She backtracked several times, trying to mess up the vivid prints she was leaving. And then, as the moon lifted higher in the sky, light snow began to fall, and she gave thanks to the Great Maker for the protection offered.

She stumbled back onto the familiar trail, numb with cold and fear. The adrenaline that had coursed so readily through her veins, lending strength and endurance, had rapidly diminished, leaving her nearly frozen, her feet clumsy and awkward.

The cougar stirred within her, restless and edgy, wanting freedom it was unused to being denied. It sensed the human was weak and in need of protection.

Kaya leashed the cat, using all her strength to ward off the shift. Not now. Not when she was open and vulnerable. Just a few more feet. She could make it. The wind picked up as the snow began falling harder. Bitter and unrelenting, it pierced her skin and the meager protection Jericho's shirt offered.

She stumbled across the smooth rock outcropping and hovered precariously close to the edge. Below was vast nothingness, shrouded in darkness. A river, shrunk down to nothing, carved its way through the valley she stood above. In the spring, it would roar with the rains and melting snow.

Weakly, she walked, and when she fell, she crawled toward the entrance to the small cave etched into the rock. It faced south, protected from the fierce north winds. On hands and knees she forced herself those final few feet until she was out of the wind and snow and into the warmth offered by the cave.

She crawled to the innermost portion and huddled against the wall, exhausted and weak. She needed to shift. Needed the warmth of the cougar's fur and much stronger body mass. But she couldn't keep her eyes open long enough to allow the cat its freedom.

Chapter Three

"Where did the crazy bitch come from?" Jericho demanded as he and Hunter pulled on boots and coats.

Hunter grunted. "This was your idea. Just remember that."

"We can't leave her to freeze to death," Jericho said patiently.

"Why not?"

Jericho stared balefully at Hunter's solemn expression. "You can't tell me that you'd doctor a wild cougar but leave a defenseless woman to certain death."

Hunter shrugged. "I didn't ask for her to invade our privacy. She let the cougar out. Nothing but trouble. And now you want to wade ass-deep through the snow so she doesn't freeze to death. Here's a newsflash for you, Jericho. She was half naked, and she took off into a snow bank. We're not dealing with the brightest bulb."

"She was scared to death," Jericho said grimly. "And she was obviously hungry. She was way too damn skinny, and she was shoveling food into her mouth like there was no tomorrow."

"You just happened to notice how skinny she was," Hunter said dryly as he finished lacing up his boots.

"It was hard to miss. She was standing in the kitchen wearing only my shirt. She was a tiny little thing. It looked like a dress on her."

"And you get on my ass about taking in strays? At least mine are the animal variety."

"I just want to make sure she's okay. These mountains are no place for a woman alone. Hell, she's probably already frozen to death," Jericho muttered. He didn't want to stop and examine his reasons for the panic that idea instilled. If he could hurry Hunter's ass out of the cabin, they could track her before the snowfall got too heavy.

Collecting the floodlights and backpacks, Hunter grudgingly

followed Jericho off the back porch and into the deep snow.

Her vivid prints made for easy tracking for the first while. Then it became evident that she'd backtracked to try and hide her trail. Jericho frowned. What the hell was she hiding from? Did she have a death wish?

With several potential trails to follow, he and Hunter split up and scoured the area. Eventually they came back together, following a single trail higher up the mountain.

The eastern sky was starting to lighten, bathing the darkness in soft lavender. Soon it would be light enough to see without the flashlights, and since the snow had stopped an hour before, her trail would be easily followed.

The prints disappeared in front of a rock outcropping, and Hunter shone a light over the surface. A small hole was carved into the face, large enough for a person to gain access if they crawled.

"More like a cougar den," Hunter said with a grunt.

"Or bear," Jericho offered.

"You're making me feel so much better."

Jericho dropped to his knees outside the small cave and pointed his flashlight inside. Seeing nothing, he started in. Behind him, Hunter sighed and followed.

He cursed when he bumped his knee on a sharp protrusion, and before he could offer warning, he heard Hunter bite out a curse as well.

"This has got to be the dumbest idea you've ever come up with," Hunter growled. "And you've come up with some doozies."

But Jericho wasn't paying attention to Hunter's bitching. He was staring at a small woman huddled against the wall of the cave, her knees drawn to her chest and her arms clutched tight around her legs. His shirt swallowed her whole and was the only barrier she had to the biting cold.

"She's here," Jericho said.

Hunter directed his light toward the woman as well. "I'll be damned. Fool woman. What the hell is she thinking? She's probably dead."

"She's not dead," Jericho said fiercely.

"Well, okay, if you say so." Hunter moved forward, holding the light on her as he made his way closer to her huddled body.

Jericho closed the distance as well, almost afraid to touch her, afraid to feel the stillness of death. When his hand found her, he flinched at the coldness of her skin, but it was still supple and pliable.

He fumbled at her neck to feel for a pulse and sighed in relief when he felt the faint *pitter-patter* against his fingers.

"Well, what now?" Hunter asked as he rocked back on his heels.

"We get her back to cabin where she can warm up," Jericho said. "We aren't leaving her here to die."

"I wasn't suggesting we do," Hunter said. He surveyed her thoughtfully then glanced up at Jericho. "This will be a lot easier if we lay out a survival blanket and drag her out of here on it. Then we can wrap her in it and carry her back."

"Let's do it, then. She's going to freeze to death while we sit here with our thumbs up our asses."

Hunter took a blanket out of his pack and arranged it on the ground at his feet. Jericho reached for the woman, picked her slight form up and set her down on top of the material.

"You go out first and pull," Hunter said. "I'll bring up the rear."

Jericho backed out of the cave, taking the ends of the blanket with him. He tried to be as gentle as possible so as not to jostle the woman, but she never even stirred, which worried him.

The sun had risen enough that they could easily see when they crawled out of the cave. Jericho glanced down at the unconscious woman as he pulled her from the opening in the rock.

She was as slight as he'd thought her to be, but what took his breath away was how beautiful she was. Long, honey-caramel hair, the color of their cougar pet. Sun-kissed skin, not too pale but not dark enough that she'd seen too many harsh sun-filled days without protection.

Unable to resist, he traced a line down her cheek with his fingertip. He brushed across her lip before tucking a strand of hair behind her ear.

Hunter knelt down and wrapped the blanket around her in a no-nonsense fashion. When Jericho reached to pick her up, Hunter gripped his arm to stop him.

"I'll carry her back. You have no business lifting with your bum shoulder."

Jericho scowled at the reminder. Hell, if he couldn't lift this little slip of a girl, then he might as well paint a "P" on his forehead and call it good.

But Hunter was already tossing his backpack at Jericho, and then he bent and effortlessly scooped the girl into his arms. Jericho shook his head and collected the packs from the ground and started after Hunter.

Nearly two hours later, they trudged up to the cabin. Jericho went in ahead of Hunter and added wood to the fire while Hunter laid the girl on the couch.

"I don't know how cold she got. We'll just have to do our best," Hunter said. "If we can't bring her around..."

Hunter didn't need to finish his thought. Jericho knew it was bad. There was no way for them to drive down the mountain with the recent snow dump and no way for them to get a helicopter to the cabin. It was at least a day's hike to get to a place where rescue might gain access.

He and Hunter were well-equipped to survive the harsh elements and the demands of the mountain. This little slip of a girl didn't have a chance. What the hell was she doing here, and where had she come from?

"Get some more blankets," Hunter ordered. "She's got to come out of this shirt. It's soaked through."

Reluctant to leave her, even in Hunter's capable hands, Jericho hesitated as Hunter peeled the blanket from around her.

"Go," Hunter barked. "Unless you want her to die."

Jericho shook himself and headed to the bedroom. When he returned, he stopped abruptly in the doorway to the living room. All his breath left him in one big whoosh. Hunter was gently rubbing the girl's naked body with a towel. He quickly and efficiently dried her hair and then swept down her body, covering every inch of her skin.

He'd called her skinny, and she *was* thin, but skinny? Skinny inferred an unattractive quality. She was fucking beautiful. Generous, full breasts, tiny waist and hips just perfect to span with his hands. He easily imagined holding those slim hips as he thrust into her.

He called back a groan of frustration and mentally slapped himself on the back of the head. He was being an asshole of the first order.

Hunter looked up and impatiently gestured for Jericho. Jericho closed the distance between them and dropped the blankets in a heap beside Hunter.

Turning away from the sight of the woman in Hunter's arms, Jericho forced his attention to the fireplace, adding more logs and stoking the glowing embers until the flames licked high and heat radiated from the core.

When he was done, he turned back to see that Hunter had wrapped her in several of the blankets and was reaching for another.

"Help me get this around her and move her closer to the fire," Hunter said as he held out her bundled body.

Jericho took her while Hunter scooted forward on the floor. When Jericho had swathed her completely, Hunter, who was now directly in front of the fire, reached for her.

Jericho hesitated and looked down into the face of the woman. "I've got her," he said softly.

"What you need to do is give her to me and find as many more blankets and pillows as you can," Hunter said. "We'll put her between us so she warms up as fast as possible."

Jericho sucked in his breath. Did Hunter have any idea what he was saying? Or the memories he dredged up? Hunter had sworn never to put another woman between them, literally or figuratively.

Beside him, Hunter cursed. "That wasn't what I meant, Jericho, and you damn well ought to know it. Look, bringing her back here was your idea, not mine. I'd just as soon she not die here."

"Keep your panties on," Jericho murmured as he relinquished his bundle into Hunter's arms.

He got up and went into the bedroom to drag the covers from his bed. Next, he hit Hunter's room and made two trips with blankets and pillows.

When he came back the last time, he saw Hunter sitting on the floor in front of the fire, the woman curled into his arms, nearly swallowed by Hunter's embrace. There was a look of determination and, oddly enough, tenderness on Hunter's face as he stroked one hand through her hair. In that one unguarded moment, Jericho saw more emotion on his friend's face than he'd seen in years.

Silently he went about making a pallet on the floor by the fire. Hunter scooted over to give Jericho room as he arranged more blankets and pillows.

When Jericho was finished, he stood and stripped his shirt off. He sat on the couch so he could pull his boots off, and he tossed them toward the front door. They landed with a thump, and he stood once again to unfasten his jeans. If he was going to be lying on the floor, he was going to be as comfortable as possible.

Stripped down to his underwear, he stepped onto the mound of blankets and gestured for Hunter to relinquish the woman. Hunter carefully leaned over and eased her into Jericho's arms. While Hunter stood to undress, Jericho positioned her to his side, lifting the blankets so that she fit flush against his body so his warmth would bleed into her.

She stirred lightly. A soft, whispery moan escaped her parted lips and blew gently over his neck. As if seeking more of his heat, she snuggled deeper into his chest, her legs twining with his.

God it felt good to have a woman in his arms again. It had been so long. Too damn long. All soft curves and swells. There was nothing like holding a woman this close.

Hunter got down on her other side and turned away from her and Jericho. Without a word, he moved until his back was molded tightly to hers. Jericho could feel the tension radiating from Hunter. It was tangible. If Jericho were smart, he'd turn his back as well. She needed their warmth and nothing else.

It was too easy to remember the last—and only—time he and Hunter had slept with a woman between them. Back when they were young and foolish and thought they had all the answers.

He glanced down at the still-sleeping woman nestled so sweetly in his arms.

"Who are you?" he murmured. "And where did you come from?"

Chapter Four

Kaya stirred but quickly stilled and held her breath. Warm. So warm. She let her breath out in a soft sigh of contentment and then opened her eyes. All she saw was human flesh. Her nose was pressed solidly against a chest. She carefully inhaled, recognizing the scent immediately.

She came fully awake as panic engulfed her.

She tried to roll but rammed into another human. Hunter. Hands came out to steady her, but she bolted upright, shaking them off and scrambling frantically away.

"Hey, easy now," Jericho murmured even as he reached for her arm.

Her gaze swept the room looking for possible escape routes. Locking onto the front door, she made her bid for freedom.

Strong arms caught her and locked her against a muscular chest. She cried out, unable to stanch the quick flash of fear.

"Shhhh," Hunter soothed.

He gripped her tightly, holding her prisoner. Her heart beat wildly, her breasts nearly flattened by his forearms. No clothes. A moan nearly escaped her. She was naked, in a strange man's arms.

The cougar howled within, worried and anxious. It took every ounce of her strength not to give over to the beast.

"No one's going to hurt you. Breathe. Your heart's beating way too fast."

Breathing was impossible around the panic swelling her throat. She stared at Jericho just a few feet away, pleading silently with him to make Hunter release her.

"Hunter, let her go."

"I can't do that," Hunter said, his breath blowing across her ear.

"She'll bolt for the door."

"She won't make it, and you're scaring her to death."

He was right. She couldn't make it to the door now that they were focused on her. She'd never get past them the way she'd done before.

Slowly, Hunter loosened his hold. She took advantage and lunged away, her knees scraping the floor in her haste. She fell forward, her palms smacking the wood as she caught herself. Jericho was there, touching her shoulder, and she rolled, instinctively putting up her hands to protect herself.

He didn't touch her again. He crouched over her, clad in only his underwear. His expression was hard, but something in his eyes comforted her. What?

"We aren't going to hurt you," he said in a low voice. "We found you in a cave, nearly dead from exposure. We brought you back here so we could warm you up and take care of you."

She scrunched her eyebrows together. "Why?"

He blinked in surprise. To the side, Hunter moved, and her gaze darted cautiously to him. But he ignored her and collected his clothing from the floor.

"Would you have preferred we left you to die?" Jericho asked.

"Why would you care?"

He cocked his head to the side. "Such strange questions. Now I'd like to ask a few, but first I think you should get dressed."

She glanced down, more aware than ever of the fact she was completely nude, sprawled on the floor. Never before had she been uncomfortable with her nakedness, but now a hot flush stole over her skin, and she was mortified.

Her arms folded over her middle, covering as much flesh as she could. Then she hunched forward so that her legs gave her additional protection.

Without a word, Hunter walked by and dropped a shirt on the floor beside her. Then he headed toward the kitchen. "I'm going to put dinner on. Let me know if she'll be staying to eat," he said in Jericho's direction.

She reached gratefully for the shirt and pulled it on, clutching at the lapels to hold them closed. The warm, masculine scent floated upward and surrounded her. Such a wonderful smell. She hugged the shirt tighter as if she could absorb the very essence of the rugged male who'd worn it.

"Now, would you like something to eat? We can offer you something better than the cold stew and cornbread you were scarfing last night."

Embarrassment heated her cheeks at his dry reminder. And even though she'd sell her soul for a hot, cooked meal, she shook her head.

"I need to go," she said in barely above a whisper.

Jericho stood and gathered his own clothing, but she saw that he kept a careful eye on her.

"Go? Where the hell are you going? Back to your cave? What in the world are you doing out on a mountain in the dead of winter running around bare-assed naked?"

Then as if the thought had just occurred to him, he stilled and his expression softened, his eyes gentling.

"Did you leave a hospital or something? Are there people looking for you, and should you be on medication?"

She stared at him in confusion. "I don't go to hospitals, and I don't take medication."

Doubt shadowed his face. "Maybe you don't think you should, but there are people who could help you."

Realization was slow in coming, but when it hit her, her mouth gaped open. Maybe she hadn't had much to do with the human race over the years, but she wasn't an idiot.

"Are you calling me crazy?"

His lips twisted sardonically. "Crazy? Naahh. It's perfectly sane to run around in the snow naked and to break into people's cabins and steal their clothes and eat their food."

"I'd say that's desperate, not crazy," she said quietly.

Now fully dressed, he returned to her and bent down on one knee. He didn't make any move to touch her, and for that she was grateful. She didn't trust herself. It had been too long since she'd had contact with another human, and she craved something as simple as touch. Skin to skin. Fingers through her hair.

A long-distant memory bubbled painfully to surface. A smiling woman brushing Kaya's hair while another girl with golden hair played close by.

Cheetah.

The word came unbidden from the dark cloisters of her mind. She felt a kinship with this girl. The cheetah running with the wind and the cougar trying to keep pace only to be left behind.

141

Left behind.

The deadness spread from her chest into her stomach. She'd been left by the humans. Her humans.

"What are you thinking?"

Jericho's softly echoed question filtered through the hazy memories. Her nose drew up and stung with unshed emotion. No, she wouldn't break. She must be strong and resilient, a worthy companion to the guardian animal spirit who shared her soul.

She drew in a steadying breath, stuck out her chin and eyed him with determination. "I'd like something to eat, and I would appreciate some pants if you have any to spare. But then I must go."

It took all her courage to face this man and lay out her demands as if she had a right to do so. She prayed to the Maker that he couldn't see how hard she was trembling.

Surprisingly, he held out a hand to her. She eyed it suspiciously, but he was patient, holding it there as he waited. Finally she took it, allowing her palm to slide over his.

He stood and then pulled her up in front of him, but he didn't let go of her hand. "First let's get you some pants. I have some thermal underwear but those would look goofy."

She shrugged. "As long as they're dry and warm."

One eyebrow lifted as he regarded her with open curiosity. "I think I have some sweats that you can tighten enough to keep around your waist. If not, I don't know if we have anything that'll work. We don't exactly keep women's clothing around here."

Again she made a motion of indifference.

He pulled on her hand, and she stumbled forward in surprise.

"I don't trust that you won't be out of here like a shot if I leave you to get the sweats."

"I won't leave until I've eaten and gotten the warm clothes," she said solemnly.

He laughed, and the shock of the deep, husked timbre of such a delightful sound rolled down her spine, making every nerve ending stand up and pay attention.

"You're an honest little thing," he said with a shake of his head.

"I'm cold and hungry. It would do me no good to lie."

They came to a stop inside a small bedroom, and she gazed around, inhaling his unmistakable scent. It was imprinted on every object. She stared longingly at the bed, at the softness of the mattress.

The covers were gone, on the floor of the living room if she wasn't mistaken.

He let go of her hand long enough to rummage in the drawer of a nearby chest, and then he yanked out a pair of black sweats.

He eyed her critically as he held the pants up next to her bare legs.

"I guess you can roll up the waist some."

She took them from him. "I'll manage."

"Okay. I'll wait right outside. You can use the bathroom through there if you need it." He pointed to the doorway leading off the bedroom.

She gave a short nod and stood gripping the pants while she waited for him to disappear. After one last look in her direction, he backed out and closed the door behind him.

Needing to feel like she had added privacy, she ducked into the small bathroom and shut the door. Before she pulled her pants on, she turned on the faucet and watched in wonder as the water slid seamlessly into the sink.

Her fingers flicked out to play with the stream, and she winced at the chill. She ducked her head, cupped her hand and pulled the water into her mouth.

Running water was a luxury she hadn't enjoyed in well over a year. She frowned as she remembered her last trip into civilization. No money, no plan. Just a desire to embrace her humanity again.

She glanced at the shower and wondered if they had a hot water heater for the water piped in from one of the nearby streams. The cabin was surprisingly modern despite its remote location.

Now that the idea was planted in her mind, she couldn't resist the lure of having hot water rain down over her body. She reached into the cubicle and turned on the water. After a few moments, she sent her fingers seeking into the stream.

A sound of absolute delight escaped her lips before she could call it back. Eager not to waste a drop, she stripped out of the shirt and stepped under the spray.

She closed her eyes and turned her face upward as water rolled over her cheeks and down her neck. This was almost as good as the promise of a hot meal.

Chapter Five

Jericho stood outside the bedroom door listening as the shower came on and then to her sounds of pleasure. She sounded almost carefree in that one moment, as though she'd been denied the simplest of comforts and rediscovered them.

What was the fool woman doing running around the mountains naked? She didn't seem crazy, just...unusual in a way that he couldn't put his finger on.

"Is she staying?" Hunter called from the kitchen.

"Yes, she's staying," he said with mild exasperation. "Where the hell is she going to go?"

"And that stopped her before?"

Jericho didn't bother with a response. Hunter usually had to have the last word anyway.

He stood there several more minutes and was about to go in to make sure she hadn't taken a dive out the window when the door cracked open and she peered cautiously out.

Those amber eyes flashed against her small face, and unbidden images of the cougar came to his mind.

"Breakfast is about done. You coming out?" he asked when she made no move to walk out of the bedroom.

She hesitated for another brief second before opening the door wider. She slipped by him with barely a whisper, and she seemed to draw in her entire body to refrain from making incidental contact. Hell, he couldn't be that scary.

But then again, in her place, he'd probably be a little worried. Being hauled out of a cave—no matter how weird that might be—by two strange men and taken to a remote cabin. No, that still wasn't more bizarre than her running naked through the Rockies in the dead of winter.

He followed her into the kitchen and nearly ran over her when she came to an abrupt halt. Hunter was standing next to the small stove eyeballing her with that piercing stare of his.

She trembled against Jericho, and despite his resolve to exercise extreme caution when it came to handling her, he reached out and folded his hands over her slight shoulders.

"He won't hurt you. He always looks like a bear with a sore tooth."

She nodded solemnly. "Bears can be very cranky creatures. I try to avoid them at all costs."

Hunter lifted one brow. "Good policy."

"Go on and sit down," Jericho coaxed. He nudged her toward the small table in the corner and gave Hunter a reprimanding glare as they walked by.

Hunter rolled his eyes as he slapped ham on a plate.

Jericho took the seat across from their guest and realized he had no clue what her name was. She sat there almost primly, ill at ease, as if with the slightest provocation she'd bolt like a deer.

"What's your name?"

"I am Kaya."

He puzzled over her stilted speech, trying to place the accent. He'd been a damn lot of places, but he couldn't remember hearing someone who sounded like her.

"You are Jericho."

His eyes widened. "How the hell did you know that?"

She paled and her eyes flashed with panic for a moment. "You told me."

"No, I didn't. We haven't exchanged names yet, sweetheart. Hard to do that when you're out cold."

"I must have heard you and Hunter talking," she mumbled.

Hunter plopped the food on the table between them and gave Jericho a look that clearly said *I told you so* before he settled into the seat next to Kaya.

She picked up both the fork and the knife and held them in tightly curled fists as she surveyed the plate in front of her. It was as if she didn't know where to start.

"Dig in," Hunter said as he speared a slab of ham and dragged it onto his plate.

She started by taking a piece of the ham as Hunter had, but then she quickly got into the spirit and spooned eggs, grabbed two biscuits and took some of the sausages as well.

There was no delicacy in her table manners. She dug in with almost scary zeal. Jericho exchanged a glance with Hunter. When was the last time she'd eaten?

He wanted to ask her questions, but he wasn't about to interrupt the killing going on in her plate.

When she'd tucked the last morsel away, she sat back with a contented sigh. "Thank you. That was wonderful."

Then to Jericho's amazement she pushed from the table and stood. "I should be going now."

He and Hunter bolted up at the same time. Hunter was less subtle than Jericho planned to be.

"You're not going anywhere," Hunter said with a growl.

Jericho wasn't sure who was most surprised by that declaration. Him, Kaya or Hunter himself.

She edged backward, her posture defensive. "I can't stay. Truly. I appreciate the clothes and the food."

"Where the hell do you think you're going to go? Back to that cave?" Jericho burst out.

Confusion darkened her eyes. "Well, maybe not that one."

Hunter was evidently through talking. He closed in on Kaya and herded her toward the living room before she could even launch a protest. Jericho followed, shaking his head at Hunter's inability to make up his mind whether he wanted the woman to stay or go.

Hunter was about to park her on the couch when he picked up her hand and turned it over. "What happened to your hand?"

Jericho got closer and noticed that there was a still-raw-looking wound in the crease of her palm. There was no blood and it was obviously healing, but it had been one hell of a gash.

She curled her fingers into a fist to hide the injury. "It's nothing."

"Seems to be your week for strays with wounded hands," Jericho taunted Hunter.

Hunter shot him a quelling look and then returned his gaze to Kaya. "Have a seat. There are some questions I need answered before I let you just walk out that door."

Kaya stared back at him in horror. He looked so...determined. "You can't keep me here if I want to go."

"Oh yeah? Watch me."

Her gaze flitted to where Jericho stood a few feet away, but the resolve framing his jaw was no less than Hunter's.

"Where the hell do you live?" Hunter asked.

"I live here," she said simply. Then she realized how that sounded. "Not *here*, I mean here. I live in the mountains. This is my home."

"Is there any reason you broke into our cabin then?" Jericho asked.

She twisted her fingers nervously in front of her. "I was hungry." And lonely. Desperate for human contact. Not just any, but theirs.

"So wherever it is you live, you obviously have no food," Hunter said grimly.

"There's food," she said truthfully. The cougar enjoyed the occasional wild game, but she'd long gone without hot, cooked food that humans enjoyed.

Hunter and Jericho exchanged frustrated glances. Then Jericho turned back to her. "Are you alone? Do you live with anyone else? I'd feel a whole lot better if I knew you weren't wandering around these mountains by yourself."

Her brows came together. "But I'm always alone. There's no crime in that."

Hunter let out a sigh, and then he leaned down, framing his hands on either side of her legs as he faced her. Their noses were just inches apart, and she blinked as she stared into his green eyes.

"Let me make myself clear, Kaya. You're staying. Until you can come up with some answers that make sense and you can convince me that you'll be okay, you're not budging from this cabin. Are we clear?"

Fear fluttered into her throat, and deep within, the cat snarled and hissed its displeasure. She wanted her freedom.

"You can't do that," she whispered.

"We've already covered this," he said in a bored tone.

Her gaze flew to Jericho, a helpless plea for him to understand. It was like meeting with a stone wall.

"Please. I have to go."

"Why?" Jericho demanded. "You look like you're about to crawl right out of your skin. We're not going to hurt you, Kaya. We want to help you."

"I don't need your help. I can take care of myself."

"What are you hiding?" Hunter asked bluntly.

The blood drained from her face. "N-nothing."

"Bullshit."

"What do you care?" she shot back. "*Let me go.*"

Something odd flickered in Hunter's eyes for a moment. Then he backed away, slowly straightening. He shoved his hands in his pockets and glanced at Jericho.

"She's right. We can't keep her against her will."

"*What?*" Jericho exploded. "Are you shitting me? You know we can't let her wander off in the snow again."

Kaya inched forward, her hands curling around the edge of the couch. Jericho jerked around to glare at her and pointed a finger in her direction.

"You don't move."

She swallowed as she watched the two men square off in front of her.

"You can't keep her," Hunter said calmly. "She's a grown woman, and from what I can tell, while maybe a little strange, she seems to be in full control of her faculties."

"You're just going to let her walk out of here in bare feet, baggy-ass sweats and my shirt?"

Hunter's teeth flashed, reminding Kaya of a wolf. It had been so long since she'd seen one. Not since her childhood in Alaska.

"Not at all. She'll stay tonight, and if in the morning she's still hot to trot to get out of here, you and I will take her home and make sure she hasn't lied to us about having a place to live."

He turned to her again and eyed her levelly. "Got a problem with that?"

She swallowed and shook her head. What else could she do or say? She cast a longing glance toward the window to where pale moonlight bathed the snow. The cougar rolled within, edgy and impatient. *Run.*

She shook off the instinct. Then she looked back up at Hunter and then Jericho. "I will stay tonight, but tomorrow I *must* leave."

Chapter Six

Jericho sprawled on the sofa in front of the fire and took turns watching Kaya pace across the floor as she alternately stared from him and Hunter to outside the window, and Hunter who observed Kaya in brooding silence.

There was enough tension to dull his sharpest buck knife.

"Hell, you don't even have any goddamn shoes," Jericho said as his gaze dropped to her bare feet.

She glanced down as if the thought had not occurred to her. "It doesn't matter."

"The hell it doesn't," Hunter growled. "Who are you, Kaya, and what the hell are you running from?"

She blinked. "I'm not running from anyone."

Jericho could see the surprised sincerity in her face. She wasn't lying. Which made it all the more puzzling. He didn't get her, and it bugged the shit out of him.

Hunter snorted. "You're trying to tell me that it's perfectly normal to run around in the snow, no clothes, no shoes. You have no food wherever it is you live. We find you in a damn cave that could be inhabited by all sorts of wild animals."

She cocked her head, and her brow furrowed as she studied Hunter. "I never said I was normal. I imagine you find me strange, but I've committed no crime. No one is after me. I simply prefer to be...alone."

A flash of pain accompanied her last words. Hunter didn't miss it either.

"What happened to you?" Hunter asked softly.

"What happened to *you*?" Kaya thrust her chin up in challenge as she stared him down. "You and Jericho live up here alone. No people for miles. You drag in at odd times and stay holed up in here until you leave again, and then you don't come back for weeks."

Both men stared at her in shock.

"How the *hell* would you know that?" Jericho asked softly.

Another look of fright scurried across her face, and she visibly retreated. "I told you I lived here. These mountains are my home."

"We're not talking about us," Hunter pointed out. "We're talking about you."

"Not anymore," she said stubbornly.

Jericho shook his head. He'd never come across a woman like Kaya. Ever. And he'd met some doozies.

Was the only reason he didn't want her to leave because he was concerned about her? Or was it a case of wanting? He wanted her.

He couldn't claim desperation. It wasn't as if he lived like a complete monk. That was Hunter's job. There was something elemental about Kaya. An earthy beauty that went far beyond the outer trappings. She was mysterious and soulful looking, a lost waif with liquid amber eyes.

Short of tying her down, he didn't see a way to keep her from leaving, and it frustrated the hell out of him. How could he just turn her out into the snow, no matter how much she wanted to go? Yet, how could he keep her against her will?

He looked at Hunter for help, but Hunter was unreadable, his thoughts closed off by his look of indifference.

"Where will I sleep tonight?" she asked quietly.

"You can have my room," Hunter said. "I'll sleep out here on the couch."

A look of wonder crossed her face. "I can have your bed?"

Hunter's lips thinned, and he frowned harder. "I said I'd sleep out here."

"Then I would very much like to go there now. I'm tired, and a bed would feel so wonderful."

Jericho started to rise, but Hunter beat him to the punch. "Would you like anything else before you go to bed?"

She shook her head. "You and Jericho have been very kind. It was nice to visit with you both."

Hunter shot Jericho a strange look. Jericho shrugged. He didn't understand this woman any more than Hunter did. She made it sound like the entire episode had been nothing more than a social call. And to think he used to believe that nothing out of the ordinary ever happened up here. Just the way he liked it.

"Come on, I'll show you to the bedroom," Hunter muttered.

Jericho sat in silence, contemplating the oddity of their encounter with Kaya. A few minutes later, Hunter returned and flopped down in the chair next to the couch.

"What the hell kind of bizarre case have we got, Jericho?"

"Fuck if I know. I've never been so goddamn confused in my life. You get the sense we're not getting the full story?"

"And what was your first clue?"

"Maybe she just wanted company for a while. If she does live up here, there aren't a lot of folks around."

"Yeah, but where does she live? I don't know of another cabin or dwelling within miles," Hunter said. "And there's the fact that we dragged her out of a cave in the dead of winter. At first I thought she was a few boxes short of a full load, but she seems okay, if a little odd."

"For someone who didn't seem to want anything to do with her, you sure were quick to tell her she couldn't leave."

Hunter scowled. "She's your stray."

"And you can't make up your mind whether you want her or not, am I right?"

Hunter's eyes flickered as he caught Jericho's gaze. "What exactly do you mean?"

"Just what I said. You seem to battle over whether or not you're going to admit you want her. One minute you're all but holding the door open for her to leave and the next you're threatening to tie her to a chair."

Hunter's scowl deepened. "If she wants to leave, I can't stop her."

"But you want to stop her."

"Shut the fuck up, man. It doesn't matter what we want."

Jericho acknowledged that with a nod. "That's true."

"She couldn't stay anyway," Hunter continued on. "We're likely to be called away any time, and she sure as hell can't go with us."

Silence fell over the living room. Hunter stared broodingly into the fire while Jericho focused his attention on nothing in particular.

"Do you ever think about giving it up?" Jericho asked.

Hunter's head whipped around. "Give what up?"

"The job. What we do."

"That's a dumbass question. We promised Rebeccah."

"Maybe we shouldn't have," Jericho said quietly. "And we didn't promise her that we'd keep running ourselves to death. We promised to support her cause. We've earned enough money for two lifetimes. When are we going to slow down and have a life?"

"You're saying you want to quit?" Hunter asked in disbelief.

"Maybe. I don't know. There has to be more to life than what we're doing. Rebeccah is gone. We can't bring her back by killing ourselves."

Hunter closed his eyes and reclined his head until he faced the ceiling. "You want to know why I keep going?"

Jericho didn't say anything.

"Because I can't remember what she looks like sometimes. I get away from the kids, the camps, and she starts to fade, but when I'm there, I can see her. Smiling and laughing. I don't want to forget."

The last was said with a note of raw agony that cut Jericho to the core.

"I loved her too," he said in a low voice. "But she's gone. We can't bring her back."

"No, but we can keep her memory alive by helping the kids she loved more than anything."

"There are ways to do it other than the way we've gone about it," Jericho said carefully.

Hunter didn't reply, and Jericho didn't chase it further. He'd said enough. Planted the idea in Hunter's head. He'd have to make the decision on his own.

Kaya woke after only a few hours. She was used to fractured sleep, taking what she could when she could. For a moment, she snuggled deeper into the covers and inhaled the firm, masculine scent that permeated the bed.

Hunter's smell was so different from Jericho's, and yet both told of powerful, strong men.

How she wished she could stay, but she couldn't go much longer without shifting. She simply hadn't spent enough time as a human over the years. The cougar was strong within her. Willful and protective. It was too easy to let the cat have her way. Already she'd been denied longer than she was used to.

Her hand slid over the pillow. "I will miss you," she whispered as if Hunter lay there next to her.

Reluctantly she rose and glanced out the window. Dawn was still a few hours away. If she were fortunate, she would be able to leave before Hunter and Jericho awakened. It would be easier that way, and she wouldn't have to offer further explanation or answer their probing questions.

She peeled away the shirt and the sweats and laid them carefully over the bed. Then with a shiver, she turned to go.

Her feet slid soundlessly across the floor with the stealth of the cougar. When she reached the living room, she spared a quick glance at the couch where Hunter slept. Then she turned to look in the direction of Jericho's bedroom.

"I will come back," she whispered.

Soundlessly she hurried to the back door and eased it open. In seconds she was through the screen door of the porch, and the bitter cold engulfed her. She stepped into the snow, wincing as the wet slush stung her feet.

She braced herself and struggled through the drifts until she was away from the house. Then she turned her face upward, eyes closed, to embrace the shift.

Chapter Seven

A week. It had been an entire week since they'd awakened to find Kaya gone. It had become habit to look out the window every time he passed. Some ingrained hope that she'd show up again.

Jericho shook his head and started to turn away when he saw the mountain lion appear from the trees on the right side of the cabin. He watched for a moment as the cat approached on stealthy feet. She was cautious, stopping every few feet to sniff the air.

"Your stray is back," he said dryly.

"*My* stray?"

Jericho turned to look at Hunter who was propped on the couch with a book.

"Your cougar pet. She's back."

Hunter immediately set his book down and got up from the couch. He went to the door and opened it, and Jericho let out a groan. Not again.

"You're insane. Tell me you aren't going to let her back in here. She's not injured anymore, and I doubt she's going to just waltz in here like a damn house cat."

The cougar increased her pace up the walkway and stopped just outside the door. Then she slowly stuck her head inside and peered at Jericho.

"Or maybe she will," Jericho murmured.

The cat padded in, her head going back and forth as she cautiously surveyed her surroundings. Hunter closed the door and she immediately went into a crouch, a low hiss sounding as she turned in the direction of the noise.

"Easy, girl," Hunter soothed.

"And we thought Kaya was crazy."

Hunter ignored Jericho and reached with a tentative hand to pet the cougar. Before Jericho could tell him what a dumbass he was for attempting something so stupid, the cat turned her head into his touch and rubbed affectionately over his palm.

"I'll be damned if that cat doesn't like you."

Hunter's lips twisted in a sardonic smile as he continued to rub her ears. To Jericho's surprise, she left Hunter and ambled over to where he stood.

She sniffed delicately at his pants and then rubbed her jowls over his leg.

"Guess maybe she likes you too," Hunter said in amusement.

Jericho reached down to touch the top of her head. When she didn't react, he let his fingers slide through her fur. She turned her muzzle up, and her eyes closed in contentment.

"Think she was someone's pet or that someone raised her?" Jericho asked. He could think of no other reason for her tameness. Mountain lions were badass fuckers.

"Could be."

The cat gave Jericho one more rub and then turned and walked toward the fireplace. She circled once on the rug in front and then settled down with an indelicate plop. She stretched out and regarded both men with lazy contentment.

Jericho made a sound of surprise. "I'll be damned."

Hunter shrugged and returned to the couch to pick up his book. "Guess she'll be staying awhile."

Unexpected anger pricked Jericho. "You know it's sad that you're more open to having a damn cougar in here than a defenseless woman obviously in need of help."

Hunter put down his book and pinned Jericho with his stare. "She's human. People come with whole different sets of problems than an animal does. The cat won't stay. Cougars are solitary creatures. Besides, I *tried* to get Kaya to stay."

The cat lifted her head and perked her ears up as she surveyed both men. She looked keenly interested, and Jericho was almost tempted to hush the conversation. How absurd was that? He shook his head and headed for the kitchen to get a cup of coffee. The way things had been going around here, he was almost hoping to get called away.

The cougar lay quietly as the fire burned down in the hearth, leaving brightly glowing embers. Outside, snow had begun to fall again, drifting downward in slow spirals. She was glad to be inside on this day. The warmth from the fire seeped into her body.

She listened to the two men talk with interest. When their conversation once again turned to Kaya, her ears moved forward again though she didn't move her head.

They argued and bickered, but the clear message was that they were genuinely worried about her. Of course they couldn't understand that she was safe and well cared for even if her existence was sparse.

The more she listened, the guiltier she felt. She should never have revealed herself to them—not that she'd intended to, but she shouldn't have taken the chance.

She licked the injured paw as she remembered the pain that drove her to seek them out. Why? For comfort? The cold, the loneliness that had been her constant companion for so long had overwhelmed her until she'd found herself staggering through the snow to the cabin that so fascinated her.

"I'm worried about her," Jericho said quietly. "No matter what she says, she's out there alone. How can she survive? Hell, she left the clothes we gave her. She's probably frozen to death."

Hunter sighed, but his expression was one of concern as well. "We looked for her, Jericho. We tracked her until the footprints disappeared. She obviously doesn't want to be found."

But I do.

The rejection of his assessment came bubbling upward in a rush of grief and long-held sadness.

I don't want to be left behind. I'm tired of being alone.

She closed her eyes. Could she trust these two men? No. She could never let them know her secret. But she could return to them as Kaya so they would know she was all right.

Worry nagged at her. It wasn't smart of her to reveal herself again. But she longed for them in a way she didn't understand. She thought that by returning as the cougar, she would be satisfied as she had in the past. But no longer was she happy with brief glimpses, a few words overheard here and there. Not now that she'd touched them. Felt their hands on her skin in human form. She craved it with frightening intensity.

If she left now, she could return before dark fell, before the temperatures dropped even lower.

Heaving herself upward, she prowled over to where Hunter sat on the couch. He regarded her warily until she rubbed her head along his leg. She let him pet her for a moment before backing away. Then she headed toward Jericho and offered him the same affection.

After allowing him to stroke her ears, she stalked to the door and paced back and forth, her tail swishing.

"Had enough, girl?" Hunter murmured as he got up from the couch.

He walked over and opened the door. Cold air burst over her, ruffling her fur. With one glance back at the two men who watched her, she loped away, disappearing into the trees.

Hunter had taken up Jericho's post by the window. Why, he wasn't sure. Jericho was the worrier, the pacer. Hunter preferred a warm fire and a good book and shutting out the world around him.

When he looked up, he was certain he'd imagined the scene before him. There was no fucking way it could be. He blinked and leaned forward, his hand against the frosty pane.

"Holy Mother of God."

He turned and ran for the door, grabbing one of the afghans from a nearby chair.

"Hunter, what the hell?" Jericho hollered after him.

Hunter plunged into the snow, racing toward Kaya who stood at the edge of the trees, naked and trembling, her arms braced around her frame as she tried to keep warm.

She looked at him with frightened eyes when he grabbed her and yanked the blanket around her.

"I'm not going to hurt you, damn it," he growled.

Not waiting for her response, he swept her into his arms and charged back toward the cabin. Jericho was at the door, his jaw tight.

Hunter shouldered past him and lowered Kaya to the floor in front of the fire.

"I'm all right, Hunter," she said in a small voice. "Just a little cold."

Jericho exploded. "A little cold?"

Hunter looked up. "Keep your cool, man."

Jericho shook his head. "What are you thinking, woman? Have you lost your mind? What the hell were you doing out there naked? Goddamn it." He dropped to his knees beside her and tore the blanket open.

"Jericho, what the hell?"

"Are you hurt?" Jericho demanded, ignoring Hunter's reprimand.

Not giving her a chance to respond, Jericho laid her back and ran his big hands over her slim body. Hunter turned away from the sight of her pale flesh all but glowing underneath Jericho's caress.

He wanted to be the one touching her, and yet he had no cause.

Kaya stared up at Jericho inquisitively. "Jericho, why are you so angry?"

Jericho's mouth fell open. "Angry? *Angry?* I'm furious! Are you trying to kill yourself?"

She was honestly puzzled over why Jericho was spitting nails. Hunter watched the confusion simmer in her eyes, and his own grew. Something wasn't right here. More than the obvious of her bizarre behavior.

"Could I...could I have some clothes?"

She stared earnestly up at both men, her arms clutched around her body to shield her nudity. Which seemed pretty damn odd when you considered that she seemed to spend her life cavorting about in the nude.

Jericho rose, his face still drawn in anger—and worry. "You stay here and make damn sure she doesn't go anywhere," he ordered Hunter.

Hunter's eyebrows rose at Jericho's tone. Jericho stalked away, and Kaya's troubled gaze followed him.

"You can't be surprised that we're angry," Hunter offered in a soft voice.

Kaya turned to him, and for a moment he was lost in the sheer beauty of her eyes. He'd looked into those eyes earlier. He sucked in his breath at how alike she and his cougar pet were.

"I did not mean to make you angry."

"Kaya," he began, "what were you doing out in the snow with no clothing?"

"I had no clothes," she said simply.

Hunter shook his head in absolute confusion. He was ready to beat his skull on the floor.

"We gave you clothes when you were here, and you left them. Why?"

Her gaze dropped. "They were not mine to keep, and I did not want them to be ruined."

"Ruined? How would they get ruined?"

She looked away, turning her face and resting it on the arms laid over her knees. Jericho stomped back into the room with the same shirt and sweats she'd worn before.

"Put these on," Jericho directed. "Then I'll make some hot chocolate. Are you hungry?"

She hesitated a fraction, looking first at Hunter and then Jericho. "I would like something to eat, yes."

"Have you eaten since you left here?" Hunter asked bluntly.

"Y-yes."

He didn't believe her. You only had to look at how slight she was to know food wasn't in abundance wherever she lived. He looked at Jericho in silent surrender. No matter what, she wasn't leaving again.

Chapter Eight

Kaya stepped into the living room after a trip to the bathroom to see both men sitting. Waiting. Hunter was on the couch, and Jericho was in a chair adjacent. They'd built the fire back up, and it licked warmly at the logs that had been added.

She walked around the couch, feeling the eyes of both men on her. Hunter wasn't reading his book. It lay to the side, page-down to mark his spot.

Without waiting for an invitation, she carefully got onto the couch next to Hunter. Drawn by his warmth, by his comforting scent, she crawled close and snuggled underneath his arm. He stiffened all over in surprise, but he didn't push her away.

Slowly his arm lowered until it curved around her, holding her against his side. She laid her head on his chest, listening to the steady rhythm of his heart.

"Hunter?"

"Yes, Kaya?" His chest rumbled against her ear.

"Why don't you like me?"

He went very still beneath her. She couldn't even feel his breath. His fingers that had been lazily making their way up and down her arm froze at her elbow.

For a moment, she thought he would lie and deny his obvious discomfort and conflict. But then his chest seemed to cave in as his breath expelled once more.

"You remind me of someone I lost," he said simply.

She sat up so that she could look him in the eye. There was sadness there. A flash of grief. She ran her fingers through his light brown, muddy blond hair. They trailed over his temple and then traced his cheekbone ending close to his mouth. "I'm sorry. I should not have come here. I don't wish to cause you pain."

He caught her hand as if to pry it away, but instead he simply held it there close to his mouth. And then he kissed the tip of her index finger. Just one light brush that sent a shiver quaking over her entire body.

"You're not causing me pain, Kaya. As Jericho has told me, it's time to let go of the past."

She turned to Jericho. For a moment she'd forgotten his presence. He sat a few feet away studying her and Hunter with stark interest. There was hunger in his eyes. She'd seen that look in many of her predator kin.

She turned back to Hunter and curled into his body once more. "Touch me," she pleaded softly.

Again his breath caught and held for a moment. His fingers once again trailed down her arm. Then he took her shoulders and pulled her down until her head was pillowed in his lap.

Like a ray of heated sunshine in the spring, his palm slid up her body, over the curve of her hip and to her shoulder.

She sighed with absolute pleasure. How wonderful his touch felt. He continued to stroke her, petting her as he'd done the cougar.

She wanted to shed her clothing and feel his hand on her bare skin. Flesh on flesh, human contact. She wanted no barriers. She twisted restlessly underneath his seeking fingers until he applied firm pressure to her hip.

"What's wrong, Kaya?" he asked.

"My skin," she whispered. "Touch my skin. I don't like the clothing."

He sucked in his breath. His legs tightened underneath her, and his groin stirred to life. She *did* affect him. Did he feel all the wild and breathless cravings that she did?

Slowly and carefully, his hand slid underneath her shirt to the smoothness of her back. His fingers danced like fire up her ribcage to the crease where her arm rested on her side. Flat down, his palm caressed and made tight circles over her shoulder blade and then traveled down her spine.

A moan, soft and needy, floated past her lips, mixing with the popping sounds of the fire.

Jericho watched from his perch on the chair, his hands curled into fists. His pulse pounded in his ears, hot, loud like a freight train.

She was his. Not Hunter's. And yet he watched with a helpless fascination as his friend opened himself to a woman for the first time since Rebeccah.

Rebeccah who had loved them both but hadn't trusted them to love her back.

It was a sort of torture watching Kaya arch with pleasure under Hunter's tentative but seeking touch. Jericho wanted to be the one touching her. Such a strange, beautiful woman. Full of mystery. Her eyes a wash of an amber sunset.

Was she as fascinated with them as they were with her?

Hunter pushed her shirt higher, revealing more of her pale skin. His hands were gentle and coaxing, almost like he was soothing a wounded animal. She quieted and settled against his lap, calmed by the caresses.

Jericho knew the moment she surrendered to sleep. She gave a delicate little shudder and all the air escaped her in one long sigh. Still Hunter continued to stroke her skin. His gaze was locked on her face, and Jericho knew he had no idea how much tenderness shone in his eyes.

"Why does she remind you of Rebeccah?" Jericho asked quietly so as not to wake Kaya. Kaya was light, a study in burnished golds and liquid amber. A lot like the aspens in fall when the trees caught fire and lit up the earth. Rebeccah was dark yet vibrant, like a storm at midnight. The two women couldn't be more unalike.

"Because she stirs me," Hunter said simply.

And there it was. No woman had stirred him since Rebeccah. Jericho could relate. It wasn't that another woman didn't have the power. They just hadn't given one the chance. Were they giving Kaya that chance?

"What are we going to do, Hunt?"

It was a simple question, and yet a wealth of meaning lay just below the surface.

Hunter met his gaze. "You want her."

He wasn't going to lie. "Yeah."

"So do I." Apparently neither was Hunter.

He blew out his breath. "Goddamn it, Hunter. We said we weren't going this route again."

"I know," Hunter said calmly.

"There's a damn lot we don't know about her."

Hunter nodded. "That's true. It would seem we've got our work cut out for us."

"What if she doesn't want to stay? She was pretty adamant before."

"And yet she came back."

"Like your cougar pet always seems to do," Jericho said.

"She reminds me of her. Her hair and eyes. Her seeming need for solitude."

Jericho rolled his eyes, but he could see why Hunter had said it.

"We're going to have to be patient. I don't know what it is about her, Jericho, but..." He trailed off as he touched her hair.

"How long?" Jericho asked. "What are we talking about here? A fling? Sex? Something more? We take off to parts unknown for weeks at a time."

Hunter frowned as he stared down at Kaya's sleeping form. "I don't know. Why do we have to have an answer now? Today? We'll take it as it comes."

Then he looked up at Jericho, his eyes burning with quiet intensity. "She needs us. That's what I know today."

"And maybe we need her," Jericho returned.

Chapter Nine

Kaya awoke, her skin crawling with the edgy need to shift. The room was bathed in the pale shadows of dawn, and the fire had reduced to a scattering of barely glowing embers. And yet she was engulfed in warmth.

She was still draped across Hunter's lap, only during the course of the night she'd turned to face him and edged upward until her cheek rested against his chest, her head tucked securely under his chin.

Both his arms were wrapped around her, his left hand cradling her hip. The reassuring rise and fall of his chest against her face soothed some of the restlessness, but still, the cougar rose.

She needed to go so the cat could run.

Regretfully, she pushed herself up only to be caught in two hands. She looked up to see Hunter staring back at her, his eyes unclouded by sleep. How long had he lain awake holding her?

"I must go," she said.

His grip tightened until his fingers pressed into the skin above her elbows. "Why, Kaya? Where are you going? What waits for you out there?"

She placed her palms on his hard chest, enjoying the muscular planes, the dips and curves, the subtle ridges.

"I will come back. Please do not worry for me."

He shook his head. "No. I won't allow it this time."

She understood his reluctance, even if his arrogance ruffled her independent spirit. Never had she answered to anyone. It was as foreign to her as having a home.

"Hunter, I have to go. I don't have a choice. Will you please trust me?" She looked beseechingly at him. "I'll return tonight, before it falls dark."

"Are you in some kind of trouble?" he demanded. "Is someone hurting you in some way? Are you threatened? Jericho and I can help you."

She smiled and slid her hand up to cup his jaw. "Will you trust me? Please? I swear to you on my honor that I will return."

He sighed deeply. His green eyes were rife with indecision. With reluctance. "I don't want you to leave, but if you must...if you *must* go, I'll understand."

Her heart lightened with relief. "Thank you."

"But," he said, holding up a finger, "you'll go out dressed and warm this time."

"But—"

She broke off at the fierceness in his eyes. It wasn't as if she could explain why she'd rather leave the clothes behind. She'd just have to get out of sight of the cabin and undress before she shifted. She could stow the clothing and return to the spot tonight to put it back on.

"No buts," he countered. "And you're going to put some damn boots on. They'll be way too big but if we put enough pairs of socks on you, they'll do, and they'll keep you warm."

"Okay," she agreed. The resolve she saw in his face told her in no uncertain terms that she'd never get out of the door unless she capitulated.

"And you're going to eat a decent meal too," he muttered.

She leaned forward and brushed her lips across his in a brief kiss. When she would have pulled away, he palmed the back of her head and held her so that his mouth could meet hers again.

Pleasure exploded in her brain. Bright and mindless. She could only follow her instincts, because every thought left her. His tongue feathered lightly over her bottom lip, and she opened her mouth. He took immediate advantage and slid inside, tasting her, leaving his taste on her tongue.

Firm and spicy, warm and so delicious. Male. He tasted wholly male, rugged and woodsy.

She broke away, gasping for air, struggling to clear her clouded senseless. He looked similarly affected, and that gave her sweet satisfaction.

"Did you like kissing me?" she asked.

He appeared surprised by her question, but his eyes darkened, his pupils dilating until only a thin ring of green surrounded the black orbs. "I like it too damn much," he growled.

"I like kissing you too," she said shyly. "Does this mean you don't dislike me so much?"

He touched her face, sliding his palm over her cheek. Then he smiled, and she watched in wonder as it transformed his entire face. She raised trembling fingers to trace the curve of his mouth.

"I've never seen you smile."

The thump of feet startled her into dropping her hand. She stared beyond the couch to Jericho's bedroom to see him walk out in his shorts. Her gaze fastened on his broad chest, to the light covering of hair along the upper portion and the thin line leading down to his navel.

He stared back at her, his eyes flashing when he saw her perched on Hunter's lap.

Hunter patted her hip. "Better get up so we can get you fixed up. Jericho's going to burst a blood vessel when he hears what I've agreed to."

Jericho strode over, a scowl on his face. "What the hell are you talking about?"

Hunter sighed and eased Kaya off his lap. "Why don't you go take a hot shower while I explain to Jericho. I'll leave some clothes out for you on the bed, and we'll get a start on breakfast."

Kaya backed off the couch and skirted cautiously around Jericho who wore an expression blacker than night.

As soon as she disappeared, Jericho rounded on Hunter. "What the hell is going on?"

Hunter grimaced, a sure sign Jericho wasn't going to like what was coming.

"She's leaving."

"You want to run that by me again?"

"You heard me," Hunter said irritably.

"Okay, now you want to tell me why the ever-loving fuck you're just going to let her waltz out of here after we agreed we weren't going to let that happen?"

Hunter sighed and ran a hand through his hair in agitation. "Look, I can't explain it, Jericho. There's something... I don't even know. I just sense that this is somehow vitally important. It's a gut instinct. She said she'd return tonight before it gets dark. She asked me to trust her. She *begged* me to trust her. What was I supposed to do?"

A rude noise blew past Jericho's lips followed by a string of curse words that blistered the walls. "Your gut. You're letting her go out alone in the bitter cold because your gut tells you to."

"I made her a promise. I won't go back on it."

Jericho threw up his hands in disgust. "Well since you two have got it all figured out, I'll just keep the hell out of your way."

He turned and stalked into the kitchen, seething in irritation. It didn't matter that Hunter was right. They couldn't make decisions for her, but they damn sure could have provided a united front. Letting her go was stupid. Hell, she'd returned stark naked. In the fucking snow. And Hunter was willing to let her just walk out again?

He yanked out the pans to start on breakfast. He was standing at the stove a few minutes later when two small hands crept around his middle. He immediately tensed and looked down as her arms encircled him.

Her cheek pressed to his spine just below his shoulder blades, and her soft breath blew over his bare skin.

"Don't be angry, Jericho," she said. "I'll be back tonight. I've given my word."

He sighed and put down the spatula. Then he pivoted in her arms until he was looking down at her upturned face.

"I guess I don't understand. Any of it. Where are you going? If I thought you were taken care of, it wouldn't bother me, but Kaya, you are *not* being taken care of."

He braced his hands on her shoulders as he said the last. Hell, he was tempted to shake some sense into her.

A sweet smile curved her lips and damn near turned him into jelly. Lord, but she was beautiful. And insanely stubborn.

"I am well taken care of, Jericho. I promise. I have a protector."

Protector? As in a man? Boyfriend? And if so then where the flying fuck was he right now? Over his dead body would she be gallivanting around in the snow, bare-assed naked, if she belonged to him.

"I see. And where is he right now?" he asked in an even voice.

Confusion clouded her face. "Who are you talking about?"

"Your protector," he said patiently. "The guy who's supposed to look out for you."

"I never said it was a he. There is no one for you to concern yourself with."

Jericho shook his head. She was making him want to pull out all his hair. It was no wonder Hunter had caved. It was give in or beat his head on the floor.

He gave it one last shot. "I'm worried about you, Kaya."

She leaned up on tiptoe. "Kiss me. Please? I want to know if it feels as wonderful as when Hunter kissed me."

Well hell. Nothing like a little pressure. If any other woman had said something like that, he'd think she was playing them against each other, but Kaya said it without artifice. She seemed genuinely curious.

With that in mind, he squelched the urge to yank her up and kiss her breathless. A little finesse wouldn't be amiss in the situation.

Slowly, so slowly he thought he'd go mad, he leaned down, gently pulling her to him. She licked her lips in nervous anticipation as their mouths danced, chasing to one side, hovering and then adjusting the angle. Finally they met in a hot, sweet rush, melting on contact.

The shock warmed him to his toes. A tingle raced down his spine, spread around his groin. His balls drew up and his dick hardened until he ached with wanting. All because she tasted like sunrise.

"How can I let you walk away?" he rasped.

Her eyes glittered, awash with the colors of autumn. Red suffused her cheeks, and her breaths came in rapid little bursts.

"I will come back to you," she said.

The words so carefully rendered were a vow in the silence of the kitchen. In that moment he believed, as Hunter evidently did, that she would indeed come back and that she would be okay.

"All right," he agreed in a quiet voice. "I'll have something for you to eat when you return."

Her smile warmed the entire room, chasing away the lurking shadows. "Oh, I'm so glad I decided to come to you and Hunter. I was afraid but so lonely. I've wanted to come for so long."

He squeezed her hands in his. "I'm glad you did. Even if it seems you're destined to drive us insane."

Chapter Ten

"It's colder than a witch's tit out here," Jericho grumbled.

Hunter's breath came out in a visible puff as the two men crouched in the snow several yards from where Kaya had stashed her clothing hours earlier.

The two men had followed her tracks, determined to find out what they could about their mysterious visitor. They'd come to a scattering of boulders where her footprints disappeared and the clothing they'd made her wear was carefully stacked among the rocks—as were the boots and three pairs of socks they'd outfitted her in.

Hunter had sworn a blue streak while Jericho had shaken his head and muttered a hundred *I told you so*s.

And now they had staked out the area, waiting for her to come back—if she indeed intended to do so. The clothes so carefully arranged gave Jericho the impression that she planned to return here and dress before going back to the cabin when she'd promised. Because she knew damn well he and Hunter would blow a gasket if she turned up naked again.

But where would she come from? Would she be alone? They wanted answers, and so here they sat, freezing their asses off, waiting for her to appear.

The sun had slipped over the horizon when Jericho looked up to see their cougar in the distance.

"Shit," he whispered.

"What is it?" Hunter asked.

"Cougar."

Hunter grunted and moved over so he could see where Jericho stared.

"Damn."

"Yeah. What the fuck are we going to do? She seems to like us fine, but if Kaya stumbles across her, the cougar could kill her."

Hunter's fingers curled into a tight fist. "We'll have to run her off."

Jericho knew it wasn't what Hunter wanted, but they didn't have a choice. After this, any trust that had been built between the cat and the two men would probably be gone.

The cat moved closer, taking measured steps through the snow. Then she froze and raised her head into the wind, sniffing, and then her ears went back. She looked in their direction. She'd scented them.

Hunter closed his eyes briefly and then raised his rifle. He took careful aim and took a shot over the cougar's head.

The cat flattened on the snow, her gaze focused on where the two men sat. Hunter rose and waved his hands.

"Get on out of here! Go on!"

He raised his rifle to take another shot, but the cat sprang away, her tail flashing as she disappeared into the trees.

Hunter settled back down, his face hard but his eyes dim with regret. "She better damn well show."

The cougar crouched in the darkness watching the silent cabin. There was no movement within. It had gone quiet in the dark, suffocating hours of predawn.

The human within fought for balance, wanted the shift. She cried out to the humans inside the cabin. But the injured cougar carefully guarded her counterpart, unsure and betrayed by the two men she'd trusted.

Pain and sorrow vied for equal attention. Finally with a shuddering growl, the cat became human, and a naked woman huddled in the snow as pain screamed through her body.

She pushed herself up with her right hand as she favored her left arm by holding it tightly against her chest. The snow burned her knees, and the cold seeped into her muscles, stiffening them and making her unwieldy.

Still, she forced herself to her feet and staggered toward the cabin only to stop in front of the door. Should she go in? She'd given her word, but they had chased the cougar away. In her fright, her animal instincts had taken over, and she'd fled. In a jump over a crevice, she'd broken her front limb. It had taken her hours to crawl her way back to the cabin, and now she didn't know if she'd made the right decision.

The cold and her pain forced her forward. At this point, she didn't have a choice. She needed warmth and rest so she could heal. She could only hope they didn't turn her away.

She stumbled when she got to the door and reached out to brace herself on the worn wood. The handle was frigid, and she fumbled clumsily at it. When it cracked open, a welcome rush of heat drifted out to envelop her.

The living room was dark. No fire burned in the hearth to her dismay. She hurried forward and shut the door behind her. It landed with a bang, and she winced.

The couch was her goal, because the five steps to it were all she could muster, and she'd be lucky to make it that far.

She'd taken two steps when light flooded the living room, and Jericho and Hunter both charged from their bedrooms.

Anger glittered brightly in Hunter's gaze. Jericho looked furious and his reaction was explosive. Her ears rang from the harsh expletives.

Jericho was in front of her in an instant, reaching for her arms.

"Don't touch—!"

It was too late. His hands curled around her broken arm.

Pain exploded through her body. Her scream was primal, rolling like a jolt through the cabin. Jericho dropped her like he'd been burned and stepped away, his fury reduced to shock.

She went to her knees, holding her arm as breathless, silent sobs billowed from her depths.

Hunter pushed by the stunned Jericho and knelt on the floor in front of her.

"What happened?"

"My arm," she gasped out. "It's broken."

"What the fuck?" Jericho finally found his voice.

Hunter curled his hand underneath her other elbow and hoisted her gently to her feet. He led her to the couch and eased her onto the cushion.

She trembled from head to toe, unsure of what bothered her most. The cold or the pain.

Jericho scrambled for a blanket and draped it around her body, taking care not to touch her arm again.

"Kaya, I didn't know. God, I'm sorry for hurting you."

She couldn't find the words around her clenched throat, but her gaze found his and she gave a short shake of her head to let him know it was all right.

She watched as they broke away from her long enough to build up the fire. Then they returned to the couch, their expressions hard. Determined.

"Who is he?" Hunter asked, his tone cold and deadly. "Is he your husband? Boyfriend?"

She blinked in confusion as her teeth started to chatter. "Who is who?"

"The son of a bitch who did this to you," Jericho said icily.

Her eyes widened in shock. "But—"

Hunter cupped her chin and turned her so that she faced him. "I'll take care of it, Kaya. I swear to you I will. Tell me who he is and where I can find him. He'll never hurt you again. We'll keep you safe. I promise."

"There is no one. I swear it."

Jericho threw up his hands in frustration.

She sank back into the couch, bracing herself for what was to come. She had to see to her arm, and though she would heal quickly, she didn't look forward to setting it.

Tired. Cold. She had reached exhaustion, the bone-deep kind that made processing her thoughts impossible.

"We've got to get her down the mountain," she heard Hunter say to Jericho.

She turned her head to bring them both into view and frowned at the intensity on their faces. They weren't talking to her. They were deciding her fate between them.

"We can take her in the sled," Hunter said. "If we can just get her down to the truck, we can drive the rest of the way provided the roads aren't too snowed under."

"Where are you taking me?" she asked faintly.

Hunter turned, his gaze softening just a bit. "The hospital, Kaya. Your arm is badly broken. We have to get you care."

"No!"

Her vehement exclamation startled the two men. Jericho frowned, and Hunter looked at her in bewilderment. Then he knelt down in front of the couch and took her uninjured hand in his.

"You're badly hurt. We have to get you to the hospital. I don't think you understand how bad that break is."

She shook her head. "No. I won't go. I can't go. Please. Just let me stay here. I will be all right."

"No, goddamn it, you won't be all right," Jericho bit out. "We're tired of doing things your way. This time we're not asking, and you're damn well not going to talk us out of doing what has to be done."

Desperation lent her strength. She couldn't let them take her to the hospital. She would be found out. Fear lodged in her throat. What would they do to her? Lock her away in a cage as they once had? Take her away from Jericho and Hunter like she'd once been taken from her humans?

She struggled upward, out of the constraints of the blankets. Hunter and Jericho both reached for her, their hands firm as she fought against them.

"Let me up," she gasped. "Please, this is important. There is something I must tell you."

God, don't let them turn away. The idea of trusting them with her secret terrified her, but how else could she make them understand that she *could not go down the mountain*?

"Kaya, stop. You're going to hurt yourself," Jericho said.

She stopped her struggles and met their gazes. She let all her desperation bleed into her expression as she pleaded with them.

"Please," she finally whispered. *"There is something I must tell you."*

Maybe the urgency finally got through to them, or maybe they realized she wouldn't participate unless they listened. Their hands fell away, and Hunter let out a long sigh.

"Tell us, Kaya. Make it fast so we can take care of your injury."

She struggled to her feet, ignoring their curses and their protests as they tried to keep her on the couch. Finally she broke free and put distance between her and them.

"Don't even think about going out that door," Jericho growled. "We won't let you go this time."

She shook her head in silent denial. That wasn't what she planned. No, what she planned was to strip herself bare in front of these two men. To tell them what she'd never told another human being. And pray they wouldn't reject her.

Chapter Eleven

It was all Hunter could do not to snatch Kaya up and haul her down the mountain. Only the knowledge that he had to tread carefully with her so as not to hurt her even more tempered his impatience.

He wasn't convinced that there was no boyfriend, husband or lover. Maybe even an abusive father. Someone was hurting her, and he'd be damned if he let her go back.

She stood between him and Jericho and the door, her slight body trembling as she held her injured arm. There was stark vulnerability on her face as if something scared the hell out of her. She kept glancing from him to Jericho with nervous eyes.

"Promise me you won't react," she whispered. "To what I tell you, I mean."

Hunter swore. Hell, was she afraid they'd hurt her?

"We promise," Jericho said in a soothing voice.

She glanced at Hunter for confirmation, and he nodded, wishing she'd just get on with it so they could get her the hell out of here.

"It will be easier if I just show you."

Hunter stifled his response and silently urged her to just do it.

She closed her eyes and tensed all over. To his shock, her knees buckled, and she fell to the floor in a heap.

"Kaya!"

He and Jericho both started forward at the same time. Hunter dropped to his knees when the unbelievable happened.

Her body arched, and a moan slipped from her lips. Her skin came to life, rippling in the low light. Instinctively he stood and backed away, unsure of what the hell was happening. He bumped into Jericho, and the two men stared in horror as Kaya's body simply changed form.

Limbs reshaped and shrank upward into her body, becoming more compact. Her mouth opened in a snarl, and she shook her head as fur raced along her neck and down her back. Fur. God almighty.

Her long silken tresses, the color of the cougar fur, became the hide of the cat. Hunter blinked and the mountain lion lay before them panting softly, her eyes glazed with pain.

"Holy fuck," Jericho breathed.

Hunter was speechless. It was his cougar. And suddenly he understood so much and so little all at the same time. The memory of what he'd done dropped him to his knees.

He crawled forward, his hand outstretched in agony and regret.

"God, I didn't know," he whispered as his hand touched her head. "I didn't know, Kaya."

The cat raised pain-glazed eyes to meet his gaze, but she lacked the strength to keep her head up. She dropped it to her paws.

He locked onto her shattered front foreleg. "I did this to you. I'm so sorry. I had no idea. I wouldn't have hurt you for the world."

He felt sick to his soul. She'd given them her trust first as the cougar and only then had she come to them as a human, and he'd betrayed her when he'd turned against her. He'd *shot* at her. In his mind he couldn't separate the fact that he was only trying to protect Kaya. Now that he knew they were one and the same, it killed him that he'd been the one to cause her fear and injury.

"Hunter, what the fuck?" Jericho demanded. "This doesn't make sense. It's not possible."

But Hunter was more willing than Jericho to accept what was so clear. So much made sense now. Everything fell into place with stunning clarity.

He turned to his friend who looked as though he were about to keel over.

"I don't know how or why or even how it's possible," Hunter said calmly. "But would you deny what's in front of our noses? You saw what I saw, Jericho."

"But Jesus Christ, this is crazy. This shit only exists in the movies. How can you be so goddamn calm!"

Shock? Regret? Disgust over the fact that he'd caused her serious injury? His and Jericho's bewilderment didn't seem important in light of what needed to be done for Kaya. She trusted them still. He didn't know why. They hadn't earned it or deserved it, but she trusted them when it was clear she trusted no one else. Never again would he betray that trust.

When he turned back to the cougar, she was valiantly trying to gain her footing. Her ears were slicked back and a sort of crazy wildness shone in her eyes. Even as he started forward, she backed away, her gaze never leaving Jericho.

"You're scaring her," Hunter growled. "Goddamn it, Jericho, get it together or we're going to lose her forever. She won't come back this time. We'll never see her again."

"That never seemed to bother you before," Jericho muttered as he moved forward, his hand outstretched in a placating gesture.

Still, Jericho obviously had no desire for Kaya to leave. Despite the reluctance of the cougar and her defensive posture, Jericho reached out to touch her. He let his fingers trail over her fur. At the first touch, the cougar hissed and withdrew, but Jericho persisted, delving his hand further into the thickness of her fur.

"I'm sorry," he murmured. "You knocked me on my ass, Kaya. It is Kaya, isn't it? You can understand me? I get why you were so reluctant and secretive, and I understand why you couldn't trust us. I hope that's changed now. We'll take care of you, sweetheart. Can you come back to us now? You have to be in so much pain. Let us help you."

The soothing timbre of Jericho's voice seemed to calm the savage beast. She relaxed, going limp on the floor as Jericho continued to stroke her with steady hands.

She let out a low growl and then her body shook and spasmed. Both men rocked back on their heels and watched in astonished horror as it happened all over again. This time, though, she went from beast to beautiful human.

Within seconds, she lay curled on the floor, naked and shivering, soft moans of pain escaping parted lips. Her arm hung broken and useless at her side, and Hunter could only imagine the agony her shift caused.

Not wasting a moment, he gathered her gently in his arms and stood, holding her close to his chest. Her pain-filled gaze focused unsteadily on him as he walked back to the couch. There was question along with fear and uncertainty.

Carefully he lowered her to the cushions and knelt in front of the couch.

"Whatever you're thinking, stop," he ordered. "We're stunned. Even wondering a little about our sanity, but we're not going to turn you out."

"But will you tell?"

Jericho growled and settled onto the couch at her head. His hand brushed across her silky locks and smoothed over her cheek.

"Of course we're not going to give away your secret, Kaya. You can trust us."

But would she offer them her trust again? Hunter was afraid to have the answer to that question. All he could remember was shooting over the cougar's head and how she ran, fear and adrenaline lending her incredible, reckless speed.

"I hurt," she whispered.

Hunter's chest tightened, and he leaned forward. "Tell us how to help you, Kaya. You should be in a hospital, not here with us."

Her eyes flashed, and she looked at him in panic. "No! I can't go. They'd know. They'll take me away." She struggled even as the words spilled from her lips.

"Hunter, goddamn it," Jericho swore. He reached down and carefully pulled Kaya against his chest, his arms tightening around her to keep her still. "Listen to me, honey. We'll figure this out, okay? No one's going to take you anywhere you don't want to go. Now talk to us, and tell us how to help you."

Slowly her struggles diminished, and she lay limply against Jericho, her face creased in pain. Hunter stood. He could do nothing right when it came to this woman. He pulled her close and pushed her away, never said or did the right thing. It was better to leave her to Jericho.

Jericho glanced at Hunter as he turned away. He could damn near see the shutters closing as Hunter withdrew. Hot and cold. Hunter didn't know what the hell he felt for Kaya, and he was fighting it tooth and nail.

With a shake of his head, he turned his attention back to the woman in his arms. He was horrified by her arm. Swollen, bruised and misshapen. It looked to be a clean break, but then how could he tell? His medical training was limited, though he'd seen enough bloodshed to last a lifetime. But that was different, somehow more distant. This was here and now, and he was frantic over how to fix it.

"Tell me what to do," he whispered. "How do I help you?"

"I have to set it," she said in a shaky voice that vibrated with pain. "If it's set, then it will heal quickly. My kind does."

Across the room, Hunter swore and turned back around, his eyes brooding. "She can't set her own arm."

Kaya nodded wearily. "You'll have to do it for me."

Jericho closed his eyes. God, he didn't want to hurt her, and there was no way to set a break like this without causing her agony.

"Just do it, please," she begged softly. "I'm so tired, and I need rest."

Jericho blew out his breath and then eased out from underneath her slight body. When he was sure she was comfortable on the couch, he strode toward Hunter, his expression tight.

"You have to help with this," he said when Hunter met his gaze. "It's going to hurt like a bitch. You can hold her or you can do the setting. Which is it?"

Hunter hesitated then looked beyond him to where Kaya lay. "You hold her. She's easier around you. I'll...I'll do the setting."

It was on the tip of Jericho's tongue to call Hunter a coward, but what would that solve?

"I'll get some linen strips and something to brace her arm. You rustle up some of that whiskey left in the cabinet. It might not help much, but maybe it'll relax her."

Jericho turned, not waiting for Hunter's acceptance, and went to collect the items they needed. He had a sick stomach over what must be done, but he swallowed against the rising nausea and methodically gathered the supplies.

A few minutes later, he returned to find Hunter settling down next to Kaya and offering her a tall glass of whiskey. She murmured a protest, but Hunter was insistent. He pillowed his arm underneath her neck and raised her enough so she could drink without choking. She coughed and sputtered, but Hunter managed to get all of it down her throat.

She sank weakly back against the cushions, her injured arm tucked protectively against her side. Her liquid eyes found Jericho, and he was astonished to find trust burning a warm, golden glow.

Hunter stood and set the empty glass on the floor a few feet away. With brusque movements, he took the strips and the two pieces of wood from Jericho and gestured impatiently for Jericho to go to Kaya.

Jericho took position at her head, lifting her gently and positioning her so that she lay across his lap and rested her head on his chest. He smoothed her hair from her face as Hunter knelt on the floor in front of the couch.

"Cry out all you want, honey," Jericho murmured against her head. "This is going to hurt like a bitch."

Hunter tensed as his fingers moved nimbly over her arm. Jericho turned away, unable to bear the sight of the arm being set. His grip tightened around Kaya as he prepared himself for her screams.

But she didn't make a sound. She coiled like a nervous rattlesnake, so tight that he could feel every quiver of her muscles. She buried her face in his chest, and when Hunter forced the bone back into place, her hot tears soaked into Jericho's shirt.

It was worse than any cry she might have made.

He kissed the top of her head, helpless to do anything but wait until Hunter was through binding the arm.

Hunter rocked back on his heels, his expression stormy. He stood abruptly then glanced down at Jericho. "You should take her to bed so she can rest."

Without another word, Hunter strode to the kitchen, and Jericho heard the clanking of dishes.

"Are you feeling any relief yet?" he asked Kaya.

Slowly she drew away until he could see her red, tear-stained cheeks. She nodded and clutched her splinted arm to her chest. "I'll be fine, Jericho. Now I must rest and heal."

As if seeking to comfort *him*, she put her free hand to his jaw, resting her fingers on his cheek.

"I will be all right."

He grasped her hand and moved it over his lips so he could kiss each fingertip. With exquisite care, he eased forward, holding her like she was precious glass. Then he stood, hoisting her up until she rested against his chest.

With a weary sigh, she laid her head against his shoulder, and her eyes were closing before he got to his bedroom. He gave thought to getting her another change of clothing, but he was too afraid of hurting her, so he put her on the bed and pulled down the covers.

She settled among his pillows with a sigh that sounded blissful. Her splinted arm rested over her side as she snuggled deeper into the covers.

How soft and utterly feminine she was. He liked the way she looked in his bed. Liked it very much. She was perfection. Slim. Long legs that sprang from rounded hips. Just a slight curve that didn't upset the lithe lines of her body at all.

A narrow waist that led up to small, high breasts with just enough plumpness to tease a man. His hands itched to touch her. To caress her and show her all the gentleness he was capable of. Lord it had been a long time since he'd ached so badly to hold a woman.

"Are you coming, Jericho?" she asked around a sleepy yawn.

He hadn't realized that he was still standing there staring down at her like a moron. Then he blinked at how normal her request sounded. Like a wife asking her husband if he was coming to bed.

Jesus. He needed some of that whiskey Hunter had given her.

He kicked off his clothing and then crawled into bed next to her. The sheets had cooled since his abrupt departure almost an hour earlier. He could feel her shivering.

As soon as he moved closer to her, she snuggled against him, fitting her slight form to his with no hesitation. Again she sighed, and her breath blew over his neck, sending forty thousand chill bumps dancing down his spine.

No matter what he may have done wrong in his life, no one deserved to be tortured like this. What kind of a sick joke was it to have a gorgeous, naked woman wrapped around him like a second skin when she had a broken arm and he was supposed to temper his raging hormones?

She was asleep in a matter of seconds while he lay there, wide awake, his body jumping through hoops while his mind tried valiantly to think of other things.

Gradually he relaxed, positioning his arm over her hip, mindful of her injury. He drew her closer until they fit together like two pieces of a puzzle.

Damn but she felt good. Right.

And now that she was asleep, he was forced to go over what he'd witnessed in the living room. The sheer impossibility of what she was, of what she'd done.

Part of him wondered if he hadn't finally gone off the deep end. Too much work. Too much stress. But that wouldn't explain why Hunter had seen the same damn thing. They couldn't both be nuts.

No matter how many times he told himself that it wasn't possible, he had to face the fact that it was. That the world as he'd known it, simply wasn't. And if he'd been wrong about this, what else was he wrong about? What else existed out there that was beyond his realm of understanding?

For a man who prided himself on his acceptance of harsh reality, there was no way to reconcile this in his mind. No, he didn't understand it. He wasn't even sure he accepted it. All he knew was that he wasn't about to let Kaya walk away again.

But she spent the majority of her time as a wild animal. How could he stop her when she decided to go?

Chapter Twelve

Kaya woke, shivering in the grip of a dream that had haunted her sleep for years. Her gaze automatically shot to Jericho who had turned over so that his back was to her. There was at least a foot of distance between them, and the urge to move closer to the heat emanating from his body was strong.

She glanced at her aching arm, unable to tell in the darkness how much the swelling had lessened. On the edges of her mind, the shadows grew. Lengthening until she swallowed against the unbearable sadness.

She feared what would happen now that Hunter and Jericho knew her secret. She hadn't gotten close to people over the years. The rapport she'd shared with these two strong, enigmatic men was the most intimate she'd had with anyone since her childhood. She hadn't allowed such a bond before.

Again she glanced over at Jericho who hadn't stirred since she'd awakened. Then, propelled by the need to see Hunter, she quietly crawled from the bed, favoring her broken arm.

The cabin was colder, the warmth from the fireplace all but gone. Outside the wind howled but no new snow fell. The windows shook and rattled as the cabin creaked and moaned against the bitterness of the elements.

She'd half expected to find him in the living room, but Hunter wasn't on the couch. He'd probably sought the comfort of his bed. The floor cold beneath her bare feet, she turned to go toward the other bedroom.

The door was closed, an unwelcoming barrier to intruders. Much like the wall he erected every time he caught himself relaxing around her.

He was a loner, like her. Something about him called to her. Even though she knew he didn't much like her—or the fact that he was drawn to her.

Carefully she opened the door and slipped inside. Pale moonlight shone through the window and bathed his face. Even in sleep, there was a seriousness, a closed-off expression that told Kaya how carefully he guarded himself from others.

For a long moment she stood over him, watching the rise and fall of his chest. She was so tempted to reach out and smooth the lines on his face, to ease the strain she saw around his eyes. He wouldn't appreciate her tenderness any more than he wanted to be tender with her. And yet he was.

Finally she walked around to the other side and quietly slipped into the bed. She wanted nothing more than to curl up with him as she had done with Jericho, but she didn't want to chance waking him and having him toss her out.

She frowned. No, he wouldn't do that, but he would withdraw. He might even get up himself so he could put distance between them. Or he might hold her as he'd done on the couch. There was no way to know how he'd react from one moment to the next, and she only wanted a few moments to absorb his heat and scent.

She settled far enough away from him that she wasn't touching him and pulled the covers to her chin. The warm blankets settled over her broken arm, irritating the sensitive skin. She twitched uncomfortably until finally she loosened her hold on the covers to allow them to slip from her arm.

Instantly, the cold skittered over her flesh and pulled goose bumps into a haphazard pattern. She closed her eyes and mentally reached for Hunter's warmth just inches away. She imagined lying flush against him.

Soon the chill slipped away, replaced by the soothing comfort of her imagination.

Hunter woke to the knowledge that he wasn't alone. He turned his head to see Kaya huddled a short distance away, her body shivering in the cold.

Emitting a soft curse he rolled, pulling the covers with him so he could cover her with the blankets. She moaned softly when the sheet

183

brushed across her arm, so he tucked the blanket carefully underneath it but swaddled the rest of her in the soft warmth.

For a long moment, he lay there, just two inches from touching her. Her gold-burnished skin glistened in the soft rays of sunshine that poured through his window, and her hair, soft brown caramel, spilled over his pillow, tickling the underside of his arm.

He'd forgotten what it was like to wake with a woman in his bed. Forgotten the contentment of knowing he wasn't alone, but he'd also managed to avoid the pain that accompanied loss.

Hell of a trade-off.

Finally he reached for her face, tracing the delicate curve of her cheek before cupping her jaw. She turned toward him, seeking his touch, her eyes never opening. She was so starved for affection. He could only imagine how lonely her life must be. What had made her trust him and Jericho when it was clear she'd avoided people her entire life?

How long could he continue to pull her close and then shove her away? He'd already admitted he wanted her. Hell, he and Jericho had had a positively civilized discussion, like she was some object to be bartered. For all he knew she didn't even look at him and see a man she wanted to be with.

She kissed as sweet and as hot as any woman he'd ever been with, but there was an innocence about her that made him question just how aware she was of her sexuality.

And he'd be a damned liar if he denied that he wanted to be the one to awaken her, to stir the flames higher and brighter, to show her just how it would be between them. Then there was Jericho.

With a heavy sigh, he rolled away to stare up at the ceiling. Jericho presented a complication. Not that he hadn't shared a woman with his friend before. They'd both loved Rebeccah, and they'd both lost her. He'd never said as much to Jericho, but he hadn't been convinced that they wouldn't have lost her anyway if she hadn't died. She hadn't trusted the bond between the three of them, hadn't believed that they could love her and not destroy each other in the process. Part of him couldn't blame her, and the other part resented that she had given her heart but not her trust. Because of that, Hunter had vowed never to get into another situation where he and Jericho were both involved with the same woman. And yet Kaya had burst into their lives and both men were drawn to her. It wasn't as easy as just deciding to back away. He knew he should, but like Jericho, he had no intention of stepping aside.

"Hunter?"

Her sleepy voice melted over him, eliciting a tenderness that he'd sworn was alien to him now. He turned to face her, watching her eyes for evidence of pain. All he saw was wariness as she watched him. Was she afraid of him?

It was a stupid question. After the way he'd acted the night before, pushing her away as soon as she'd revealed her secret, she probably had no idea what he was thinking or how he felt.

"Are you hurting?"

There was strain around her lips, and then she licked them, parting them as her husky voice slid over his ears. "Yes, but it will get better. Already I'm healing."

He reached out to run a finger over the broken arm. The bruising had already faded, and the swelling had gone down remarkably.

"Why did you come in here?"

As soon as the question was out, vulnerability flashed in her eyes. He could see her withdrawing as she braced herself for his rejection. He wanted to reassure her, apologize for the brash way he'd blurted out the question, but he was genuinely curious as to why she'd left Jericho's bed to come to him.

"I wanted to be with you," she said simply. "I'm sorry. I'll go back to Jericho."

She started to slide toward the edge of the bed.

"No, don't go. I didn't mean it like that."

She paused and stared back at him. "Are you still angry with me, Hunter? I'm sorry I broke my word. I was coming back to you and Jericho."

"Angry with you?" He was astonished. "Kaya, it's you who should be angry with me. I shot at you, for God's sake. I'm the reason you broke your arm."

She touched his lip with her fingers. He kissed them hungrily, and for the first time allowed all of the desire to well, unfettered and free. It overwhelmed him in a rush. He hadn't allowed himself to feel since Rebeccah, and it was frightening in its intensity.

He shook with his need, with wanting. Beside him, Kaya studied his expression, her head cocked to the side in gentle curiosity.

"Will you keep my secret, Hunter?" she whispered. "I've never told anyone. It frightens me because now I feel powerless."

He moved closer to her, careful not to touch her arm. Their mouths were now so close that he could feel the warmth of her breath on his chin.

"You can trust me, Kaya. I'll protect you, take care of you. No one will ever know but me and Jericho. I swear."

She touched his cheek with light fingertips. "Thank you." And then she kissed him. Just one sweet brush of her mouth to his. It was the lightest of sensations, like a butterfly's wings, but it electrified him.

Her eyes were glowing when she pulled away, and he stared, mesmerized, into her liquid depths.

"Will you tell me about the cougar?" he asked.

"Yes, I will tell you and Jericho. Could I...could I eat first?"

His stomach clenched. It sickened him to imagine how many times she'd gone without food or shelter.

"Do you want me to bring you something in bed?"

"I can get up. I want to see Jericho too."

He reached over to help her sit up. She kept her arm flat against her chest, and her lips tightened into a fine white line as she swung her legs over the edge of the bed.

They met at the foot of the bed and stood staring at each other. She regarded him with understandable wariness, and yet he was shedding the protective layers he'd worn for so long.

"Come here," he said in a low voice as he reached for her.

She settled against his chest at an angle where she could keep her arm from pressing against him. He wrapped both arms around her and simply absorbed the sensation of holding her. Emotions long buried fought their way to the surface, raw and painful, and yet he welcomed them like the spring thaws after a long, harsh winter.

She made a sweet sound of contentment that rocked him to his soul. Somehow she belonged. Here. With him and Jericho. He should deny that fact. He should push her away, but he could no more do that than he could stop the flood of want.

It wasn't just sexual desire. It transcended the simplicity of lust and passion. He needed her and that scared the hell out of him. How could he need this slip of a girl who encompassed the soul of the cougar?

"Come on so I can get you something to eat. You're too thin."

He felt her smile against him. "I am hungry."

He took her hand, unable to resist touching her. And then he dropped it, disgusted by his weakness.

She didn't let him leave, though. She stopped him with an outstretched hand. Her fingers curled trustingly through his, lacing them together. She squeezed as if she understood the battle he was waging with himself.

"It will be all right, Hunter," she said solemnly. "I know what it's like to hurt, to be alone."

Somehow he believed that. She'd suffered enough hurt and loneliness, though. If he could help it, she wouldn't hurt again.

Stunned by the implication of his wayward thoughts, he pulled her toward the kitchen. Had he just committed himself to her well-being? It was more than that. He'd just locked his future with hers.

Fool. He knew nothing about her. She could leave tomorrow, and here he was forming attachments he had no business forming. The sad thing was, in the few days he'd known her, he'd already given her the power to destroy him as soundly as Rebeccah had.

And he only had himself to blame.

Chapter Thirteen

Jericho looked up when Hunter and Kaya entered the kitchen. He fought to keep his expression neutral. When he'd awakened to find Kaya missing, he knew she'd gone to Hunter. It shouldn't bother him, but it did. This wasn't new territory for him and Hunter, but with Rebeccah it had been different. The three of them had always just been. Theirs was a comfortable relationship. The way he felt about Kaya was wild and decidedly uncomfortable.

Kaya's gaze met his, and she studied him with a hint of unease, almost as if she could read his thoughts. He stared back, holding his breath as he waited. For what he wasn't sure, and then she told him. With her actions.

She walked directly to him, her courage bolstered and burning brightly in her warm eyes. Mere inches away, so close he could feel her slight warmth, she stopped. Her broken arm was clutched tightly against her body, but her free hand glided up his arm and then over his chest.

He caught her fingers, unable to resist touching her as she touched him. Curling his hand around hers, he brought her palm up to his lips and pressed a kiss to the pad of her thumb.

A soft little sigh escaped, and she leaned into his body.

"Kiss me, Jericho."

Forgetting all about Hunter who stood a few feet away, Jericho gathered her gently in his arms and lowered his mouth to hers. Her lips were crushed petals, as sweet as a spring flower.

His grip tightened, and her whimper escaped into his mouth. He released her immediately and cursed his lack of care.

"I'm sorry. I didn't mean to hurt you."

She smiled ruefully down at her arm. "I will be well soon."

"How soon?" Hunter asked.

She turned as if she too had forgotten Hunter's presence.

"A day, maybe two." A frown wrinkled her brow. "Could be longer. I've never broken an entire arm."

Despite her serious tone, Jericho had to laugh at the way she'd said it. "An entire arm? What have you broken, then?"

"A finger," she said as she flexed her index finger on her right hand. "I had to set it, but it didn't hurt as bad as last night."

She seemed surprised by that fact, and he and Hunter just shook their heads at each other.

Hunter moved forward, nudging her gently toward a chair at the table. "Have a seat, Kaya. Breakfast will be up shortly, and you need to eat before we ask you twenty questions."

"Only twenty?"

At first Jericho thought she was teasing, but there was solemnity on her face that suggested she had no idea it was a joke.

"Well, maybe a few more," Hunter said with a smile.

Jericho cocked his head in Hunter's direction. He seemed a lot more relaxed this morning. More accepting. As if he'd gone ten rounds and finally scored a knockout in the final seconds. Try as he might, he couldn't catch Hunter's gaze to verify his suspicions. Oh well, he'd just see how it played out this morning. He had a feeling he wouldn't have to wait long.

Kaya settled down and fussed a few minutes as she tried to get comfortable with her clunky splint job. Jericho turned back to the stove and forked out the last of the frying bacon.

Hunter ambled over to get plates and forks while Jericho finished putting the food on the table. Kaya looked at all the food with what Jericho could only describe as sheer wistfulness.

"Dig in, honey. Get as much as you want," Jericho said as he plunked down on the chair beside her.

He and Hunter watched as she piled her plate high with eggs, bacon and toast. After a few minutes fumbling awkwardly with the fork, she forewent utensils and ate with her fingers.

What should have been slightly barbaric turned into an erotic exercise that was destined to drive both men insane. After each tiny bite, she licked delicately at her fingers, sometimes sucking the tip between her lips only to release it with a slight pop.

When she was finally done, neither man had eaten much and

Jericho quickly cleared the table of the dishes.

"Let's go into the living room, and I'll add some more wood to the fire," Hunter said. "We can talk there."

Kaya hesitated and looked back at Jericho, her eyes gleaming with questions.

"Go on. I'll be there in a minute," he said.

She seemed to relax as Hunter ushered her away. Jericho tossed the dishes in the sink and decided to take care of them later. There were a hell of a lot of questions he wanted answered, and he wanted to make sure Kaya didn't get any crazy ideas about leaving again.

Kaya settled onto the couch and watched as Hunter added more logs to the fire. When it crackled and blazed higher, he came back to the couch and sat down on the end. There were at least two feet of space between them. She fidgeted, going back and forth between staying where she was and moving closer to Hunter. But if he'd wanted her close, he would have sat next to her.

Jericho suffered no such compunction. When he entered the living room, he went straight to the couch, picked her up and settled her onto his lap. Surprised by his show of affection, she snuggled into his chest and let out a contented sigh.

Her cheek resting on Jericho's shoulder, she gazed over at Hunter who regarded them intently. What was it about these two men that compelled her so solidly? They'd drawn her out of the mountains, caused her to risk discovery. She couldn't stay away. It was as if some invisible force guided her back to them time and time again.

Perhaps it was the Maker's way of ensuring she wasn't left alone forever. For that she was grateful.

"Two mates," she whispered in wonder. Was it possible?

"What was that, honey?" Jericho asked.

She shook her head. "Nothing." She didn't know their intentions, and the last thing she wanted to chance was rejection.

"Will you tell us about yourself, Kaya?" Hunter asked. "We have so many questions."

She tensed against Jericho, and he pressed his lips to her hair in a reassuring manner. "Don't be afraid."

"It's not that. It's just…"

Her voice trailed off as painful memories, long buried, welled to the surface. Unexpectedly, tears stung the corners of her eyes.

Hunter scooted forward on the couch and carefully brushed away a tear with his thumb. Then he cupped her cheek in his palm. "Whatever it is, we can help you."

She braved a shaky smile. "The memories are painful for me. Once I had a home and a family."

Hunter's expression darkened. "Did they turn you out because of what you are?"

Her brow crinkled in confusion. "No, at least I don't think so. I don't really know."

Jericho squeezed her shoulder then brushed her hair over her shoulder. "Tell us. We're listening."

"I had a sister. She was a cheetah. She's all I remember, really. I mean, I know I had a mother and father, but so many years have gone by. Their faces are so dim."

"There are more of you?" Hunter asked in astonishment.

"She was beautiful and fast. So graceful. I remember wanting to be like her. She always left me behind when we ran. One day we ventured farther from our home than we should have. We were just cubs then. Mischievous and anxious to explore our surroundings. I was caught in a trap and the people took me away. They said I didn't belong there."

"Where was there?" Jericho asked.

"Alaska."

Hunter raised a brow. "I can see why they didn't think you belonged. Did they see your sister?"

Kaya shook her head. "No, I don't know what happened to her. I was taken here to the mountains. For a while I was kept in a cage. Maybe they intended me for a zoo. I'm not sure. I was terribly frightened, so I stayed in cougar form until I could escape."

"How old were you?" Jericho asked.

"Four, maybe five."

Hunter swore. "You were just a child!"

She nodded. "After I escaped, I hid for a long time, afraid that if I came out, they'd take me again. Then, when I was able and older, I made my way back to Alaska only to find the house deserted. I was nine or ten."

Tears welled again and Jericho's grip tightened around her.

"They were gone. They'd left me. I waited and waited but they never returned. So I went back to my mountains."

"How long?" Jericho asked. "How long have you lived alone up here?"

Kaya frowned as she considered for a moment. "I've passed thirteen winters. Maybe fourteen since the time I came back here. It's hard to keep count."

"Jesus," Hunter murmured. "How the hell did you survive?"

She shrugged. "The cougar is a very good hunter. She took good care of me."

"You talk like she's separate from you," Jericho said.

"In a way she is. We are one and yet we aren't. She is who guided me to you."

"How is it you can change?" Hunter asked softly. "I didn't think people like you existed."

"I don't remember a lot of my heritage," she said sadly. "I know the animals are gifts from the Great Maker. Our souls are united when we are still in our mother's womb. The cougar is my caretaker and I am hers. We have to strike a careful balance between the human and the animal. We have great healing power, but we must shift often. I chose to stay in animal form to stay safe, and it's taken a toll on me. Even now, the cougar cries out to be set free. Embracing the change is what aids the healing process."

"Amazing," Jericho said in an awed voice. "I'm speechless."

"Same here," Hunter echoed.

She found Hunter's gaze then tilted her head to look up at Jericho. "Does it bother you?" she asked hesitantly.

Jericho touched her cheek and then lowered his mouth to hers. His kiss was soft and sensual. Warm and so loving.

"No," he said against her mouth. "Nothing about you bothers us. We want you to stay."

Her eyes widened in surprise as she pulled away. Then she turned to look sharply at Hunter. Surely he couldn't be included in the invitation. She'd seen the hurt in his eyes. She reminded him of someone he'd lost. He wouldn't want her as a constant reminder.

As if sensing her rioting emotions, Hunter leaned forward again, his eyes intensely focused on her.

"I want you to stay, Kaya. Somehow, someway, we'll work it out. I don't want you out there alone, in the snow, cold and frightened. I want you here where Jericho and I can take care of you, make sure you have food and warm clothes."

She frowned a little. "Is that all? You just want to take care of me?"

Jericho nudged her chin until she was forced to look at him. "I think you know that's not true, honey. We just don't want to push you. I can't even be in the same room with you without wanting you. We'd like you to stay so that we see where this takes us."

Two mates. It was more than she'd ever dreamed. After so long on her own, of having no one, that she'd have two strong mates was more than she could conceive.

"I'll have you...both?" she asked, still disbelieving what they were offering.

"Do you want us both?" Hunter asked quietly.

"You are both here," she said, raising her uninjured arm until her hand curled into a fist over her heart.

Hunter's expression softened, and he reached for her fist, raised it to his lips and kissed each knuckle. "Yes, you'll have us both. If that's what you really want."

She smiled. Smiled so big that she felt like bursting. "Two mates," she said, loud enough that this time they heard.

Jericho chuckled. "We can be hard to live with, Kaya. You might change your mind."

She shook her head vigorously. "If you can accept the cougar then there is nothing about you and Hunter I cannot accept."

Jericho kissed the top of her head again and settled her against his chest. "We accept you, honey. I'm still dumbstruck by what I saw you do, but I accept it and you."

Chapter Fourteen

Hunter sat reading his book in front of the fire, the cougar sprawled on the couch beside him, her head resting on her paws. Jericho sat on the opposite end, his hand lying over the cougar's soft fur.

Several days had passed since Kaya had broken her arm, and it was nearly healed. She'd shifted periodically, and the two men had watched in agony, wincing in sympathy as her body contorted and went through unspeakable torture.

With each shift, the break healed more. The splint was gone, and all that was left was residual tenderness and limited motion.

Absently, Hunter stroked the cat's ears, and then he turned the page of his book. He settled his hand back on her head as he resumed his reading. Underneath his fingers, she trembled. Hunter looked up at Jericho.

"Get a blanket and her clothes. She's been colder coming out of her shifts. I'll build up the fire."

In another minute, Kaya lay shaking beside Hunter. She raised her arm and flexed it, rolling her wrist as she bent her elbow back and forth. As she raised her head, Hunter had already laid aside his book, and he reached for her.

She went willingly, curling into the warmth of his body. He savored these moments, when she came out of her shift like a spindly colt trying to get its legs underneath it. In that moment, she depended on him and Jericho. She always sought them out, cuddling into their warmth. Her trust humbled him. She trusted them not to hurt her, and she made Hunter want to keep that unspoken promise.

Her bare skin pressed flush against his flannel shirt, and he cursed having anything on at all. He wanted to feel her against him. He and Jericho had not made any moves toward her in the days following her injury. He had no idea what Jericho's thoughts were on the matter, but it was important to Hunter that she trust them completely and that they not take advantage of her.

When he made love to her, he wanted her whole, completely yielding and understanding. Hell, he didn't even know exactly how old she was, just that she was young and innocent, somewhere around twenty-three or twenty-four, and he was old and jaded. He wasn't even sure she'd ever had a lover. How could she when she'd led such a secluded, isolated life?

The idea that she was a virgin terrified him and appealed to him in equal parts. That she'd never belong to anyone else was a fact he relished, but at the same time, he didn't want to hurt her, was terrified of not being gentle or tender enough.

Jericho returned with a flannel shirt and the sweatpants they'd altered to fit her. At some point they'd have to go down the mountain into town to buy her better clothing, but as long as the snow kept coming down, they were stuck in the cabin.

She stood shivering, laughing as she yanked on the clothes in jerky motions. When she was finished, she dove into Jericho's waiting arms while Hunter stood to tend the fire.

Hunter turned and chuckled as Kaya tried to burrow underneath Jericho. Jericho's face was a study in tenderness as he looked down at Kaya. His hand brushed lightly over her hair and down her cheek.

How odd that they both had vowed to never get involved with the same woman after Rebeccah, and yet here they were, inexorably tangled. With Rebeccah it had just been understood. They'd always been friends, and when she died, they hadn't just lost a lover, they'd lost a part of their past.

Kaya...Kaya spoke to a part of his heart that hadn't been previously opened. He was hard-pressed to explain it, and he wasn't sure exactly the extent of his feelings for Kaya. They were too new, too raw. With Rebeccah, things had been easy. Fun, a little wild, even tumultuous at times.

Kaya was sweet, and she called to his protective nature. Rebeccah hadn't needed him and Jericho. She never had. Kaya was strong, but she needed them, and he couldn't control the surge of satisfaction that gave him.

Jericho watched the range of emotions flickering in Hunter's eyes. Eyes that had been cold and unfeeling for so long. As conflicted as

Hunter was about Kaya, Jericho knew that he'd made a firm decision that he didn't want to let Kaya go, even if he didn't yet know what he felt for her.

Kaya stirred restlessly against him, her slim arms wrapping around his waist as she rubbed her cheek over his chest. He smiled and pressed a kiss to her temple. A sense of contentment gripped him. Contentment he hadn't experienced in a long time.

She felt...right.

It went beyond simple lust. He hadn't taken her to bed yet, but she settled him. He was happy. And God, when was the last time he could say that? When had either he or Hunter been able to say that? They'd made a practice of existing from one assignment to the next.

Kaya's fingers touched his cheek softly, and he looked down to see her staring up at him, her eyes questioning.

"What are you thinking?" she asked softly.

"That you're beautiful."

She flushed a delightful shade of pink, but her eyes shone with happiness.

"I'm glad you find me beautiful. No one has ever thought I was beautiful." She said the last in a wistful tone that twisted a region deep inside his chest.

"Would you like me to show you just how beautiful I find you?" he asked huskily.

Her eyes glowed brightly, shadowed only by returning desire.

"You wish to mate with me?"

He arched one eyebrow. It was asked in such an innocent way that he suddenly felt uneasy about making love to her. Was he taking advantage of a complete innocent?

"Do not worry, Jericho," she said, her tone slightly chiding. "I understand mating." She turned to cast a wistful glance in Hunter's direction. "Is it possible to mate with both of you?"

Jericho could almost hear Hunter's groan. Lord, but the woman was going to be the death of both of them.

"Honey, look at me."

She turned back to him while Hunter stood rigid in the background, his eyes glittering with need.

"Have you ever...mated before?"

She shook her head solemnly. "I would not let a man near me. I was too afraid."

"And you're not afraid now? Of us?"

Her brow furrowed, and she looked almost angry. "Why would I be afraid of you? You are my mates. I trust you. You would never hurt me."

"It's not hurting we're concerned about," Hunter said gruffly. "We don't want to take advantage of you. We have to be damn sure you know what you're getting into."

"Oh. I see." Then she smiled. "Would it be better if I did the mating?"

Jericho damn near swallowed his tongue. He'd eligible for sainthood if he survived this.

Hunter closed the distance until he stood over Kaya. He looked very much like a hungry predator. Jericho instinctively curled a protective arm around her waist.

Hunter cupped her chin in his hand and smoothed a thumb over her cheek. "Just tell me you want this, Kaya. Tell me you know what you're doing and that you understand what's about to happen."

She closed her eyes briefly and leaned into Hunter's touch. She nuzzled his palm before opening her eyes again.

"You're going to undress me and touch me. Kiss me and love me," she whispered. "I'm going to take you inside me until we become one."

Hunter reached for her hand, holding his palm up. "I'm going to do a hell of a lot more than that."

Chapter Fifteen

Kaya could no longer control her erratic breathing. Images of the two men touching her, covering her body with theirs captivated her mind. Slowly, Hunter pulled her upward until she was free of Jericho's hold.

She stood in front of the couch, between both men. Where she belonged.

The idea of mating had never frightened her. It fascinated her. She'd seen many instances in the wild, though she knew that humans did it far differently. Still, the innate savagery of beasts mating was somehow beautiful and unspoiled.

Hunter and Jericho would be far more loving and gentle, and she craved being cherished by both.

Hunter slid his fingers down the column of her neck and around to the buttons on her flannel shirt. One by one, he unfastened them, parting the lapels as he went. There was no urgency in his motions, just a practiced ease that she knew was intentional. How she loved him for taking such care.

Behind her, Jericho stood and gripped her shoulders in firm hands. He bent to nuzzle her neck as Hunter tugged her shirt away.

Tiny prickles danced across her skin. She shivered and leaned back, wanting more of his heated kiss. And then Hunter knelt in front of her, his hands pulling away her bottoms as his mouth found the turgid peak of one breast.

Her legs buckled, but she was caught between them. Safe. Supported.

"You're so beautiful," Hunter whispered. "So golden and tawny like the cougar."

The cat purred within, and Kaya threaded her fingers through

Hunter's short hair, pulling him to her breast. With her other hand, she reached to pull Jericho back to her neck. Their mouths drank from her, tasted and teased her.

She wanted to taste them back.

She swiveled in their arms, turning to face Jericho. Her breasts pressed against his muscled chest as she frantically tore at his shirt. He helped her, shrugging impatiently from the confines of his clothing. Her mouth met his flesh, and she moaned in sheer delight.

She pushed, and he ceded to her power. Falling back on the couch, he took her with him. Her mouth found him again, licking and kissing her way up the hair-roughened hollow of his chest.

Behind them, she heard the rustle of Hunter's pants hitting the floor.

Before she could really get into her exploration of his body, Jericho pulled her up by her shoulders until their mouths were level. Their breaths came hard and fast as they dodged and parried. Finally their lips met, and she sighed in utter contentment.

Hunter's mouth pressed to the small of her back, and a shockwave sizzled through her veins at the sensation of two mouths heating her skin.

His hands cupped and kneaded her buttocks just as Jericho's found her breasts. She threw her head back while he thumbed both nipples forced outward by his grip.

"I want you both so much," she whispered. "I love you."

Both men went still. So still she thought she'd made a mistake by being so honest with her feelings. And then Hunter scooped her up into his arms and strode toward the bedroom. Jericho followed close behind, arriving just as Hunter tossed her down on the bed.

She looked up in anticipation as both men towered over her, their eyes lean and hungry. How proud and strong they looked, their legs slightly parted, their erections jutting upward. She imagined them sliding into her body, over and over until she quivered in anticipation. Slowly, she raised her hands in supplication.

Hunter came down over her, his body pressing against her softness. She marveled at their differences, how hard he was, and yet how careful he was not to hurt her.

Jericho reclined on the bed next to her, his fingers threading through her hair as Hunter suckled at her breasts. Her eyes closed in contented bliss when Jericho tenderly kissed her temple.

"We don't want you to be afraid, Kaya," Jericho whispered next to her ear. "If we move too fast or do something you don't want, just stop us."

She turned her face to him, seeking his lips with hers. "Nothing you do will frighten me. I want you. I want this."

Hunter moved down her body, his mouth open as it grazed along her midline. His breath was scorching against her, his tongue warm and slightly rough. His hands followed, firing her senses. Her back bowed as she arched into him, seeking more of his mouth, of his touch.

All her breath left her when he parted her legs and his fingers carefully found the sleek, damp flesh at her heart. He stroked and then spread her folds wider as he lowered his head.

"Oh..."

She closed her eyes and twisted restlessly as his tongue found her. Electric currents raced from her pelvis to her breasts, tightening them to puckered buds.

Jericho traced a damp trail around one with his tongue, lapping and then finally sucking the point between his teeth. He gave her a little nip just as Hunter's tongue delved into her very core.

The most amazing thing happened. A flood of the most indescribable pleasure she'd ever known washed through her like a raging river. It happened so quickly she wasn't prepared. It was overwhelming, and yet she wanted it to go on and on.

She was still battling the fire when something hard nudged at her entrance. She opened her eyes to see Hunter braced over her, his expression one of intense pain.

She reached out to touch the harsh lines across his face, wanting to ease the tension etched there.

"Come to me," she whispered. "Fill me."

"I don't want to hurt you."

"Never."

He closed his eyes and eased forward. She opened around him, and she marveled at the delicious sensations that pulsed in her groin. Her body surrounded him, inviting him further, clinging like a second skin.

"Hold onto me," he rasped. "I'll make it quick."

She had no idea what he meant, but she gripped his shoulders, determined to please him. With one powerful surge, he thrust into her body. She felt a slight tearing, and her mouth fell open in shock, but almost as quickly as she became aware of the pain, it faded to the background.

There were so many things she could feel. Slight discomfort as her body fought to accept his intrusion. But also the stirrings of something wonderful. She felt itchy, alive, like she could crawl right out of herself. She needed him to move.

Wrapping her legs around him, she lifted her hips higher, desperate to appease the ache deep within her. Jericho's mouth was on her breast. Hunter's hands were tight at her hips.

"Please," she begged.

Hunter groaned. It was the sound of the sweetest agony. And then he finally began to move. He withdrew, but before she could protest, he thrust again, seating himself deeper than before. Her gasp echoed across the room.

"Am I hurting you, honey? I'll stop."

"No! Please. I need you, Hunter. Please, I ache so much."

"Ahh, Kaya. You're so sweet. I'll take care of you, honey. Just hold onto me tight."

She would have done anything for him in that moment. He began to move harder and faster. More demanding. Taking but giving back with each thrust. She went slick around him, and suddenly he didn't seem quite so large inside her passageway.

The friction became unbearable, and she feared she'd burst. Higher and higher she climbed. She gripped him with a fierceness alien to her. Every muscle tensed in anticipation of something so sweet, so pleasurable.

And then she tumbled out of control, her body flying in a hundred different directions. She quivered around his thick shaft as he pushed and strained against her.

With a breathless groan, he withdrew from her and collapsed onto her, his arousal throbbing against her belly. Something hot and liquid pulsed onto her skin.

"You're so beautiful when you come," Jericho murmured. "So expressive, so wild."

She slowly turned her head to see him smoothing away the hair from her cheek. Hunter's mouth rested against the hollow under her ear, and she could feel the rapid stuttering of his heart against her chest.

"Now you," she whispered as she reached her hand to Jericho.

He smiled and caught her fingers in his gentle grip. "Not now, honey. I don't want to hurt you."

"But you won't—"

He shook his head. "Not intentionally. Your body isn't used to having a man inside you. You're too tender right now to take me."

"He's right." Hunter agreed.

She glanced down in confusion at the wetness on her belly and Hunter's still semi-erect shaft. She knew enough about the elements of mating to know this wasn't right, but she couldn't form the right words to question it. Why hadn't he remained inside her?

Hunter seemed to sense her confusion, and he touched her cheek, his eyes soft as he looked down at her. "Jericho and I don't keep condoms here. It's not as if we ever expected to have a woman here."

"Condoms?" she echoed.

"They're sheaths that go over our..." He looked down and she quickly got the idea. "They protect you from pregnancy—and diseases."

"Diseases?" She was beginning to feel very stupid about this mating business.

"You don't have to worry about diseases," Jericho growled. "It's been a long damn time for both of us, and there was only one woman we didn't wear condoms with."

His response didn't really answer her confusion, and now she wondered about this other woman. Maybe later she'd have the courage to ask about her.

"I'll go start a shower and be back for you in just a second," Hunter said as he backed off the bed.

She watched as he walked nude across the room and disappeared into the bathroom.

"Are you all right?" Jericho asked as he pulled her into his embrace.

She nodded and snuggled deeper into his arms. "I don't like having to wait to take you inside me."

He laughed softly. "I guarantee I don't like it any more than you. We have all the time in the world, though, and I want it to be perfect for you when it happens."

She sighed in contentment. She liked the promise of having time. It made it sound like he had no intention of being parted from her.

Chapter Sixteen

Kaya stood in the small bathroom as Hunter rubbed her dry with a warm towel that Jericho had held in front of the fire while she and Hunter showered. When he'd finished, he pulled her close, warming her with his body heat.

"Hunter?"

He pulled away and looked questioningly at her.

"Jericho didn't...that is he didn't have any pleasure." She frowned slightly as she wrapped her mind around what it was she was trying to ask.

"I'd say he got a lot of pleasure from watching you," Hunter said. "But ultimate satisfaction, no he didn't. Not yet."

Her brow wrinkled in consternation. "Isn't there anything I can do to give him pleasure?"

"There is," he said carefully. "But I think it might be best if we took things slowly."

"Tell me," she insisted, latching onto his first statement and ignoring the last. "I want to please him."

Hunter sighed. "A man likes it very much when a woman takes him in her mouth. He could achieve satisfaction without hurting you."

Her pulse jumped in excitement. "Show me."

Hunter shook his head. "I don't think it would be a good idea."

Kaya gripped his arms. "Show me, Hunter. Please. I want to do this for Jericho." Then another thought occurred to her. She cocked her head to the side. "Would it bring you pleasure to watch me satisfy Jericho?"

"Yes," he growled. "Very much so."

Her breasts tingled and began to ache in anticipation. "Show me what to do."

He hesitated for a moment and then carefully pushed at her shoulders until she went down on her knees in front of him. She was eye level with his groin, and she began to understand what it was he was trying to tell her.

He placed one hand on top of her head and he grasped his cock with the other hand and slowly guided it toward her mouth.

"Open for me, honey. Let me inside your mouth."

Her lips parted instantaneously and he slid inside, just as he'd done earlier between her legs. Only she could taste him. Inhale his masculine scent and feel his hardness on her tongue.

"Be careful of your teeth. Suck but not too hard. Relax and let me slide all the way in."

She listened carefully to his instructions, but she soon grew impatient and began to move on her own. He grew larger and harder between her lips, and she explored each ridge and vein with her tongue.

He groaned even as he thrust to the very back of her throat.

All too soon, he withdrew, his heavy breathing fogging the mirror again.

"Why did you pull away?" she asked around swollen lips.

"Because I liked it too much and you wanted to do this for Jericho. He'll be in the living room. Go on out and find him."

She rose but reached out to fondle the heavy sac between his legs. Her fingers explored the texture and softness of the puckered, hair-covered skin.

"You're going to kill me," he said in a strangled voice.

"Are you going to watch?" she asked curiously.

"Oh yeah, I'm going to watch and fantasize that it's me you're sucking off."

Satisfied that he'd in some way be included, she left the bathroom, still nude, in search of Jericho. She found him on the couch, dressed. She smiled in anticipation of removing those pants.

He looked up when she walked around in front of him. His eyes glittered when he saw her naked body, but he quickly tried to mask his arousal. Her lips twitched as she fought her smile of triumph. He didn't want to chance hurting her, but he had no idea what she had in store for him.

She knelt on the floor in front of him and wiggled between his parted knees. She rested her elbows on the tops of his legs and studied him for a long moment, absorbing the way he looked at her.

Then her gaze dropped to the discernible bulge at the juncture of his jean-clad thighs. Placing her palm on the inside of his leg, she ran her hand up to cup his groin. He sucked in his breath then reached to pull her hand away.

"Please, honey, have mercy. There's only so much a man can take."

She stared at him from underneath her lashes and carefully extricated her hand from his grasp. His pupils flared in reaction when she unbuttoned his jeans and eased the zipper down.

"Are you going to help me?" she asked softly. "Or do I have to do all the work myself?"

"Holy hell," he breathed.

He lifted his hips and allowed her to peel the denim away. His underwear came with it, and his erection sprang free then lay heavily on his lean belly.

Rising to her knees, she leaned down and ran her tongue up the length of his arousal.

"Kaya, what are you doing?" he groaned.

"She wanted to pleasure you," Hunter said from across the room.

"I asked him how," she said as her hand curled around the base.

Jericho's brown eyes gleamed in amusement. "So I have Hunter to thank for this?"

"I'll try not to suffer too much over here," Hunter said dryly.

Jericho tucked his hands behind his head and leaned back, his eyes narrow slits as he stared down at Kaya. "By all means, don't let me interrupt your fun."

She levered his stiff erection downward, tucking the head just inside her mouth. Her tongue circled the crown then lapped over the slit at the tip. She drew away in surprise as a bead of moisture slipped onto her tongue.

"See what you do to me?" Jericho asked huskily.

Tentatively she flicked her tongue out to catch another droplet, savoring the taste.

"Take him slow and deep," Hunter said. "Just like I showed you, honey."

Lulled by the arousal in both the men's voices, she guided him inside her mouth, sucking lightly as she drew him as far in as she could. Jericho arched his hips off the couch, his entire body bowing. His eyes closed, and deep lines appeared with the strain.

His hands flailed and then caught in her hair. His fingers immediately gentled and stroked against her scalp, separating each strand as she worked her mouth over his cock.

"Deeper," Hunter ordered huskily. "Yes, like that. Now hold it. Breathe through your nose and swallow."

Jericho moaned and trembled violently against her when she followed Hunter's instructions. Delighted by his response, she went through the process all over again.

"She's a quick study," Jericho rasped out.

Hunter's low chuckle sent a thrill down her spine.

Firming her grip around the base, she rolled her hand upward, following her mouth.

"Oh yeah, just like that. Harder, just a little harder," Jericho breathed.

She chased her hand with her lips, swallowed against the tip and then withdrew again. Foregoing her teasing, she picked up the pace, exerting firmer pressure as she tormented him with her tongue.

His hands flew down to the couch. His fingers curled into the cushions, going white around the knuckles as he clenched harder.

"Kaya, honey, I'm going to come."

She realized this was her warning, that he meant to spare her if she didn't want him to release in her mouth. She was equally determined that he give it to her. All of it.

She fondled his swollen testicles with one hand while she gripped his cock with her other. Breathing deeply through her nose, she sank down over him, swallowing convulsively when he bumped the back of her throat.

He tangled his hand in her hair, gripping so tightly that she winced as it pulled at her scalp. He held her in place as he took over the pace. No longer was she controlling the movements. He thrust in and out of her mouth in a near frenzy, and then he stopped, locked deep in her throat.

Warm fluid spilled onto her tongue, filled her mouth. She drank deeply, tasting him, swallowing the very essence of him.

Jericho caressed her hair, stroking her as she stroked him with her tongue. Then he looped his hands underneath her armpits. "Come here," he said as he hauled her up against him.

Their mouths met in a fiery clash. He kissed her, hot and breathless, his tongue dueling with hers. With a quick motion, he turned her and laid her on her back on the sofa.

He was spreading her legs even as he lowered his head. A lightning bolt shot through her pelvis when he licked from her entrance to the fold of her soft hood.

"Come in my mouth like I came in yours."

She shuddered against his lips, but he held her firm, covering her with tiny kisses, nips, then soothing her sensitive flesh with laves of his tongue.

"Jericho!" she cried.

And suddenly Hunter was there, his hands threading through hers and pulling them over her head. His mouth found her breasts while Jericho tormented her endlessly.

It was all so new to her. These sensations hadn't existed until the first time she'd seen the two men. From the first, they'd stirred something to life in her that had lain dormant. They called to the woman when for so long, the beast had ruled.

"Come," Jericho whispered again.

Her hand curled into Hunter's hair as every muscle tensed in preparation for the explosion. The room blurred around her.

"Oh, please."

She didn't even know what she was begging for. Mercy? More?

Their names came out in a sob. Her body convulsed and she felt their hands on her, soothing and calming. They kissed her and murmured to her, their voices soft and husky.

Her entire life she'd wanted this. A sense of belonging. The sheer rightness she felt overwhelmed her.

And then Jericho raised her, picking her up into his arms. He tugged her down as the two of them lay on the couch, their legs entwined. Hunter moved away, content to let them have their moment as he tended the fire.

"Thank you," Jericho murmured against her hair.

She smiled. "Thank Hunter. He taught me."

Jericho chuckled. "You'll forgive me if I refuse to thank another man for the best damn blowjob I've ever gotten."

She snuggled deeper into his arms, sated and complete. His steady, reassuring heartbeat thudded against her ear.

"I love you," she whispered.

Chapter Seventeen

Two days later, Kaya's patience had reached its limit. Though the men were exceedingly tender with her, neither had made a move to mate with her again. She wanted the same bond with Jericho that she'd established with Hunter. Taking Hunter into the most intimate part of her body had established a permanence in their relationship, at least in her eyes.

The cougar lay curled on the couch between the two men as the fire crackled in the hearth. The human inside waited impatiently until finally she could wait no longer. The cat rose and jumped from the couch, her paws silent on the wood floor.

The two men moved as she shifted, and Hunter held out a blanket as he always did when she came shivering to form, but this time she ignored him and walked straight into Jericho's arms.

She fused her lips to his and twined her arms around his neck, telling him precisely what it was she wanted—no, demanded.

Jericho groaned. "Ah, honey, you make resisting you impossible."

She drew away and stared into his warm eyes. "Why are you resisting me? It's been two days. I want you inside me. Please, Jericho. I need you so much."

In response, he swung her into his arms and strode toward his bedroom. Leaning over the bed, he laid her on the mattress and rested his hands on either side of her body as he looked down at her.

"You're so incredibly beautiful," he murmured. "I don't even know where to start. I want to taste and touch every inch of you."

Warmed to her core by his words, she reached for him, pulling him down to her mouth.

"Start here," she murmured against his lips.

He smiled and then kissed her deeply, letting his tongue roll over hers. So warm and loving. A deep sigh slipped from her as his mouth skidded down her jawline to her ear. Her soft sound of contentment hiccupped into a moan when he nipped at her lobe then dropped lower and sank his teeth into the column of her neck.

Sweet heaven, she wanted to bite him back. Something dark and feral rose from deep within. Wild and forbidden with an edginess that consumed her.

Her mouth found his shoulder, and she nipped playfully, marking a path to his neck. When she found the strong pulse, she bit. Hard.

He jerked against her and swore.

She immediately pulled away. "Did I hurt you?"

"Hell no, do it again."

"I will as soon as you take off your clothes."

He backed from the bed and hastily pulled at his shirt and pants. She watched in avid fascination as his body was bared to her view. It was a sight she never tired of, all the muscles, the masculine hairiness of his chest and legs. He had an odd assortment of scars, some fresher than others. No part of his body seemed untouched by violence, and to her, the marks signaled his strength.

His erection jutted upward and bobbed as he climbed onto the bed. She reached automatically, wanting to touch the satin length, but he reared back.

"Oh no, you touch me, I'm gone, and I want this to last."

She smiled but didn't protest when he straddled her thighs and lowered his big body over hers.

"Bite me," he whispered. "Mark me. Make me yours, sweetheart."

She licked from his shoulder to his neck, enjoying the way he trembled underneath her mouth. His taste burst onto her tongue, salty, strong and so masculine. Her nostrils flared as she inhaled his scent, savored it and let it go again. Prompted by the need to do just as he asked and mark him, she sank her teeth into his neck.

His entire body tensed and then went wild against her. His hands slid down her sides to her hips and lower to her thighs. He pulled almost frantically at her, and she helped him by spreading her legs.

His fingers slipped between them, delving into her wetness as if testing her body's readiness. Afraid he'd regain his senses and decide to take things much slower, she bit him again, harder this time, licking at the small wound she inflicted then moving higher to just underneath his ear and biting again.

"Holy hell," he gritted out.

His hips jerked against her, and his hardness settled into place. She arched into him, opening to him, inviting him.

"Take me," she ordered, surprised at her fierceness. She followed up her directive with one more bite.

He surged into her in one hard thrust. She gasped, unable to process all the different sensations that crashed into her.

He stilled immediately, pulling his head away to stare down at her. His eyes were worried and anxious.

"Did I hurt you, honey? Goddamn it—"

"Shhh," she said, placing her finger over his lips.

She wiggled underneath him, testing her position.

"Ah hell, you have to stop that," he groaned.

She brought her legs up, tilting her buttocks up slightly. The position sent him deeper, and she sighed in absolute contentment.

"Okay?" he asked huskily as he dropped a kiss on her lips.

"I will be if you'd move," she said desperately.

"Lock your legs around my waist," he said. "Take me deeper."

She did as he asked, and they both cried out when he slipped further into her body.

"Give me just a second," he rasped out.

He leaned his forehead on hers and closed his eyes, his face creased with strain.

"Why do you stop?" she asked curiously.

He reopened his eyes and pulled away just enough so their gazes met. "Because if I don't, I'm going to come, and I want to make sure you come with me."

"Are you going to put your seed on my belly like Hunter did?"

"If you're asking if I'm going to pull out, then yes. Where it goes is directly proportional to how fast I pull out," he said with a laugh.

Her lips pursed as she considered his words.

"You could..."

She trailed off, not sure she had the courage to suggest what she was thinking. It wasn't as if she hadn't taken him in her mouth before, but this was different, wasn't it?

"I could what, honey?" he asked gently.

"Could you put it in my mouth, I mean before you spill?"

He swallowed hard and swelled even larger inside her. He liked the idea, and now that she knew that, she was determined to make it happen.

"I could," he said carefully. "If that's what you want."

She nodded.

Slowly he withdrew, the rippling sensation in her sheath sending the most pleasurable shockwaves through her body. He pushed forward again, and she moaned at the friction. It felt so tight, almost as if they couldn't possibly fit, and yet he glided through her body with ease.

A hard ball formed deep inside her core, knotting tighter and tighter with each thrust of his shaft. She held her breath as the tension grew more unbearable, and it was only at his gentle insistence that she breathe that she expelled the air in a long whoosh.

She wasn't entirely sure what was happening, but she knew she didn't want him to stop. She kept her legs locked around him and arched to meet his demanding thrusts.

His muscles rippled beneath her mouth. His scent grew stronger, more intoxicating. She licked, catching the sheen of sweat that glistened on his flesh then bared her teeth to bite him again.

"No," he said hoarsely. "Honey, if you do that I won't be able to stop. You first. Let me take care of you."

So she took his mouth instead, kissing him fiercely as she dug her heels into his back. Then she turned her head away, baring her neck for him as she spiraled out of control.

He pressed his lips softly to the spot just below her ear and then nipped hard, holding her with his teeth.

She went liquid around his thick, pulsing shaft and then simply exploded. Shattered. She fell apart in his arms and blinked in bewilderment when she couldn't focus her vision.

Sweet, unending pleasure flowed like rich honey through her veins. She shuddered and gripped him tightly, alternately pushing and pulling as her release became nearly unbearable.

She became aware of him stilling within her and of his hands smoothing over her face and her breasts, soothing her as he murmured reassurance.

For several long moments, he lay over her, kissing her and nibbling delicately at her jaw and lips. Finally her vision cleared enough so that she could see him looking at her. She blinked in confusion, and he smiled tenderly.

"Hi," he said huskily. "You okay? No, don't move," he said when she started to shift beneath him.

Her entire body hummed, throbbed almost painfully. He leaned down to kiss her again, and he tentatively moved inside her.

She sighed in contentment, liking the weight and fullness of him. Gradually he picked up his speed, his hips meeting hers. His eyes closed, his jaw grew tight, and then suddenly he pulled out of her.

"Move down," he rasped out, tugging at her hand.

She scooted down the bed as he moved up her body toward her mouth. His hand slid behind her head, cupping the back of her neck and pulling her up to meet his thrust.

She opened her lips to receive him, reveling in the shock of hard, male flesh filling her mouth. After the second thrust, warm saltiness spilled over her tongue, and she swallowed as he sank deeper.

He towered over her, so strong and muscular, his hand gripping her head as he held her to him. His fingers flexed at her nape, and she marveled at how strong he was and yet how restrained he was, how careful he was not to hurt her.

Slowly he lowered her head down to the mattress and moved to the side, taking her with him and into his arms. She went willingly, curling against his chest, wrapping her arms around him to hold him as tight as he held her.

He kissed the top of her head. "Okay?" he asked again.

She smiled. "Very okay."

Chapter Eighteen

The next weeks followed a predictable course. The days were spent with the cougar in front of the fire until she shifted back to human and went shivering into Hunter's or Jericho's arms.

At night, she and Jericho made sweet love in front of the fire, their shadows transposing erotic images on the wall. And though she couldn't always see him, Hunter watched from those shadows. Sometimes she left Jericho's arms to find Hunter waiting. He took her into his bedroom and mated with her with such urgency that it was like lighting a wildfire inside her body.

She had learned much from these two men, but she also had good instincts for what pleased them. Yet, despite the fact that that they'd made love to her together the first time, neither had made an effort to make it happen again.

Why it was so important to her, she wasn't sure, but even when each made such sweet love to her separately, she felt she was missing a vital part of herself. She wanted—needed—both of them to complete her.

Tonight, the two men sat in the living room with her as they watched the glow of the embers in the hearth. It was the perfect opportunity to appeal to them both.

She rested in the crook of Jericho's arm, her head pillowed on his broad chest. "Jericho?"

His fingers trailed lazily down her arm. "Yes, honey?"

"Why haven't you loved me together? Like the first time..."

Her gaze drifted to Hunter as she spoke, and he went still, his eyes burning into hers. Hungry. It was the only word she could come up with to describe the gleam.

Jericho's hand stopped its casual trail over her arm.

"Do you not wish to do so?" she asked softly.

Hunter lifted his gaze to Jericho. She was aware of the silent communication between the two men, and she wondered at the sudden tension that filled the room.

"We want to very much," Hunter finally said. "We just wanted to give you time. In so many ways you're still such an innocent, Kaya. We've got a hell of a lot more experience than you."

"Do we really?" Jericho asked softly. "Want to, that is?"

Kaya turned her head up to see Jericho staring intently across the distance at Hunter. She frowned, not understanding what was going on between the two men.

"Yeah," Hunter said.

"Are you sure?"

Again, Hunter nodded.

"Jericho?"

Jericho looked down at her softly spoken entreaty and ran his fingers over her cheek. "What is it, honey?"

"What is going on?"

Jericho sighed then looked over at Hunter who slowly got up from his chair and walked over to the couch to sit on the other side of Kaya. Hunter took her hand and linked his fingers with hers.

"I'm not sure how much of human relationships you understand, but having two...mates...is not normal."

"I know," she said solemnly. "It's why I feel so fortunate."

"Before we knew you, there was a woman that Jericho and I both loved."

"Rebeccah," she said softly.

"Yes, Rebeccah," Jericho said.

"You lost her."

"Yes, we lost her."

"How?" she asked.

"She was killed in a rebel uprising in Africa. She...her foundation...furnishes medical aid to villages caught in the crossfire, particularly the children. Jericho and I provided the muscle—the firepower, so to speak. We often led a team in front of hers to clear the way so she could get into the places no one else could—or would—go."

"And this is where you went when you left the cabin each time?"

Jericho nodded. "At first, before Rebeccah died, we stayed with her. After she was killed, we came here. It seemed easier. We could face going back if we had the distance between assignments each time."

"You do it to honor her memory," Kaya said in understanding.

"We made a promise," Hunter said grimly.

She smiled and touched his cheek then turned to offer the same affection to Jericho. "You are noble men."

"At any rate, we both swore we'd never put another woman between us again," Jericho said, ignoring her statement. "That's why I was making sure that Hunter is okay with this."

"But why?"

Hunter sighed. "It's complicated. Rebeccah...she didn't trust our relationship. She was in essence waiting for it to fall apart. To fail. She didn't believe we could continue on, two men loving—sharing—the same woman."

Kaya stared at him in dismay. "She didn't trust you?"

"She didn't trust the situation," Jericho corrected.

"She didn't trust us," Hunter said in agreement with Kaya.

Jericho went silent, his face turned away from them both.

"I'm sorry," Kaya said quietly. "No wonder you didn't want to involve yourselves with me."

Hunter ran his finger up the underside of her arm. "But we do, Kaya. Despite our vow never to become involved with the same woman. You came into our lives, and neither of us is willing to let you go now."

"We didn't plan it," Jericho said. "But we aren't going to fight it. We want you, Kaya. With us."

She reached up to palm his cheek. "And I want to be with you. Both of you."

Jericho captured her fingers and slid her hand over his mouth. He kissed the pad of her thumb and then each finger.

"Do you trust us, Kaya? Do you believe we won't hurt you or do anything to frighten you?"

She smiled. "Just love me. I want you both."

Hunter slid from the couch and reached to pick her up. He strode toward the bedroom, Jericho just behind him. He laid her on the bed and took a step back to stand beside Jericho.

For several seconds, both men stood over her, staring as she lay submissively, waiting for what they would do next.

Jericho stripped off his shirt and hastily dragged his pants off.

215

Hunter was more methodical, though, watching Kaya as he slowly undressed. Button by button, he bared the smooth texture of his chest and abdomen.

He parted the lapels and pulled them back, the material sliding over his shoulders and down his arms. It fell away, and he reached for the button of his jeans. It popped open, and the sound of his zipper rasped over her ears.

Jericho was completely naked now, and Hunter pulled his pants over his hips, freeing his cock from constraint. When he stepped out of the jeans, Jericho moved onto the bed, crawling onto the mattress beside her. He palmed her belly then slid his hand up her midline and then under one breast. He ran a thumb over her nipple, brushing back and forth until it tightened unbearably.

She turned her head with a gasp when Hunter settled on the other side of her, his fingers sliding through the soft folds between her legs. She sucked in her breath again when he tucked one finger inside her opening. He left it just inside for a moment before easing deeper. He withdrew, added another finger and then opened her a little wider.

"One of us will be here," Hunter said as he stroked the inside of her sheath. He withdrew his fingers and ran them lightly up her belly, over her chest and up to her lips. They were damp with her moisture when he pressed them over her tongue. "And one of us will be here," he said as he slid his finger deeper into her mouth.

Her eyes widened at the images his words evoked. Hunter over her, thrusting. No, that would be awkward. Behind her, mounting her like her animal brethren. A low shudder worked through her frame as she imagined being mounted like an animal. Jericho in front of her, using her mouth as a second sheath.

Both men closed in on her, lowering their heads until they each took a nipple between their teeth, sucking and nipping at the sensitive buds. She floated free of the bed, staring up at the ceiling. Dreamily, she ran her hands through their hair, holding them against her breasts.

Then she closed her eyes, content to just feel, to experience the love these two men offered.

Their mouths scorched over her skin. Hot. Breathless. Their ragged breaths filled the room, blew over her flesh. They turned her until she lay belly-down, and then their hands and mouths resumed their lazy seduction.

One moved over her, pressing his body to hers. Hunter. His rigid cock settled in the cleft of her behind, rubbing up and down, dipping between her legs. He thrust against her, not gaining entrance, rather teasing her with what was to come.

Beside her, Jericho turned her face until her cheek rested on the mattress and her mouth was accessible. Holding his cock, he brushed it across her lips, teasing like Hunter, but not gaining entrance. The tip grazed her cheek, then slid over her mouth and back again.

"You're so beautiful," Jericho whispered. "Stretched out between us, your hair like silk."

She smiled, deep contentment sliding like velvet through her veins.

Hunter spread her legs and gently pulled her backward until she was half off the bed.

"Up on your knees," he said.

He helped to get her in place, his hands caressing, soothing and calm. His fingers found her again, delving deep into her wetness, pressing against the sensitive nerves in her passage.

"I want you ready," Hunter said. "I don't want to hurt you in any way."

She turned her head to look at him over her shoulder. "You won't hurt me, Hunter."

Careful hands turned her chin back until she faced Jericho. He pushed back her hair, stroking her cheek with gentle fingers.

"Tell me if anything frightens you. We'll stop immediately."

"I don't want you to stop," she whispered.

He held her face in his hands as Hunter positioned himself between her parted legs. Hunter brushed the tip of his cock against her entrance and then carefully tucked it inside. Slowly he pushed forward as Jericho held his gaze locked to hers.

There was something extremely soul-stirring about this shared moment when Hunter was connected to her physically and Jericho was connected to her spiritually.

Hunter found his way deep inside, his movements so light and caring that her heart ached. It was as if they were discovering her all over again for the first time.

She reveled in their tenderness, but something wild inside her strained to be set free. Rising hunger, burning need. She was a volcano waiting to erupt.

She stared up at Jericho and parted her lips in sultry invitation.

His hands tightened at her jaw, and one hand left to grasp his cock. He didn't have to instruct her. Her need for him was inherent, a primal instinct that had nothing to do with the beast inside her. No, this was the woman within, screaming for what was hers.

After so many years of restraining her human needs, of ceding to the cougar, she was poised to break free, to live. Really live and bask in her femininity.

She sucked him hungrily inside her mouth. Both men reached their depths inside her body at the same time. They stilled as she absorbed the sensation. She trembled around them, her heart swelling, aching, loving.

Their hands petted and coaxed her, caressed her and told their own story of their love for her. Fingers tunneled through her hair, ran sensuous lines down her back and over the slope of her buttocks.

She moaned and stirred restlessly between them, moving back and then forward, encouraging them, pleading with them to take her.

Hunter's hands gripped her waist and held her in place as he plunged, harder now. Jericho tilted her chin upward, angling so he could thrust deeper into her mouth. She closed her eyes and gave herself over to their care, her trust in them complete.

She couldn't know how beautiful she looked, Hunter thought. Her neck arched to accept Jericho, her back in a delicate bow as she raised her hips to take him. Her hair cascaded over her shoulders and trailed down her spine, dripping from her skin like honey.

He was completely taken by her even though it was him doing the taking. The desire to protect her and cherish her overwhelmed him, filled areas of his soul left barren. How had she done it?

Her trust in them awed him. She had no reason to trust anyone, let alone two rugged men who came and went with the wind. And yet she accepted them unreservedly.

He ached for release, but it was more than physical. This time he wouldn't just give her his lust. He'd give her his heart and soul.

He leaned over her as he plunged into her welcoming depths. His lips brushed her shoulder and then the thin line of her spine and down to the small of her back. And then he threw his head back as his orgasm swelled and burned in his groin, tightening his balls as he prepared to explode.

The wet, sucking sounds of her mouth around Jericho whispered erotically over his ears, and he opened his eyes, wanting to watch as they both came, as she took what they both had to offer.

Jericho's expression was drawn tight in ecstasy, his hand tangled in her hair, his fingers clenched at the top of her head. He held her head in place and thrust one last time.

Hunter began to unravel. He yanked out of her, his cock slapping against her bottom, and then his release surged onto her skin.

Kaya existed in a hazy world of intense, sharp sensation. Her mouth filled, and still, Jericho thrust. His semen slipped down her throat. Some of it spilled down her lips as he withdrew, only to plunge again.

Hunter held her hips tightly in his hands as the last of his seed pulsed onto her back. For a long moment, neither man moved, until she struggled and gasped for breath. Jericho released her immediately, and she sucked in big mouthfuls of air. Hunter moved from her then returned and wiped the moisture from her skin.

Then he pulled her back against him, turning her so that he cradled her in his strong arms. He smoothed her hair, his hands everywhere, on her, stroking and loving.

"Did we hurt you? Frighten you?"

She twined her arms around his neck, wanting him close, needing his strength and his heat.

"I am complete," she whispered. And for the first time in her life, she knew she had come home.

Chapter Nineteen

The cougar bounded through the snow, her feet kicking up the powder as she forged ahead of Hunter and Jericho. She looked playful, not at all like a lean, powerful predator.

She disappeared from sight, but then doubled back as if telling them to catch up.

"Whose idea was this again?" Jericho grumbled.

"Mine," Hunter said when they stopped at the rise overlooking a deep ravine below. "I'm not comfortable letting her run free out here. Too many hunters. She could get shot."

"She's survived for a lot of years out here."

"And I intend to see that she survives a lot more years."

"She wouldn't be happy that you don't trust her survival skills."

Hunter blew out his breath in frustration. Jericho just grinned. It was fun to yank Hunter's chain. He was way too easy a mark.

"It's not that I don't trust her. I worry..."

"Yeah, I hear you. I was just messing with you, man."

Hunter looked around with a frown, his gaze scanning the snow-covered terrain. "Where the hell did she go now?"

Just then a blur of caramel colored fur blew past Jericho and knocked Hunter on his ass. Jericho doubled over laughing as he watched Hunter being licked to death by an extremely playful cougar. She was standing between his legs, her front paws on his chest as he tried to fend her off.

"Damn it, Kaya, enough with the licking," he growled.

She lunged off him and sauntered over to Jericho, rubbing against his legs and circling as if sharing a laugh with him. Hunter rolled to his side and pushed himself up from the snow, glaring at both Jericho and the cougar as he dusted all the snow and ice from his clothing.

Kaya lay down in the snow and then rolled over onto her back.

"Yeah, yeah, you've got natural insulation," Hunter said darkly. "I'm going to freeze my ass off once this wet gets to my skin."

She went still and began to shake and tremble.

"What the hell? Hell, no. Kaya, don't you dare. I'll kick your scrawny ass."

Despite Hunter's ridiculous threats, a moment later a naked Kaya lay shivering in the snow, her eyes gleaming with mischief.

Hunter fell to his knees beside her, tearing at his coat to cover her. He sputtered and cursed while Jericho tried valiantly to keep from laughing.

Hunter was about down to just a shirt and his pants when Kaya rolled away and shifted back to the cougar.

"You little... You did that on purpose."

Jericho snorted. "Of course she did. You're so easy. She has you wound up like a clock."

Hunter picked each item of clothing off the ground, bitching and moaning the entire time.

"Playtime's over. I'm going back to the cabin where most normal people are on a day like this. Inside."

"Just remember it was your idea," Jericho said mildly.

Hunter stopped in his tracks then swung around to stare accusingly at the cougar. He stuck out a finger and closed in on her, wagging it like an old schoolmarm. "You set me up. You did this so I wouldn't want to come out with you next time. Devious heifer."

The cat sank onto her belly and laid her head on her outstretched paws. She managed to look positively sorrowful as she gazed up at Hunter with those amber eyes.

"I'm going to buy you a collar and a leash. Then we'll see who has the last laugh."

Jericho lost the battle and died laughing. He laughed so hard, he had to clutch his middle as cramps knotted his midsection.

Hunter threw up his hands and stalked toward the cabin.

When Jericho had calmed down enough to catch his breath, he knelt on one knee in the snow and put his hand on the cougar's head. "Come on, girl. We better get back to the cabin before he has a hissy fit."

She picked up her head and eyed him balefully.

"Yeah, yeah, I know, he's already pitched one hell of a fit."

Still, he rose and started back toward the cabin, hoping Kaya had had enough romping around in the snow for the day. He and Hunter were gratified that she was spending less and less time in cougar form as the days passed. They liked it a lot better when they knew exactly where she was and that she was safe.

She trailed alongside him until the cabin came into view. Then she bounded ahead of him and butted against the slightly ajar door.

When Jericho entered, he saw Hunter wrapping a blanket around a shivering, naked Kaya. Jericho picked up the change of clothes they kept by the door and started toward her.

Something in Hunter's gaze stopped him.

"Go get dressed, honey," Hunter said in a low voice as he turned her toward Jericho.

Jericho frowned and held out the clothes to Kaya as he continued to stare at Hunter.

"K-man radioed. We've been called out."

Jericho froze. It wasn't entirely unexpected. They lived with the knowledge that they could be called away any minute of any day. But they'd spent the last weeks in denial of that possibility.

"Are we going?" Jericho asked evenly.

Hunter's eyes held a whole lot of regret. "Yeah. We are. It's a bad one. Members of Rebeccah's medical team are trapped in a village being attacked. The U.S. basically told them if they went in not to expect any help. This one will be off the books."

Jericho swore. "What about Kaya?"

Kaya, who'd remained a silent observer, stepped forward, still draped in the blanket Hunter had wrapped around her.

"You're going away?" she asked quietly.

"You could stay here," Hunter said to Jericho.

"Fuck that," Jericho said rudely. "I'm not letting you go in alone."

"I wouldn't be alone."

"Forget it. Not happening."

They both turned to Kaya who watched them with uncertain eyes.

"We have to go away for a little while," Hunter said. "We won't be long. No more than a couple of weeks. Just like always."

She drew into herself, her eyes flashing soft vulnerability. "Will you come back?"

Jericho swore under his breath and reached for her, pulling her into his arms. She trembled against him and clutched at his chest with small hands.

"We'll be back, Kaya. Always. You're ours. We want you to stay here. There's plenty of food, and it's warm. You'll have shelter. When we return, we'll bring more supplies and some decent clothing for you."

She nodded against his chest, but he wasn't sure if he'd convinced her.

Hunter cupped his hand under her elbow and pulled her away to look at him. He stared down at her, his expression utterly serious. "Promise me you'll be careful. Stay close to this cabin at all times. No jaunts over the mountains as the cougar, and when you're in human form, don't step outside this cabin."

"I promise," she said solemnly.

Kaya sat on the couch in front of the fire, her knees hugged to her chest as she watched the two men prepare to leave. They worked methodically, as if they'd done this a million times before. And they had, she knew. She'd watched them from a distance as they'd donned their pack gear and hiked down the mountain.

Only this time they were leaving her, and it frightened her.

When the last of their supplies were packed, they turned to her. The moment she'd dreaded was here. The goodbye.

"Come here, honey," Jericho said in a low voice.

She flew off the couch and into his arms, hugging him fiercely. He covered her mouth with his, kissing her with unrestrained passion. Then he tore his lips away and rested his forehead against hers.

"We'll be back soon. You won't even miss us."

"I'll miss you."

He smiled. "We'll miss you too. Take care of yourself until we can come back and do it ourselves."

He walked around her to stand by the door and allow Hunter his goodbye.

For a long second, she and Hunter stood staring at one another. Her heart swelled and ached with every beat. She didn't want them to go. Selfishly, she wanted to beg them not to leave her, not to go fulfill the legacy of a woman they'd loved before her.

A tear slid over her cheek before she could wipe it away.

Hunter closed the distance between them and pulled her to him.

"Don't cry. We'll be back before you know it."

She reached up to frame his face in her hands and then pulled him down to kiss her.

"I love you, Hunter. Hurry back to me. I'll miss you both so badly."

He kissed her lingeringly, touching her face with gentle hands.

"Be careful, Kaya. I don't like leaving you like this."

"I know," she said sadly. "Now go."

Jericho opened the door, and the two men walked out into the snow. She stood at the window watching until they disappeared down the mountain. The cougar protested, wanting to bound into the snow after them, but she squelched the urge before it could take over.

Her hand pressed against the frosty glass pane.

"I love you," she whispered.

Chapter Twenty

Kaya paced the confines of the cabin restlessly. Her skin crawled and itched with the need to shift. Every day after Hunter and Jericho had left, the cougar had tracked through the snow to a rocky overhang that afforded her a prime view of the path they'd take back up the mountain. And she waited.

Today when she'd called to the cougar, the cougar had not risen. For the first time she couldn't shift.

What was wrong with her? Why was the cougar lying dormant? It frightened her. Made her feel insecure and uneasy. How could she protect herself if she couldn't call on the beast?

She sensed the cougar had withdrawn. Why? She was still there, but she had settled deep within, refusing to be drawn out.

If only Hunter and Jericho would return. Then she wouldn't feel so scared. Maybe she'd feel more herself. Maybe the cougar would return.

The shadows had lengthened and dusk settled over the cabin. They wouldn't return tonight. Dejected, she went into the kitchen and consoled herself with a hot meal. The novelty of cooked food hadn't worn off.

Her gaze took in the canned goods in the cabinets. Plenty of food to last several more weeks. Jericho and Hunter would return well before then.

Feeling marginally better after filling her belly, she went into Jericho's room and crawled under the blankets. They still held his scent, and she inhaled deeply to allow it to surround her. She alternated sleeping in their beds, wanting to keep them near at all times.

Tonight, she was asleep almost as soon as her head hit the pillow.

Deep and dreamless. In the recesses of her mind, she became aware of a comforting warmth. Gentle sunshine and a touch so light that it carried her along before she realized she was floating.

A smiling woman, familiar and yet strange, with long dark hair. She carried a blanket-wrapped bundle in her arms. When she stood in front of Kaya, her expression filled with love and joy. Then she lowered the tiny bundle into Kaya's arms.

Kaya looked down to see a baby. The child opened her eyes and their gazes connected. Immediately, Kaya was filled with indescribable pride and happiness. Her finger carefully touched the little one's cheek. The baby turned, trying to suck the finger into her tiny mouth.

A sound forced Kaya's gaze beyond the baby. A beautiful silver wolf stood a few feet away. Strangely she felt no fear for her or her child. The eyes were familiar.

The wolf lowered its head and walked slowly toward the baby. Its nose pressed against the baby's cheek and then both baby and wolf looked up at Kaya again and she saw their eyes were identical blue. Ice blue.

And then the wolf disappeared. But Kaya understood. This was her child. The Maker was gifting her child with the spirit and soul of the great wolf.

The child squirmed and turned toward Kaya, rooting until it found her breast. She latched on and began to suckle as Kaya tenderly kept watch over her.

Kaya came awake with a start, her hand flying to her stomach. She sat up, sweat beading her forehead even though a heavy chill lay over the cabin.

Could it be? She rubbed her belly, but she now knew why the cougar had refused her. Knew why the Maker had come to her in a dream.

A baby. Her daughter.

She slid her legs over the side of the bed and sat there, both hands covering her still-flat stomach as she stared down in wonder.

A child. She was pregnant with Hunter and Jericho's child. A child who would grow to be a great silver wolf. Strong and majestic. Would it anger Hunter and Jericho that their daughter would be like Kaya?

No, she didn't think so. It would cause them endless worry, but they would embrace her heritage as they had embraced Kaya's.

She smiled as tears of happiness welled in her eyes. They had given her their love and she would give them a daughter. She would have her own family. A tiny circle of people who she loved and who loved and accepted her.

She couldn't wait for Hunter and Jericho to return so she could share her wondrous news.

"I don't like this," Hunter muttered.

Jericho stared through the scope of his rifle and grunted his agreement. "It's too easy."

Hunter held up his hand as the rest of their team fell in behind them. He positioned the tiny mic close to his mouth and addressed the others.

"This stinks to high heaven. I want everyone on their guard. Jericho and I will go in first. K-man, you and Dierks swing around and come in from the north. The prisoners are being kept in the middle of the camp. Make sure they aren't compromised. The rest of you split into two teams and take out the guard towers to the east and west. Get in and get out. Fast."

K-man and Dierks disappeared from sight while the other team members moved noiselessly left and right. Keeping their weapons up, Hunter and Jericho crept forward.

No noise emanated from the encampment. Only the sounds of distant predators filled the night. The eerie laugh of a hyena sent a shiver over Hunter's skin.

Something wasn't right. It was all too pat.

Jericho moved ahead before Hunter could motion him back. Jericho laid aside his rifle and hauled the makeshift trap door up a few inches so he could peer inside the pit.

"Hunter, the west guard tower is empty."

The words echoed in his ear just as Jericho made a slashing motion to indicate the pit was also empty.

Christ. "Pull back," Hunter hissed into the receiver. "Get the hell out. Now!"

Jericho dropped the door. Before he could pick up his rifle, the world around them lit up.

"Get down!" Hunter shouted as he lunged to cover Jericho.

The two men went down as a blaze of orange filled their senses. Heat. Then pain. Then nothing.

Chapter Twenty-One

Kaya stared dully out the window over the newly reawakened earth. The snows had melted and in their wake, green burst from the ground and the trees.

And still Hunter and Jericho hadn't returned.

She folded her hands over the swell of her belly, reassured by the steady kick of her daughter.

Her supplies were exhausted and with the ability to shift gone until her baby was born, she had no way to feed her or her child.

Left behind.

Abandoned.

All the feelings of her childhood bubbled up, only these were sharper. They cut. They made her bleed.

She dropped her head and closed her eyes. Why hadn't they kept their promise? The days had turned to weeks, and the weeks into months. Winter had given up its stranglehold on the mountains, and wildlife was on the move all around her.

Her belly had swelled as the life within her grew. How she'd longed to share these moments with Hunter and Jericho, but they hadn't come back, and now she was forced to face the uncomfortable truth.

They weren't going to.

She would have to venture down to the town below. The idea terrified her. While she'd walked among humans, she'd never had to try and play by their rules. She needed food and clothing, and she had no idea how to go about getting either. All she knew was that she couldn't get it here.

Knowing she was only putting off the inevitable, she moved from her position at the window. She took special care in her appearance, or as much as she could manage. She used the men's brush and worked the tangles from her hair until it sparkled and shone.

The sweatpants fit her a little better now that her belly had grown larger, and the flannel shirt hit her at mid-thigh instead of falling to her knees. She looked somewhat normal.

Then she looked down at her bare feet. She had the boots that Jericho had made her wear, but they were far too large for her and would look ridiculous if she tromped into town with them. Maybe she could find shoes later. For now she would make do.

She let herself out of the cabin and looked sadly back at the place she'd considered her home if only for a short period of time. She wouldn't be back. There was nothing here for her any longer

"Help me, Maker," she whispered. "I'm so afraid."

Jericho opened his eyes and blinked when everything stayed blurry. His head ached like a bitch. Then he realized that he couldn't feel much more than the vile ache at the base of his skull and the burning of his eyes.

He looked down, trying to see the rest of him. His arms, his legs, something.

"Ahh, you're finally awake. You had us worried, Mr. Hartley."

He turned blindly in the direction of the voice. "Jericho. No one calls me Mr. Hartley."

"Okay, Jericho."

"Who are you? Where are you? I can't see you. Where am I?"

"One question at a time." The voice was soothing. Feminine. "My name is Susan. I'm the nurse assigned to your care. Give yourself a few minutes to orient yourself. Your vision should clear soon."

"Hunter," he croaked. "Where's Hunter?"

"Your friend is alive."

That didn't say a whole lot. What the hell had happened? He strained to remember, but all he could summon was an image of fire. An explosion so loud it had split his ears. And then nothing.

"Oh, look, someone is here to see you."

Jericho turned again, blinking, furious that he couldn't make out more than a fuzzy shape moving toward the bed.

"Hey, man. God am I glad to see your ass awake. I was sure you'd decided to take a permanent vacation on us."

"K-man."

"Yeah, in the flesh. Can you see me?"

"Move closer."

The blur came into sharper focus, and some of the burning in his eyes eased. He could make out K-man's face. See his eyes even. They looked worried.

"How long have I been here?" he asked. "What about Hunter? The others."

"Several months, dude. You've been out of it for a long while. We weren't sure you were going to make it."

Months.

Panic kicked him in the gut and crawled up his throat until his chest felt like it was going to explode.

"Months? Months? Tell me you're joking, K-man. Don't bullshit me. This is too important. I need to know exactly how long I've been here."

K-man touched him on the shoulder. "I wouldn't lie about this. We brought you in four months ago. You'd just about bled out, had enough shrapnel in you to build a missile, and you had more broken bones than bruises."

"Kaya," he whispered. Dear God, what was Kaya thinking? They'd told her they'd be a few weeks. They'd left her alone with only enough food for a few months.

"I've got to get out of here," he said as he sat forward.

Immediately, pain speared through his chest, leaving him gasping for air. He tried to swing his legs over the edge of the bed, but they didn't cooperate.

"Whoa, man, chill out. Are you trying to kill yourself?"

Jericho found himself held down on both sides. He struggled against the constraints. "I have to go. You don't understand. I've got to get back."

K-man got in his face, his eyes blacker than night. "What I understand is that I'll sit on you if I have to. Lay back and keep your ass in bed, or I'll have you physically restrained. You got me?"

"Kaya. She's alone. You've got to let me go, K. This is important."

"I can't do that, Jericho. Not until the doc clears you. You almost died. I doubt you could walk out of here if you wanted."

Frustration beat painfully at his temples. His jaw clenched until his teeth ached. "I'm only going to ask this once, K. And you better be straight with me."

"You know I will."

K-man relaxed his hold on Jericho and nodded at the nurse, who also let go. She backed away. "I'll be outside if you need me," she said quietly.

"I need to know exactly what's wrong with me, and I want to know what happened to Hunter."

"You're pretty busted up. Ribs. Left leg. Dislocated shoulder. Concussion. Numerous cuts, burns and bruises. They put you in a drug-induced coma for a long time until the swelling in your brain went down."

"And Hunter?"

"Pretty much the same. He was paralyzed for a while. We worried it would be permanent, but they removed a piece of shrapnel from his spine and when the swelling went down, he regained feeling in his legs. He's been out of it. He keeps calling Kaya's name. Interesting that you mentioned her as well."

Jericho's lips pressed together in a tight line. "I need to see him."

K-man shook his head.

"Don't tell me no," Jericho said fiercely. "I don't care how it happens. I have to see him. Get me a wheelchair or help me out of bed. Just get me in there."

"I think it'd be easier to have him come here," K-man said dryly. "At least he can walk."

"Get him. I don't care how it happens. And then we're getting out of here."

K-man stared hard back at Jericho. "What's going on here, Jericho? What's so important that you'd risk leaving when you're not even close to being ready? We're a team. You know if you need something, you only have to ask. We'll take care of it."

Jericho closed his eyes. What K said was true. If it were anything else, he wouldn't hesitate to ask K-man to take care of it. But he couldn't ask him to go to the cabin and get Kaya. It was too risky. He'd given his word that he'd never share her secret with anyone. He wouldn't risk her that way. He had to talk to Hunter, and they had to get the hell back to Colorado.

Chapter Twenty-Two

Kaya stood outside the small general store, her heart pounding thunderously. Her palms were damp, and her stomach rolled and heaved. How silly that the thought of going inside terrified her so. She belonged in this world just like everyone else did.

But humans had a history of letting her down.

She jumped when a man came out of the shop in front of her. He stood there, holding the door open as he looked at her. It took her a moment to realize he was waiting for her to go in.

"Thank you," she murmured as she hurried by.

She was immediately assaulted by a barrage of smells. Meats, so many different kinds. Her first priority had to be food. Clothing could wait. She had no money, and so she could only take what she could easily hide, which wasn't much given her flimsy shirt and burgeoning belly.

Making sure she wasn't being watched, she walked toward the back. If there was no one in the rear of the store, she could simply duck out the service entrance with whatever she could grab fast.

When she was sure she was unobserved, she slipped a packet of ham in the elastic band at her waist. She reached for two more that she placed at her sides, disguised by the loose fit of her shirt.

Behind her, she heard the roll of a grocery cart, and she bolted for the doorway leading to the back of the store. Her fingers were on the door when a hand reached out and captured her wrist.

She let out a startled cry and stumbled back, staring up at the man who held her.

"Ma'am, would you come with me?" he asked politely.

Oh no. How had he seen her? Where had he come from? A policeman, of all things. To her further horror, the packages of ham slipped down her leg and fell out of her pants onto the floor.

He didn't look angry. There was an odd expression in his eyes. He gently helped her to her feet, and to her further surprise, he led her out the back way instead of making her run the gauntlet to the front and onto the street where she would be in plain sight of anyone passing.

But her fear of discovery shattered her.

Numbly she allowed the officer to lead her out the back door into the cool spring morning air. Her gaze darted left and right, and she decided her best escape route was to her right where a clump of aspens led to a denser grove of trees.

Seizing her moment when his grip loosened on her wrist, she twisted and struck out with her foot, kicking him in the back of the knee. His leg buckled, and he let her go. She ran for the trees as if her very life depended on it.

Behind her, the policeman cursed and gave chase. She was nearly to the trees when he grabbed her arm and pulled her up short. She started to go down, but he cradled her body into his and rolled so that he took the brunt of the fall.

She landed on top of him and their eyes locked. She started to struggle, but he held on tight.

"I'm not going to hurt you," he bit out. "I didn't want to haul you to my office in cuffs but if you don't cease and desist immediately, I'll not only cuff you but I'll carry you back over my shoulder."

She went still, her eyes welling with frustrated tears.

"Aw now, don't cry," he said in obvious discomfort.

He stood and helped her to her feet, maintaining a tight grip on her arm at all times. His scent hovered over her nostrils, strong and masculine—but there was something else, something faint that stirred a distant memory.

"My name is Duncan Kennedy. I'm the sheriff here. I'd like us to go to my office so we can have a talk about what you were doing back there."

What was she going to do? He led her along the back side of several businesses before he ushered her inside the fourth building down. She quickly realized his "office" was in fact a cage where they kept humans.

She panicked, backing away, twisting her arm to try and gain her freedom. Duncan grabbed her around the middle, trapping her arms against her sides. Then he simply picked her up and carried her the rest of the way inside.

He set her down in a chair against the wall and then reached back to drag another one over until he sat directly in front of her, preventing her from getting up and going anywhere.

"Now, perhaps you can start by telling me your name."

She stared back at him, the knot of fear swelling in her throat.

"No? Okay, then tell me why you were stealing food."

When she remained silent, he let out a sound of exasperation.

"Look, lady, I can't help you if you won't cooperate." He glanced down at her belly, and his gaze softened. "When are you due?"

How strange a question was that? Due for what? She focused on a point beyond his shoulder, refusing to meet his gaze again.

Duncan sighed. "I didn't want to have to do this, damn it."

He reached for a set of keys attached to his belt. Carefully lifting her arm, he pulled her upright and led her over to one of the human cages. He inserted the key and opened the door just as she realized his intention.

"Nooooo!"

Her wail caught him off guard, and she wrenched away from him, running for the back door. He caught up to her, placing his hand on the door in front of her face so she couldn't get out.

He picked her up as she struggled and flailed. She hit at him, doubling her fist. He didn't seem bothered by her resistance in the least. He strode back toward the cell and promptly set her down inside.

Before she could launch herself at him again, he shut the door with a clank and locked it.

She stood there stricken as he stared at her from the other side of bars. Her hands cupped her arms and moved up and down as a deep chill settled over her skin.

"It's not my habit to lock up pregnant women. Especially one as desperate as you seem," he said grimly. "But you haven't given me a whole lot of choice in the matter. When you're ready to give me some information, holler, and we'll have a talk. Until then I'll see about getting a meal sent over for you."

She watched in anguish as he walked away. She ran to the bars, gripping them tightly in her hands. Shaking until the rattle echoed over the bare floors, she vented her frustration and her abject terror.

Once again, she was caged, deserted by humans, locked away like an animal. This time she had a child to nurture. Her hand went to her belly as panic flooded her all over again. What would happen to her baby?

She pressed her forehead between the bars and closed her eyes. Why hadn't Hunter and Jericho come back to her? Why had they broken their promise?

The helicopter touched down a mile from the cabin. Hunter and Jericho both leaned forward in anticipation. K-man turned around to look at the two men.

"I don't like this, damn it. You're in no shape to be out of the hospital, much less for me to leave you alone on this damn mountain. If you need this Kaya so bad, let me go get her for you."

"No," both men said into their receivers.

"No," Hunter said again. "We appreciate everything, K, but we gotta do this ourselves."

K-man swore but he didn't say anything more. Hunter and Jericho ducked painfully from the helicopter. Hunter glanced over at Jericho as they headed to where their truck was still parked. K-man lifted off, and soon the helicopter disappeared in the distance.

"You okay?" Hunter asked when they reached the truck.

Jericho was pale, his forehead beaded with sweat, but his lips were drawn tight in determination.

"I'm fine," he said shortly. "Let's get the hell back to the cabin."

Hunter quickly switched out the battery, connected the cables then slid into the driver's seat.

Neither man voiced his biggest concern, but it lay between them as Hunter drove up the switchback. When they reached the trail that led to the cabin, he turned off the road and bounced over the rocky terrain.

Jericho grunted but didn't offer any complaint.

If they hadn't both been so sick with worry over Kaya, Hunter would have never allowed Jericho out of a hospital bed. K-man hadn't wanted either of them out of the hospital where they'd been pieced back together by talented surgeons, but Hunter could walk, and walk he had.

He breathed a sigh of relief when they topped the rise and the cabin came into view. He roared up to the front door and cut the engine. Jericho was already stumbling from his seat.

"Kaya!" Jericho called as he hurried inside.

Hunter went in behind him, but his nape prickled as soon as he entered the cabin.

He looked around as Jericho went to search the bedrooms, but he knew Kaya wasn't here. The cabin was too still, too shut in. He went straight to the kitchen. His fingers clenched into tight fists when he saw the empty cabinets. A few cans lay on the counter, tipped over, and empty bread wrappers were piled neatly in the corner.

Jericho rushed into the kitchen behind him, his eyes wild.

"She's not here, Hunter. Goddamn it, she's not here!"

"She ran out of food," Hunter said in a quiet voice. "She had to have gone hunting. She'll be back."

She had to be back.

"What the hell do we do? She's out there alone, probably thinking we ditched her like her family did."

The desperation in Jericho's voice matched Hunter's own mounting panic.

"You're in no shape to go out after her," Hunter said. "You stay here in case she comes back, and I'll go out on the mountain to see if there are any tracks."

"Find her, Hunter. Find her and bring her home."

Hunter nodded and let himself out the back. It wasn't as easy as it had been in winter with over a foot of snow on the ground to yield its secrets. He searched for hours, and only when it became too dark to see did he return to the cabin, praying the entire time that Kaya had returned ahead of him.

Jericho sat on the couch in the living room and looked bleakly up at Hunter when he walked in the door.

"She's gone," Jericho said. He covered his face with a hand and rubbed almost violently through his hair, hair that was still growing back. "She thinks we left her just like her family did. I wonder how long she stayed here, telling herself we were different."

Hunter didn't want to agree with Jericho. He wanted to argue, offer false hope, say stupid things like she'd be back in the morning, but Jericho was right.

"I searched the den, the mountain, every hiding place I could think of."

Jericho nodded but turned his face away so Hunter couldn't see the naked emotion burning in his eyes.

How the hell were they supposed to find her? She could be anywhere. She could have been shot by hunters. Killed by another mountain lion. Or she could have simply gone away, moved to another area. There was no way to know. No way to find out. She lived in a world where she didn't exist.

The only thing they could do was stay here in case she returned. No way did he want her coming back to find the cabin deserted like she'd once found her childhood home.

"I'll go into town in the morning for supplies," Hunter said.

Jericho nodded, but neither of them said another word about Kaya. Theirs was a silent agreement that they would wait. As long as it took.

Chapter Twenty-Three

For Duncan Kennedy, it was another bad day, and it could only get worse. He stared across his desk to the jail cell that housed the young pregnant woman, and he felt like pond scum all over again.

Hell, he was probably doing her a favor, but all he could see was the abject terror in her eyes as he'd placed her in the cell.

The door opened and his deputy Nick strode in. He was halfway across the room before he took notice of the woman in the jail cell, then he did a rapid double-take. When he got to Duncan's desk, he flopped down in the chair in front of him.

"We're jailing pregnant women now? What the hell did she do?"

Duncan raised his brow at the anger in Nick's voice. "For all you know she could be a serial killer."

"Is she?"

"No."

"Then what the hell is she doing in jail?"

Duncan sighed. "I wish I knew. Caught her stealing food. She freaked on me when I tried to talk to her. Tried to escape twice. She looked tired and hungry so I brought her here, but she hasn't uttered a peep. I ran her fingerprints and got squat. She won't tell me who she is or where she lives or if she has a place to live for that matter. I don't want to just let her go. Hell, she's barefooted."

"Damn," Nick muttered. "Is Aliyah still at her folks visiting?"

Duncan nodded.

"Too bad. Maybe another woman could talk to her. She might just be terrified of men."

"I didn't think of that," Duncan murmured.

Nick chanced another look across the room at the woman huddled on the cot in the cell. "She looks scared to death."

"Yeah, I know. I don't know what the hell to do, to be honest. I can't really hold her here. Margaret isn't pressing charges for the packages of ham she tried to lift, but I feel like I'll be doing the wrong thing if I just let her go. What if she has no place to go? I'd like to help her if she'd just talk to me."

"Hell of a note when a pregnant woman ends up alone and having to steal food to eat," Nick said darkly.

"Maybe I'll do down and see Margaret. Your idea of having a woman talk to her is a good one. Margaret has a soft streak a mile wide."

He stood and grabbed his hat, plunking it on his head as he started toward the door.

"Why don't you see if you can get her to talk to you while I'm gone?"

Nick cast him a doubtful glance but nodded.

Hunter pulled up to the general store and cut the engine. He was beyond exhausted, and what he really wanted was about three straight days of sleep, but every time he closed his eyes, he saw Kaya frightened and alone, thinking he and Jericho had abandoned her.

Would he sleep until they found her, and would they ever find her?

He nodded at Duncan Kennedy, the sheriff, when they entered the store at the same time.

"Hunter, it's been a while. Have to say, you look like hammered horse manure."

"Thanks," Hunter said dryly. "Just got back from an assignment."

"Get some rest. Looks like you need it. I'll see you around, okay? I need to talk to Margaret."

Hunter dipped his head in acknowledgement and then went to do his shopping. A few minutes later, he walked through the produce section to see Margaret stocking bananas while Duncan stood next to her, a frown on his face.

As he neared, he couldn't help but overhear their conversation.

"If you could just come down and talk to her," Duncan said. "I'm at my wit's end. She won't say a word to anyone. She just sits in that cell looking terrified."

"Poor thing," Margaret said, her face creased with pity. "Of course I'll come down. You did tell her I wasn't pressing charges for stealing food, didn't you?"

An uneasy prickle took hold of Hunter's neck. He edged closer, pretending interest in the apples.

"Yeah, I did, but I hate to let her go until I know who she is and that she has somewhere to go. I know she's scared witless, but at least she has a dry place to stay and food to eat."

The gnawing in his gut had become too much to bear. Dropping his basket, he bolted down the aisle toward the front door, Margaret's and Duncan's startled exclamations ringing in his ears.

He ran down the street toward the sheriff's office, pain jolting up his spine the entire way. He heard Duncan's shout from a distance, but he ignored it and burst through the doorway of the jail.

His gaze registered several things. Kaya lay huddled on a cot while a deputy stood over her, his hand reaching to touch her shoulder.

With a snarl, Hunter lunged for the open jail door, yanking it wider and leaping inside. The deputy tried to reach for his pistol, but Hunter was on him too fast.

"Get away from her," he snapped.

His hands gripped the deputy's shirt, and he slammed him against the bars opposite where Kaya lay. She didn't even flinch.

"Hunter, what the hell do you think you're doing?" Duncan demanded.

Hunter looked up to see Duncan standing on the other side of the bars, his pistol raised and aimed at Hunter.

"Let him go. Now."

Hunter slowly released the deputy and took a step back, purposely putting himself between them and Kaya.

"Nick, out of the cell."

The deputy cast a wary glance in Hunter's direction before heeding Duncan's order.

"Now suppose you tell me what the hell's going on," Duncan said when the cell had been cleared.

"She's mine," Hunter said in a near growl. Then, ignoring the gun pointed at him, he turned and fell to his knees in front of the cot.

"Kaya," he whispered. "Kaya, honey, it's me, Hunter."

He ran his hand up her slight body and then stopped when he

saw the delicate line of her distended belly.

"Oh God."

Pregnant. They'd left her pregnant. Alone. No food.

Carefully he gathered her in his arms. Finally she turned her head, her amber eyes flashing with pain and recognition.

"Hunter," she whispered. "I prayed you would come, but you never did."

He held her tightly against his chest, his breaths coming out in stuttered hiccups.

"I'm sorry. I'm so sorry, honey. We didn't mean to frighten you. I swear if we'd known you were pregnant, we would've never left you. We'll never leave you again."

She clung desperately to him, her tears wetting his shirt. "I'm so scared. They kept me in this cage. I couldn't escape. I think I'm in trouble."

"No, honey. I'll get you out of here, I promise."

He turned to stare at Duncan who was watching them with interest. "I want her out of here. Now."

Duncan sighed but backed away from the door, allowing Hunter to carry her out of the cell.

"Don't get any ideas," Duncan said. "You can take her into my office, but neither of you is going anywhere until I get some answers."

Hunter glared at Duncan as he passed, but he didn't try to walk out of the station. The sooner they got this over with, the sooner he could take her back home where she belonged.

Once in Duncan's office, he eased Kaya into a chair. "Comfortable, honey?"

She nodded, but her eyes were still sad and wary. And very frightened.

Hunter stood and met Duncan at the door. "Any conversation we have will be outside this office. I won't have her upset any more than she is."

Duncan raised one brow but backed way and allowed Hunter to shut the door.

"Now suppose you tell me what the hell is going on here?" Duncan said when the two men were alone.

"Why is she in jail?" Hunter asked, ignoring Duncan's question.

"I caught her stealing food. Truth is I had no intention of holding her. I wanted to help her, but she wouldn't say a word, hasn't said a word since I brought her in. No name, no nothing. I couldn't in good conscience let a pregnant woman go when she'd been desperate enough to steal food. She doesn't even have shoes, for God's sake."

He looked accusingly at Hunter as he said the last.

Hunter closed his eyes and sighed. "It's a long, complicated story. One I'm not at liberty to divulge. Jericho and I left her in our cabin when we went on our last assignment. There was plenty of food to last the amount of time we thought we'd be gone. But a bomb changed our plans. As a result, we've been gone several months. We didn't know she was pregnant when we left or we'd have never gone for any reason. But we're back now, and we're not going to leave her again."

"Okay, let me get this straight. This woman is in a relationship with you? Why the hell wouldn't she just tell me that? Why didn't she just ask for help if she'd run out of food? There is something extremely fishy about this, and my bullshit meter is beeping like a motherfucker."

Hunter sighed. "She's different, Duncan. She's been alone most of her life. She doesn't trust anyone. She hasn't had much contact with other people. She doesn't understand the rules."

Duncan's eyes narrowed. "You didn't take advantage of that, did you, Hunter?"

Hunter stiffened. "I'm going to pretend you didn't ask that. All you need to know is that that is my woman in there, and she is pregnant with my child. If you aren't pressing charges, I'm taking her home with me right now."

"Hell no, I'm not pressing charges," Duncan said in disgust.

"Then we'll be on our way."

"Fine. But buy her some damn shoes, for God's sake."

Hunter walked back into Duncan's office and carefully approached Kaya. She stared up at him, uncertainty written on her face. His heart ached at the loss of trust. Before she'd given herself and her trust with no reservation. Now he and Jericho were going to have to work damn hard to get it back.

He knelt on the floor in front of her and took her cold hands in his. "Are you ready to go home, honey?"

"Where is Jericho?"

There was a fearful look in her eyes, as if she was afraid that Jericho hadn't come back for her.

He cupped her cheek in his hand, rubbing tenderly. "He's at the cabin. We'll explain everything when we get there. I swear."

Slowly she nodded.

"But first we're going to go buy you some decent clothes and shoes."

She glanced down at her bare feet. "Okay."

He took her hand in his and carefully helped her to her feet. "Come on, honey. Let's go home."

Chapter Twenty-Four

The drive back up the mountain was silent and tense. Hunter had a thousand questions burning his brain, but he owed it to Jericho to wait so he could hear it all as well. He was impatient to get Kaya back to the cabin. Jericho had been out of his mind with worry, and he was still badly in need of recovery time.

As they neared the cabin, Hunter reached over and took Kaya's hand in his. The touch was more to reassure him than her. How close they had come to losing her. If Duncan hadn't stashed her in the jail, no matter how terrifying for her, they likely wouldn't have ever seen her again.

The back of the truck was filled with food and clothing. He hadn't taken much time with the shopping. He'd grabbed what they needed immediately and left an order to be filled with Margaret. He'd go back to get the rest. From there, he'd gone to the small clothing store and grabbed everything off the rack he thought would fit Kaya. And shoes. He'd sized her small feet and bought tennis shoes, slip-ons and a pair of boots.

As they pulled up to the cabin, Jericho stepped onto the porch, leaning against the railing for support. Kaya stiffened, her hand going to her mouth as a gasp escaped.

Jericho strained to see the inside of the truck, hoping against hope. When Hunter stepped out, his heart sank. He closed his eyes as despair swept over him. Where was she? Was she alone? Afraid? Hurt or in trouble?

Hunter walked around the front of the truck and to the passenger side. Jericho's breath caught and held, swelling in his chest, when Hunter opened the door and reached inside.

Seconds later, Kaya stepped from the truck, tucked into Hunter's protective hold. The two figures went blurry in his vision, and he quickly scrubbed at his eyes with the back of his sleeve.

Then he noticed the small swell of her stomach and how she palmed it protectively. Her nervous gaze sought his, and he could read fear and uncertainty in her eyes.

Pregnant.

Indescribable joy swelled in his soul until he thought he'd burst. He had to grab at the railing again as he swayed like a sapling in the breeze.

She was here. She was pregnant. They had a child.

Hunter slowly walked her forward until they stood a few feet away. She stared hard at Jericho, her lips turned down into a frown.

"What is wrong, Jericho?" she asked.

He held open his arms and she hurried forward, burying herself against his chest.

"Nothing," he said in a choked voice. "Now that you're here, nothing in the world is the matter."

She held him for a long moment before finally pulling away to stare up at him, concern etched into her eyes.

"What happened to you? You're in pain, and you don't look well."

Jericho found Hunter's gaze. "You didn't tell her?"

"We have a lot to talk about," Hunter said wearily. "I waited until we got here. She was down in Duncan's jail."

"What?" Jericho exploded.

Kaya jumped against him, and he gentled his touch, soothing her with his hands.

"Let's go inside," Hunter suggested. "We all need to sit down."

Unable to let her go even for a moment, Jericho held her tightly against his side as he started for the living room. He stumbled when his leg didn't cooperate, and Hunter grabbed him to steady him.

"Thanks," Jericho muttered.

"Jericho, what happened?" Kaya asked.

Her anxious eyes found his, and all he could do was kiss her. He lowered his head to find her lips, closing his eyes as her sweetness enveloped him. Finally. Finally he was home.

With Hunter's help, he got to the couch and sat, pulling Kaya down beside him. He kept her anchored against his side, afraid to let her go even for a moment.

"What happened, Kaya?" Hunter asked gently. "I need you to tell us everything."

She withdrew and twined her fingers in her lap, twisting nervously.

"I stayed as long as I could. I ran out of food, and since I couldn't shift, I had to go to the town to try and get something to eat. I thought...I thought you weren't coming back."

Hunter swore, and Jericho closed his eyes.

"Why couldn't you shift?" Hunter asked.

"Because of the baby," she said softly. "It's too dangerous. I didn't know at first. One day the cougar wouldn't respond to my call to shift. I was so frightened. I thought she had deserted me too."

"Oh honey, I'm so sorry," Jericho whispered against her hair. "We didn't desert you. We'd never voluntarily leave you. I know how it must have looked, but we wouldn't have left you for the world."

She swallowed. "Then I had a vision from the Maker bestowing his gift on my daughter, and I understood. I realized I was pregnant."

"Gift?"

"Daughter?"

Both men voiced their questions at the same time.

She nodded and framed her hands around her belly. "She will be a great silver wolf. I saw it in my vision. She will be free and beautiful."

The men stared at each other in disbelief. A wolf. Jericho couldn't wrap his brain around it. How the hell did a cougar-shifting woman give birth to a wolf-shifting daughter?

She looked up at them, her anxiety a living, breathing thing hovering in the air. "Are you upset about the baby?"

Hunter's mouth fell open, and Jericho squeezed her against him, his heart beating double-time.

"Upset?" Hunter asked.

"Hell no." Jericho's hand covered hers, cupping the swell. "I'm only upset that we left you here to fend for yourself, alone and pregnant."

"Honey, how do you know she'll be a wolf? And how is that possible when Jericho and I...we aren't shifters."

She offered a shaky smile. "It was the Maker's choice to gift our daughter with the wolf. She will grow to be strong and beautiful."

"Like her mother," Hunter said softly.

"What happened after you found out?" Jericho asked.

She stiffened again at his side. Her small fingers curled and uncurled. She seemed to be grappling with her emotions.

Sliding away from him, she rose to pace in front of them her eyes glowing, her face creased in consternation.

Kaya sucked in her breath, praying for wisdom, but her anger was quickly building. It surprised her, this rush of rage, her feeling of betrayal. She'd held so much in for so long because she'd been so afraid, but now with the two men in front of her, she seethed like a cauldron.

She turned to face them both. "Why?"

Jericho looked tortured, his face a mask of pain, both physical and mental. Hunter looked away, his body tense.

"You said you'd return. You led me to believe you would only be away a few weeks. You *left* me."

She palmed her belly again and rubbed in agitation.

"I had no way to feed myself. I had no money to live in the human world, and when I tried to feed myself and my child, I was taken and locked in a...in a...*cage*," she choked out.

She covered her face in her hands as sobs spilled out. Her shoulders shook violently as she tried to keep the raw noise from escaping.

In an instant she was enfolded and surrounded by both men. They held on to her while months of fear and grief erupted. She clutched at them, simultaneously furious and overjoyed that they were here, holding her.

"I'm so sorry, honey," Jericho murmured. "When I realized how long we'd been gone, I went crazy."

She went still and then pushed away so she could look up at him. "What do you mean?" She took in his haggard appearance, the weight he'd lost, the pallor of his face and the unmistakable evidence of pain. All the things she'd seen when he'd appeared on the porch, looking weak. "Jericho, what happened to you? Why wouldn't you know how long you were gone?" She clutched frantically at his chest. "Tell me what happened!"

Hunter gently pried her away from Jericho and led her back to the couch. Jericho came with her and collapsed beside her on the cushions, looking for the world like the last of his strength had been sapped.

"Come here," Jericho said, holding his arms out to her.

She went willingly, her earlier anger evaporating as the sweetness of his embrace surrounded her.

"We were set up. When we arrived in the encampment to rescue the medical workers, no one was there. There was an explosion. Hunter and I didn't get out in time."

She gasped. "No!" She touched his face frantically then ran her hands down his chest, searching for evidence of his injuries, wanting to know how bad they were.

Then she turned to Hunter as Jericho's words sank in. "You too? You were both hurt?"

Hunter gave a short nod.

"I'm so sorry. I had no right to be angry, no right to yell at you."

Hunter thrust his hand in her hair, smoothing the strands with his fingers. "No, honey, we understand. You were alone and afraid. For all you knew, we'd abandoned you like your family did."

"But it was you who were alone," she whispered. "How bad was it, and don't lie to me."

Both men sighed.

"Jericho nearly died," Hunter said.

"Goddamn it, Hunter."

Kaya's stomach fell to her feet. She swallowed the rising nausea. If he had died, she would've never known.

"And you?" she whispered to Hunter.

"For a while I couldn't walk. I was paralyzed when a piece of shrapnel lodged in my spine. I'm just lucky they were able to remove it. We were both beat up pretty bad, but we made it, Kaya. We came back to you."

She threw herself into Hunter's arms, burying her face in his neck. "I'm sorry. I'm so sorry. I had no right to feel as I did. I didn't know you were hurt."

He stroked her hair and held her close. "No, honey. You had every right. But we're home now, and we're never going to leave you again. Do you understand that?"

Slowly, she pulled away and reached for Jericho's hand, wanting to touch him and gain reassurance that he was here and whole.

"You aren't going away again?"

"Never," Jericho vowed.

"But, it's what you do," she said. "It's how you honor Rebeccah's memory."

"No, it's what we *did*," Hunter said quietly. "But not anymore. Rebeccah is gone. We loved her, but now we love you."

She went completely still. "You love me?"

Jericho nudged her chin until she stared back at him. His eyes were alight with emotion. *Love.*

"You're everything to us, Kaya. You're what kept me alive. We fought to get back to you."

She threw herself into his arms as she had done Hunter. "I love you too, Jericho." And then thinking better of her actions, she jerked away, her hands running down his chest. "I'm sorry. Are you all right? Do you still hurt?"

To her surprise, he laughed and captured her hands with his. He brought both up to his mouth and kissed her palms. And then he looked down at her belly, his laughter dying as a look of intense longing filled his eyes. Love softened his entire face, and if she ever had doubts as to whether he welcomed the idea of a baby, she shed them now.

He lowered his hands to her belly, cupping it through the thin layer of her shirt.

"I want to see," he said huskily. "Will you show me?"

She glanced over at Hunter to gauge his reaction, and his eyes went soft as he followed the direction of Jericho's hands.

"Show us our child, Kaya," Hunter said.

She wiggled from between them and turned on the couch until she was on her knees. Then she raised her shirt and pushed down her pants until she bared the curve of her belly.

Strong, blunt fingertips tentatively pressed into her sides.

"You won't hurt her," she said gently.

"You're so sure it's a girl?" Jericho asked.

She nodded solemnly. "She will have blue eyes."

"We have to talk about her, your pregnancy, I mean," Hunter said. "You need care, Kaya. You haven't been eating properly. You need extra vitamins. Tests. Sonograms. A doctor."

She stared curiously at him. "Sonograms? Tests?"

"He means you'll need help when it comes time to have the baby," Jericho said. "A hospital."

She shook her head vehemently. "No. You know I can't do that."

Hunter's hand tightened on her belly. "We'll figure something out. We'll take care of you and our daughter. You have our word."

"I'm so glad you're both home," she whispered. "I missed you so much."

She went forward, snuggling into both of their bodies. To be happy now after living so many months in fear overwhelmed her. If she closed her eyes, would this all be a dream? Would she wake back in the cage?

Her heart pounded at the thought.

"What's wrong, honey?" Hunter asked gently.

She didn't respond at first.

He pulled her onto his lap and carefully framed her face in his hands until she looked him in the eye.

"You know we love you, don't you?"

She nodded.

"And you also know we'll never leave you again."

She hesitated a fraction.

Hunter pulled her down to kiss her lovingly on the lips. "I don't blame you for not accepting it right away. But we'll prove it to you. We're not going anywhere. You have our word."

Tears trailed down her cheeks, and he wiped them away with his thumbs.

"I love you too. So much. I just want to be with you and Jericho."

"Then we'll take it one day at a time. Jericho and I both have some healing to do. Just like you do. We'll do it together."

She smiled through her tears and leaned in for another kiss.

"I'll take very good care of you and Jericho," she promised.

"And we're going to love you for a very long time," Jericho said.

"I'll start by making dinner," she said. "Hunter bought supplies in town, and I taught myself to cook while you were gone."

Hunter smiled. "Let me go out and get the groceries, and I'll meet you in the kitchen."

Chapter Twenty-Five

Duncan drove toward his cabin after a long-ass day of work. He was tired, the day had been filled with bullshit calls, and what he really wanted was his wife. But she wasn't due home until the next day.

He pulled up, cut the engine and sat there for a long moment, mustering the energy to get out and go inside.

He had one leg out the door when his cabin door flew open and Aliyah tore out of the house, her golden hair flying behind her.

Suddenly finding a hell of a lot more energy, he stumbled out of the truck about the time his wife hit him square in the chest. She leaped into his arms and wrapped her legs tight around him. Her lips crashed over his in a sweet, honeyed rush that left him breathless.

"God, I'm glad to see you," he groaned as he cupped her ass in his hands.

She went completely still against him and inhaled deeply. She drew away and frowned and inhaled again, her nostrils flaring.

"What the hell is wrong with you?" he asked in amusement.

"Your scent is different," she said sharply.

Then she lowered her head, sniffing his neck and his shirt. When she pulled back again, her eyes glowed strangely, and her body quivered, signaling an impending shift.

"Aliyah, get it together. You can't shift out here, for God's sake. Anyone could be watching."

She blinked several times before the feral light in her eyes subsided.

"Who have you been around?" she demanded. Her expression was utterly serious as she slid from his arms.

He frowned. Aliyah wasn't usually the jealous type. Hell, she'd scented plenty of women on him before. Hazard of the job. But she'd never reacted this way.

"Honey, the only people I've been around are Nick and a bunch of crazy-ass hunters who decided to get drunk and go spotlighting."

She shook her head vehemently. "A woman. Who is she?"

"The only woman I've been around I picked up for trying to steal food from Margaret's. She wouldn't tell me her name or anything else for that matter so I held her at the station until Hunter came for her. Come to think of it, I still don't know her name," he added with a frown.

"Where is she now?" Aliyah demanded. "This is important, Duncan."

"I suppose she's with Hunter up at his cabin. He was the only one she'd talk to. Nick and I tried hard enough to get anything out of her. What the hell is going on, Aliyah? It's not like you to get so freaky about a woman."

Aliyah's face was strained and worried, and she'd gone pale underneath the golden sheen of her skin. "Her scent, Duncan. I know it well. I should. It's Kaya."

His brow furrowed. "Kaya? Who the hell is Kaya?"

"My sister. Don't you remember me telling you about her?"

"Yes, honey, but you said she disappeared years ago, when you were just a child."

"Exactly. And now I smell her on you and you tell me a woman was in your jail, a woman who would tell you nothing of herself. She was probably frightened out of her mind."

Understanding dawned. "Holy fuck. She's a shifter? I know you told me she was a cougar, but are you sure this is your sister? I mean, honey, it's been a lot of years. Are you certain you aren't mistaken?"

"I'd know her smell anywhere," Aliyah said quietly. "Take me to her, Duncan. I have to see her. I have to know if she's my sister. I have to know what happened to her."

Duncan sighed. "If it is her, it would explain a hell of a lot. Hunter's protectiveness of her and why they were so damn secretive. You have to be prepared for the possibility that she won't remember you and that they won't welcome you asking questions."

"I have to see her for myself," Aliyah said fiercely.

"I know, sweetheart. We'll go in the morning."

"No. We go now. I won't sleep until I see her."

Duncan studied her in resignation. She was stubborn as hell when she set her mind to something, and if he didn't take her, he knew she'd shift into a damn cheetah and take off without him. And that was going to happen over his dead body.

"All right," he said with a sigh. "We'll go now. But you have to promise me you'll stay behind me until I say it's safe. Do you promise?"

She nodded solemnly and then ran around to get into the passenger seat of his truck. Duncan blew out his breath and climbed back into the driver's seat. So much for a nice evening at home and maybe some welcome home sex.

Chapter Twenty-Six

Kaya lay on the couch between Hunter and Jericho as a fire blazed in the hearth to ward off the evening chill. She was tired and wanted nothing more than to drift off to sleep surrounded by their heat and their love, but she didn't want the night to end.

They'd talked long into the evening. Hunter and Jericho had told her about the days in the hospital. Hunter's despair when it looked as though he wouldn't walk again and when he thought Jericho was dying. And then Jericho waking to discover so many months had passed and his panic that Kaya wouldn't be there when they got back.

They talked about the coming baby and how excited they were at the prospect of having a daughter to spoil and protect. Hunter and Jericho had a million questions about raising a child who could shift to an animal. How were they to prevent the same thing happening to their daughter as what happened to Kaya? The idea terrified them all, and Hunter had quickly changed the subject when he'd seen the upset it caused Kaya.

The room had grown quiet, and the fire had burned down to a glowing bed of coals when a knock sounded at the door.

Hunter went stiff as a board.

"What the hell?" Jericho bit out.

"Stay here," Hunter ordered in a steely voice. "I'll go see who it is." He cast a look at Jericho, and Jericho nodded as the two communicated silently. As Hunter got up to go to the door, Jericho was already getting up and moving Kaya across the room toward the shadows of the kitchen and in proximity of the back porch.

Hunter retrieved his pistol from the mantel and went to the door. He opened it an inch and peered through the crack into the night.

"Hunter, it's me, Duncan."

Hunter relaxed but still kept the door as a barrier between him and the sheriff.

"What brings you up here at this time of night?"

Duncan sighed. "Can I come in?"

Reluctantly, Hunter opened the door and allowed Duncan inside. Jericho moved in front of Kaya, and Hunter positioned himself between Duncan and Jericho.

It wasn't lost on Duncan.

"Look I understand your caution, but I'm not here for any trouble. I just need to ask you a few questions."

"Like?" Hunter asked.

Duncan glanced over at Jericho who stood unsmiling in the shadows.

"About Kaya."

Hunter frowned. "I'm pretty damn certain I never told you her name, and I know she didn't say anything to you. Want to tell me how you came up with it?"

"I need you to answer some questions for me first. Actually I'd prefer it if Kaya would talk to me herself."

Hunter shook his head even as Jericho bristled menacingly.

"Not going to happen," Hunter said evenly.

"Look, I understand. Believe me, I understand. I wouldn't allow Aliyah in this kind of situation either."

"Who the hell is Aliyah?" Hunter asked.

Behind Jericho, Kaya stiffened and curled her fingers into Jericho's shirt. He reached behind for her hand and squeezed reassuringly. Holding onto his hand, she moved from behind him to stare at Duncan. Duncan looked back at her expectantly, as if he were waiting for a reaction.

Hunter cursed and moved closer to Kaya, so that he and Jericho flanked her protectively.

"Aliyah is my wife," Duncan said evenly. "Aliyah Carver was her name before she married me. Does that ring a bell, Kaya?"

"Why the hell should it?" Jericho snarled.

Kaya put a reassuring hand on Jericho's arm and then moved forward into the light.

"Why are you asking me about this woman?"

"Do you remember her?" Duncan asked in a gentle voice.

Her brow furrowed. "Why should I remember her?"

"Damn good question," Hunter muttered. "I don't like this. Duncan, get to your point or get the hell out. I don't want you upsetting Kaya. She's already been through enough."

"Because she's like you," Duncan said, ignoring Hunter.

Kaya froze and retreated behind Duncan and Jericho once more.

"Get out," Hunter said in a dangerously low voice.

Jericho put both his arms behind him, pulling her against his back. She laid her cheek against his shirt, her breaths sticking in her throat. How had he known? What would happen to her now? Was he here to take her?

"Let me call Aliyah inside," Duncan said evenly. "I'm not about to put my wife in danger any more than you're going to place Kaya in danger. Aliyah wants to see her. It's important, or believe me, I would've never allowed Aliyah up here."

Without waiting for an answer, he went to the door. Kaya watched around Jericho's arm, frightened and intrigued at the same time. He'd said his wife was like her. How could that be?

Duncan leaned out the door and motioned with his hand. A few seconds later, a beautiful young woman walked in, and like Jericho and Hunter had done with Kaya, Duncan tucked her behind him, his gaze wary as he looked over at Hunter and Jericho.

"Where is she?" Aliyah demanded.

Duncan pointed to where the two men stood, and before he could hold her back, Aliyah hurried forward. She stopped in front of Hunter, her expression pleading.

"I won't hurt her. I have to see her, though. She's my sister."

Kaya gasped, and Hunter merely closed the distance between him and Jericho, forming an impenetrable wall between the two women.

"If you're her sister, you've already hurt her enough," Hunter said darkly.

"What are you talking about?" Aliyah asked, hurt in her voice.

Kaya's heart thundered against Jericho's back. Was she telling the truth? She closed her eyes, reaching for the memory of the cheetah. A girl with long golden hair and golden eyes and a beautiful smile.

"Her family abandoned her," Jericho growled. "We're her family now. She doesn't need you."

"That's not true!" Aliyah gasped. "Kaya, please, talk to me."

Racing side by side and then the cheetah spurring ahead, leaving her as she raced across the Alaskan terrain. The two girls laughingly playing tag. The memories tumbled through Kaya's mind. Was this her? The cheetah?

Tears formed, and Kaya swallowed them back. Slowly she pushed at Hunter and Jericho until she was visible in the space between them.

"I remember you," Kaya said in a low voice.

Aliyah made a small sound of joy as the two sisters stared at each other. Duncan was right behind Aliyah, his hand protectively at her shoulder as he watched Hunter and Jericho warily.

And then Aliyah's gaze fell to her belly. She rounded on Duncan, her eyes accusing. "You didn't tell me she was pregnant! Duncan, how could you? She must have been so terrified. You know how our kind feels about cages."

Duncan sighed patiently. "I didn't know who she was, Aliyah. And I put her in a cell so she'd have a warm place to sleep and food to eat. She looked as if she was badly in need of both."

Aliyah turned her accusing stare on Hunter and Jericho. "Why was that? Why haven't you taken care of her?"

Kaya ignored everything but the woman standing in front of her. Tentatively she stepped forward, reaching out to touch a strand of golden hair. She inhaled deeply, allowing herself to be surrounded by this woman's scent.

As she fingered the strand of hair, her sad gaze found Aliyah's. "Why did you leave me?" she whispered.

"Oh, Kaya, we didn't leave you."

Impulsively, she hugged Kaya, wrapping her slim arms around her as she squeezed. Kaya closed her eyes as more buried memories roared to the surface. The two girls sitting cross-legged on the floor of a house. Trading dolls as they combed each other's hair.

When Aliyah pulled away, her eyes glittered with tears.

"You still have the most beautiful eyes," Kaya said solemnly.

Aliyah reached for Kaya's hands and squeezed. "Can we sit on the couch? There's so much I need to tell you and questions I want to ask." She looked to Jericho and Hunter as if seeking their permission.

Kaya also looked at her two mates. "I will be fine."

Reluctantly, Hunter nodded, but they both stayed close as Aliyah led Kaya over to the sofa.

"Why do you think we left you?" Aliyah asked when both women had found comfortable positions.

"I went back," Kaya said. "When I was able, I made my way back home. The house was empty. I waited and waited, but no one ever came."

Aliyah's eyes filled with tears. "This will destroy Mama and Papa."

Kaya cocked her head to the side. "I don't remember them. Are they like us? I always thought my family was human except for you."

Aliyah shook her head. "No, they are like us. Mama is a great eagle and Papa is a Kodiak bear. When we lost you, they were devastated. They were afraid the same would happen to me, so we moved to Africa until I grew older and more restrained. You must have returned to Alaska while we were there."

"They wanted me?" Kaya asked in a small voice.

"Oh, Kaya, they've mourned you since the day you went missing. Not a day has gone by that we haven't thought of you. They're going to be so thrilled when I tell them that I've found you. You can't imagine what this is going to mean to them."

Again her gaze fell to Kaya's stomach. "Is your child going to be like us?" she asked softly.

Kaya smiled and started to reply, but Hunter stepped forward, his expression fierce. Kaya's mouth snapped shut. Hunter didn't want her to trust Duncan and Aliyah, especially when it came to their daughter's safety. He was right. She should exercise the same care she always had when it came to other people.

Aliyah sighed, and then her gaze found Duncan's. Whatever it was he saw in his wife's eyes, he didn't like it.

"Oh no, Aliyah. Hell, no. Don't you dare."

She ignored him, rising as she started to pull at her clothes. Duncan descended on his wife, hiding her from the others' view as her clothes fell away.

Kaya watched in fascination as Aliyah dropped to the floor, her body contorting. She couldn't remember seeing another person shift before, and now she realized how she must look to Hunter and Jericho. No wonder they watched her in such agony.

Duncan whirled around, his gun drawn, his eyes cold as ice. "Make one move toward her and it'll be your last."

A cheetah arose where Aliyah had fallen. The cat padded over to Kaya and rubbed against her leg. Her childhood playmate. Kaya dropped to the floor on her knees and threw her arms around the cheetah's neck. Her purrs filled the room, and she licked Kaya's cheek.

Kaya buried her face in the cheetah's fur and held on as tears slid down her cheeks.

The men weren't unmoved by the sight. Duncan slowly put away his pistol and Jericho and Hunter both moved forward, their faces softening as Kaya wept.

The cheetah waited patiently as Kaya clung to her sleek body. When her sobs quieted to silent hiccups, the cheetah retreated and went back to the shelter of Duncan's body. Shielding her from the others, Duncan waited as she shifted back to human form, and then he hastily helped her into her clothing.

Aliyah returned to the couch and held out her arms to Kaya. The two women embraced, both crying noisily while the men looked on in discomfort.

"How did she know?" Hunter asked Duncan as they watched over their women.

"She scented Kaya on me and freaked. Demanded I bring her up here immediately." His expression grew serious. "Her folks are good people, Hunter. They didn't willingly abandon Kaya. They thought they'd lost one child, and they didn't want to lose another."

Hunter just nodded as he and Jericho continued to watch over Kaya.

Aliyah pulled away and smoothed Kaya's hair from her face. "It's funny. You're the older sister, but I've always felt as though you were the younger. Even when we were children. I guess I didn't look out for you well enough, though," she said sadly. "How did you survive, Kaya? Where did you go?"

"It's not your fault," Kaya said in a low voice. "I haven't lived much in the human world. I spent most of my time in cougar form. Until I met Hunter and Jericho, I rarely shifted to human."

Aliyah stole a glance at the two men hovering so closely to Kaya. "Are they good to you, Kaya? Did one of them father your child?"

Kaya almost smiled at her sister's surly tone. "They are very good to me, and they are both the father of my daughter."

Aliyah gasped softly. "Daughter?"

Kaya nodded. "She will be a great silver wolf."

"Oh, that's wonderful," Aliyah said as her eyes teared up all over again. "Mama and Papa are going to be so happy."

"How is it that you're all so different?" Jericho asked in a bewildered tone. "Your mother is an eagle, your father a bear. It doesn't make sense."

Duncan grinned and clapped him on the shoulder. "Why don't we step outside and let the girls do some catching up and I'll tell you all about the family you're taking on."

Chapter Twenty-Seven

Kaya was still awake as dawn crept over the sky. She sat on the porch steps watching as the earth came to life around her. Birds sang, and the rustling of smaller animals in the undergrowth could be heard as they set about their day.

The air was still chilled enough that she could see her breath escaping in a small cloud, and she wrapped the blanket tighter around her.

A family. She had a family. And they hadn't abandoned her. It was hard for her to change her way of thinking after believing for so long that they hadn't wanted her.

She couldn't remember her mother and father, try as she might. Had she blocked them out on purpose? She could clearly remember Aliyah, but could not conjure images of the people who had given her life.

The door opened behind her, and Jericho stepped outside. He eased awkwardly down onto the steps beside her and handed her a cup of hot chocolate. She smiled as she took it. One of the things she'd developed an intense craving for was sweets, and the hot, sweet drink was one of her favorites.

"You shouldn't be out here, honey."

She looked in concern at the lines on his face. "Neither should you."

"I was worried about you," he said quietly. "How are you handling everything?"

She sipped the chocolate and stared out over the rugged terrain. "I don't know," she said truthfully. "It's all a little hard to comprehend."

"We'll take you to Alaska if that's what you want."

She immediately shook her head. "No. I don't want to leave here."

She turned back to look at him again. "I know it sounds silly, but I feel safe here, and I don't want to go back to the place I found empty so many years ago. It holds too many unhappy memories."

Jericho touched her cheek and then leaned in to kiss her forehead. "Then we'll stay here. Your folks can come visit you whenever they like."

"I don't remember them," she said sadly. "Do you think it will make them angry?"

Jericho slipped his arm around her and hugged her close. "No, honey. They're going to be so happy to see you. They'll understand. You've been alone for such a long time. No one will expect you to remember."

His hand slipped underneath the blanket and molded to her belly. "How is our little one this morning? Is she kicking yet?"

Kaya smiled and set aside her cup. She placed her hands over Jericho's and moved it upward until it was in just the right spot. "Feel here."

A tiny little bump, barely more than a muscle twitch, pittered and pattered against his palm. His entire expression transformed to one of intense awe.

"That's her," he whispered.

She leaned forward and brushed her lips across his. "She's glad to see you."

When she pulled away, Jericho leaned down and kissed the spot where the baby had been kicking.

"Good morning, sweetheart," he murmured against Kaya's belly.

Kaya tangled her hands in his hair, holding his head as he nestled it against her belly. The future was a very uncertain thing indeed, but she held to the one thing she knew. Jericho and Hunter would be with her. They would take care of her and their daughter. She'd never be alone again.

A sound made her look up, and she saw Hunter standing there, holding a cup of coffee as he stared down at her and Jericho.

Wordlessly, she held up her hand, an invitation for him to join them. Hunter set his coffee on the railing and settled on the other side of Kaya, his arm going around her. She laid her head on his shoulder and closed her eyes as she held Jericho's head in her lap.

"I love you both so much," she murmured. "I think I loved you from the first moment I saw you."

Hunter kissed her forehead and stroked her hair. "I love you too. More than I imagined ever loving another person. It scares me sometimes."

She smiled and nestled closer as she ran her fingers through Jericho's hair.

"I'm tired. I think I would like nothing more than to go to sleep with my mates."

Jericho raised his head and stared into her eyes. "Your mates would like that very much."

Hunter ran his fingers down the curve of her arm and around the swell of her breasts. "And who says we have to sleep all the time?"

She caught his lips with hers. "I like the way you think."

Chapter Twenty-Eight

"How long is it going to take?" Hunter asked with a scowl. "And why the hell did she ask us to wait out here?"

Aliyah smiled at him and patted him on the arm. "I imagine the poor midwife was thoroughly intimidated by you and Jericho hovering over Kaya like you'd cut off the arm of the person who dared touch her."

"We aren't that bad," Jericho muttered.

Duncan snickered but didn't move from his perch against the wall.

"Like you'll be any better when Aliyah is pregnant," Hunter said in Duncan's direction.

"You two have lost any and all good sense," Duncan said in disgust.

Aliyah checked her watch again. "Mama and Papa should be here soon. Oh, I can't wait for them to see her. I don't think Mama has stopped crying since I called her."

Hunter wished he could share Aliyah's enthusiasm, but the fact was he wasn't as excited over Kaya's parents' arrival, and he knew Kaya was scared. He would have honestly preferred for the reunion to take place after the birth of their child. Until then he wanted to keep her as happy and as stress-free as possible.

Jericho sighed impatiently and dug his hands into his pockets. "Do you think something's wrong? This was supposed to be a routine exam. Shouldn't be taking this long."

Hunter frowned. They'd arranged to take Kaya to a midwife after much argument from her. They'd sworn the midwife would do nothing more than examine her, offer advice, make sure she was as healthy as she needed to be. Her secret would be safe, and moreover, they'd never allow anyone to take her from them.

It was a vow they gave often in an attempt to reassure her. Though she'd forgiven the circumstances that kept them away from her for so long, she hadn't forgotten the terror she'd lived.

Finally the door to the tiny exam room opened and Kaya stepped out, her cheeks blooming with a smile. Her gaze instantly found Jericho and Hunter, and her smile widened as she hurried over to them.

"I got to hear her heartbeat," she exclaimed. "Oh, Jericho, it was wonderful. The midwife had this little machine, and she put it on my stomach, and it made the most amazing sound."

Hunter smiled at her excitement and reached out for her hand, unable to keep from touching her. She responded by leaning into him. He didn't even know if she was cognizant of doing it, but it thrilled him all the same how she instinctively sought him out. Somehow, he and Jericho hadn't lost her trust. God knew they'd deserved to. They'd made mistakes with her, mistakes that almost cost them everything, and yet her trust in them was whole.

"Is everything okay with the baby?" Jericho asked anxiously. "And with you? She told you that you should be eating more, didn't she? She probably thinks we're not taking very good care of you."

Kaya laughed and reached up to touch Jericho's cheek which immediately halted his tirade. "I'm fine. Our daughter is fine."

"Is that all?" Hunter asked, directing her attention back to him.

"Well, she did mention my weight."

"I knew it," Jericho muttered.

"But she said I was strong and healthy and that she couldn't foresee any problems with the pregnancy."

"Good," Hunter said in satisfaction. "Jericho and I can certainly fatten you up."

Kaya blushed and squeezed his hand, her fingers curling around his in a little flutter. Her gaze went to where Aliyah and Duncan stood across the room, and her hand began to shake in his.

"Relax, honey," Hunter murmured soothingly. "You don't have to do this, you know. We can go back to the cabin. You don't have to see them at all."

She shook her head. "No, I want to see them. I'm just scared."

He smiled and pulled her into his arms. "Don't be scared. Jericho and I will be with you the entire time."

She looked up at him, her eyes shining. "I know. I love you."

He dropped a kiss on her lips then turned her toward the door. It had been agreed that the reunion would be held at Duncan and Aliyah's. That way if Kaya needed to escape, they could simply leave and return to the cabin, and there would be no awkwardness of expecting her parents to leave.

Jericho took her hand as they walked outside to get into their vehicles. The breeze blew over them, lifting her hair at the ends. She turned her face into the sun and closed her eyes, and Hunter was struck by how utterly beautiful she was. And she was his.

He found himself praying when he thought he didn't believe in prayer anymore. Just a whisper to God to help him to love and keep her and their daughter from harm. If the sun shone a little brighter over her upturned face, he was sure it was a coincidence.

A brief memory flashed across his mind. Rebeccah smiling, her face soft with love. For a moment he grabbed on and held tight...and then gently let it go, watching as it was carried away on the waves of his past.

It didn't hurt so much anymore. The shadows slowly dissipated. For the first time he looked to his future with such hope and joy that his heart positively ached.

"Thank you," he whispered, and felt the tight bands around his chest loosen and fall away. Freedom was such a sweet, sweet gift. Love? That he be granted a second chance to love and be loved was more than he could have ever asked for. He was going to grab it and hang on for all he was worth.

Kaya paced the interior of Aliyah's living room despite repeated pleas from Jericho and Hunter to sit down. They worried, she knew, but she couldn't sit down. Not when her stomach bubbled like a cauldron. It was all she could do not to go to the bathroom and be violently ill.

"They're here," Aliyah said softly.

Kaya froze, her legs trembling. Jericho and Hunter were immediately beside her, their touches light and reassuring.

Aliyah went out, closing the door behind her. Kaya appreciated the buffer because she was terrified. These people were strangers. And yet they were her parents. They loved her. Aliyah had told her how they suffered, how they all suffered after she'd disappeared in Alaska.

"Are you all right?" Jericho asked.

She nodded then stiffened all over when the front door opened.

A young-looking woman with long, dark hair stepped hesitantly into the living room. Her gaze locked with Kaya's, and tears filled her eyes and spilled down her cheeks.

Kaya stared in wonder. She knew this woman. It was the woman from her vision, the one who had placed Kaya's daughter in her arms. Her *mother*.

"Mama," she whispered.

"Kaya!"

With a broken sob, her mother moved forward, her arms outstretched. Kaya stumbled into them, absorbing the warm feeling of homecoming. She inhaled deeply, comforted by the familiar scent.

Her mother stroked her hair as Kaya's face lay buried in her neck. Oh, there was nothing better than a mother's hug. So much love, unfettered acceptance. So much that she had missed over the long years.

"Kaya, my daughter," her mother whispered softly against her hair. "At last, you've come back to us."

Kaya pulled away to stare at her through watery eyes. "I tried. I came back as soon as I could. I waited and waited."

A strangled noise came from behind her mother, and she looked to see a large man standing just inside the doorway, tears streaking unabashedly down his face.

"Papa?"

He held out his arms for her and she ran forward, suddenly spurred by memories of doing the same thing when she was a girl. He'd catch her and whirl her around, a huge grin on his face. Only now he gathered her against his massive chest almost as if he were afraid she'd disappear.

"My baby," he said brokenly. "I'm so sorry we weren't there, little one. You don't know what it did to me when Aliyah told us what had happened. I've died a thousand deaths knowing my little girl needed me and I wasn't there."

Any anger or sadness lifted and was carried away as love filled her heart. "You're here now," she whispered.

He scooped her up in his big arms and hugged her tight against him. When he finally put her down, she was once more enfolded into her mother's embrace.

"How beautiful you've grown."

Her mother's words hummed gently over her hair, and Kaya closed her eyes as she stood between the two people who had given her life.

Her father cupped her cheek and kissed her before pulling away and turning his attention to Hunter and Jericho. His gaze held both curiosity and concern. Kaya stepped back into the shelter of the two men and smiled tentatively at her parents.

Her father held out his hand to Jericho. "I'm Lawrence Carver, Kaya's father. This is my wife, Merry."

Jericho returned his shake. "Jericho Hartley." He nodded at Merry when she offered a smile.

Lawrence turned to offer his hand to Hunter as well.

"Hunter Caldwell," Hunter said grimly.

"Our family is growing," Merry said, her eyes glistening with tears.

Jericho stared at her in disbelief. Just like that, she accepted his and Hunter's place in Kaya's life. There was subtle wariness in Lawrence's expression, but nothing in his body language suggested he took exception to either him or Hunter.

Kaya took his hand then reached for Hunter's. She pulled them forward until they stood flush against her sides. "Mama, Papa, these are my mates."

Kaya shifted nervously against them, her hand shaking in Jericho's grip. He squeezed to reassure her. She wanted her parents' blessing, and for her sake, he hoped they gave it, but their disapproval wouldn't stop Jericho and Hunter from having a life with Kaya.

Merry smiled gently at her daughter. "It is obvious they love you. They have my gratitude for caring for you well."

"And mine," Lawrence said.

"Now tell me of your little one." Merry stepped forward to place her hand on the bulge of Kaya's stomach.

Jericho watched as Kaya lit up like a Christmas tree and told her parents of the Great Maker's gift to her daughter—his daughter. Hunter's daughter. It all seemed surreal, something out of a bizarre dream to listen as shape-shifting was calmly discussed as if it were an everyday occurrence. But then for these people it was.

And now this was his family. He stole a glance at Hunter who looked as nonplussed as Jericho was. For two guys who had isolated themselves from the world, they were growing a damn big circle of people.

To his surprise, it felt pretty damn good.

Kaya rose on tiptoe and brushed her lips over his ear. "I love you," she whispered.

He smiled and squeezed her hand. Somehow she knew just what to say and when. She moved to Hunter, and he let her go, knowing she'd return. As she settled into the crook of Hunter's arm, Hunter's arm came snug around her.

She laughed and smiled, her eyes bright and shining. The haunting loneliness was gone from her gaze.

The loneliness was gone from Jericho's soul. The pain and fatigue eased from his body, replaced with warmth that went bone deep.

And then Kaya turned her beautiful amber gaze on him, and his heart was lost all over again.

About the Author

To learn more about Maya, please visit www.mayabanks.com. Send an email to Maya at maya@mayabanks.com or join her Yahoo! group to join in the fun with other readers as well as Maya. http://groups.yahoo.com/group/writeminded_readers.